AUG 2018

FL

THE
DARK
BENEATH
THE ICE

THE
DARK
BENEATH
THE ICE

AMELINDA BÉRUBÉ

sourcebooks
fire

Published by Sourcebooks Fire, an imprint of Sourcebooks, Inc.
P.O. Box 4410, Naperville, Illinois 60567-4410
(630) 961-3900
Fax: (630) 961-2168
sourcebooks.com

Library of Congress Cataloging-in-Publication Data

Names: Bérubé:, Amelinda, author.
Title: The dark beneath the ice / Amelinda Bérubé.
Description: Naperville, Illinois : Sourcebooks Fire, [2018] | Summary:
    Marianne has felt a supernatural presence since she stopped dancing, and
    is afraid that she is following her mother into mental illness until a new
    friend, Ron, helps her find the truth.
Identifiers: LCCN 2018010614 | (hardcover : alk. paper)
Subjects: | CYAC: Supernatural--Fiction. | Anxiety disorders--Fiction. |
    Mentally ill--Fiction. | Divorce--Fiction. | Aunts--Fiction.
Classification: LCC PZ7.1.B46495 Dar 2018 | DDC [Fic]--dc23
LC record available at https://lccn.loc.gov/2018010614

Printed and bound in the United States of America.
WOZ 10 9 8 7 6 5 4 3 2 1

To Robert Knipe, Shirley Black, Lila Pulos, and Janet Cover,

because enthusiasm is caught, not taught.

1

THE SILENCE STILL CLINGS TO me.

If I close my eyes it's there waiting for me, filling my mouth, heavy as water. Ready to swallow me again.

I rest my forehead against the window, willing the ordinary sounds around me to wash the memory away: the windshield wipers, the spatter of the rain, the rattle in the wheel well. In the driver's seat beside me, Mom breathes in little hitches, trying not to sound like she's crying.

I risk a glance at her; she's wiping her eyes. Her hair is usually tied up in a neat sweep of gleaming black, silver threads glinting through it. Today she's yanked it through an elastic, pieces straggling dull and stringy around her face. Before I can look away again her gaze meets mine and she attempts a half smile.

It hurts to see it. I study the flowers in my lap: lilies—big, splashy orange ones. The smell is giving me a headache. They're for Aunt Jennifer, for taking care of me. It's not like I haven't been to Aunt Jen's overnight before, not like it's some huge favor. How long is she planning to leave me there?

Mom slams on the brakes, and I clutch the bouquet to stop it from sliding to the floor. She grates out a few choice swear words at the car ahead of us.

"I left your father a message," she says. "I sure hope he calls you."

I take the words in like water—like an icy lake, swallowing their impact without a splash, letting them sink. I turn back to the window, watch my reflection slide over the river and the low-slung clouds. My face is thin and pale, my eyes dark hollows. I look like a ghost.

Mom heaves a sigh, yanks a tissue from the box sitting between us. She won't tell me where she's going. She won't tell me why. Not that I've pressed her for details. There's a traitorous piece of me that's relieved. Mom's always been unpredictable, prone to wild mood swings she apologizes for later, and Hurricane Laura, as Dad puts it, has been howling full blast these past couple days. We used to joke about battening down the hatches, waiting out the storm. But this time, Dad's the reason she's in pieces.

And he left me to pick them up by myself.

I won't think about it. Just like last night—whatever happened last night. It's a stone, and it's vanishing into the water, leaving me serene. Unmoved.

Aunt Jen's building is long and low, brick and stucco, a little shabby at the edges. It's a strange contrast with the palatial homes on the next street, but that's what this whole neighborhood is like. The boat launch at the end of the road is barricaded and piled high with sandbags to keep the river from swallowing the pavement. Right beside it, half a dozen two-story row units are surrounded by a high cedar hedge. Aunt Jen's is the last one before the water. As the car crunches to a stop in the driveway, the sun comes out, as if from behind a veil. Suddenly, over the seawall, the river is all blue glitter, the trees drooping over the end of the street glowing golden-green, the last drops of rain sparkling as they drip from the leaves.

We sit silently in the car for a long moment. Seagulls wheel overhead, crying.

"Wait here," Mom manages eventually, taking the flowers. She slams the door without waiting for me to respond and hurries over to Jen's gate in the hedge, where a flush of pink roses shine in the sun.

I get out more slowly once she's disappeared behind it. Their voices drift toward me: Mom's barely muffled wails, Jen's reassurances. I can't make out words from here, though. I kick at a rock, following it down to the end of the road toward the seawall.

The river shouldn't be this high. Behind the seawall—a chest-high barrier that zigzags behind the imposing homes lining the waterfront—the water is brown, choppy, slapping at the concrete a foot below the top, an occasional wave sending spray sloshing over onto the grass. By now it's usually fallen low enough that the boat launch stands open to the river; later in the summer it drops all the way down to a stony outcropping that makes for a great place to skip rocks. It's hard to imagine that now.

The rain hasn't stopped for more than a couple of hours at a time this past week; I can't even remember the last time the sun was out for this long. It won't last. The news has been talking endlessly about record precipitation and the threat of flooding, images of picnic tables standing in the water and empty outdoor swimming pools with their surfaces pocked with raindrops. The DJs hosting the radio morning shows, in between laughing at their own jokes, moan about how summer is never going to come. Usually I love the peace and softness of rain, its soothing murmur on the roof. But it's starting to feel oppressive lately. Inescapable.

I turn my back on the water, breathe in its green, weedy smell, and tell myself to relax. Aunt Jen's place has always been cozy, a haven of good memories going back to when I was little. I used to play "inflatable Auntie" with her, pretending to blow her up like a beach ball. She would puff up obligingly and then deflate again, sagging in her chair and making a loud raspberry noise for full effect. I tried that game once with my mom, but she put on a pained smile and told me she didn't like it. I think she was worried I was implying she was fat. Aunt Jen, comfortably plump compared to Mom, doesn't seem to care about that sort of thing; she keeps her graying hair cut short, doesn't wear makeup, and lives in jeans and sweaters unless forced to dress up, when she just drapes herself in something long and flowy.

The gate creaks, and Mom hurries out toward me, folds me into a tight hug. She's not even trying to hide that she's crying now. Aunt Jen follows behind her but heads to the car, popping open the trunk, although she casts a worried look our way.

"It's only for a little while," Mom whispers. "Just a little while. It's not you, sweetie, I just can't deal with this, not on top of everything else."

"With what?" My voice breaks too, and despite my resolve, they come bubbling up: all the questions I haven't dared to ask. "Mom. Please tell me. Did something happen last night?" She lets me go, half turns away, wrapping her arms around herself as if I punched her, her face crumpling. "Mom, *what happened?*"

"Nothing," Mom sobs. "Nothing. Nothing."

She draws a fierce breath, then another, and grips my shoulders, fixing me with a tearful glare.

"Nothing happened, Marianne!" Her fingers dig into my arms. "Understand? It's not you. I just need to get some help. I'm going to get some help, all right? I'll come and get you as soon as I can, and… and we'll figure everything out. Okay?"

I nod. There's nothing else I can do. The sun is gone again. I'm cold from the tips of my fingers to the hollow of my back, despite my sweater.

"Okay," Mom repeats. Her lips tremble. "I love you."

She pulls away, takes long steps back toward the car, and yanks the door open. She folds her arms over the steering wheel and rests her head on them for a moment while her shoulders shake. With the glass between us, I can't hear her sobbing.

"Come on, Mare-bear." It's Aunt Jen's arm around me now, a band of warmth, pulling me close. "Let's go inside."

We step into Aunt Jen's living room, a cool, leafy cavern. Gray light filters through plants that spill from shelves and dangle from hanging planters. The piano, a mass of dark, carven wood, is the only surface that isn't draped with fronds or vines. The little radio on the side table next to the old maroon couch fills the room with earnest, thoughtful conversation.

"I've set up the spare room for you," Aunt Jen says, pulling the patio door closed behind us. "You can get yourself settled in a bit, and then we'll have a cup of tea."

Hugging my pillow, my laptop case banging against my leg, I follow her up the stairs. There are empty spots on the wall where pictures of my parents used to hang. I feel for my phone in my pocket. Dad hasn't called. I hope he will. I hope he won't.

The room hasn't changed: the window looking down onto the garden and the river beyond it, a twin bed with a threadbare quilt, moss-green walls, a white dresser topped with a menagerie of little china animals—a tiger, a monkey, a turkey, a horse. Mom told me they belonged to my grandmother, who died when I was still a baby. I used to play with them when I was little.

"There's plenty of space in the dresser if you want to unpack," Aunt Jen offers tentatively. "It's never fun living out of a suitcase."

I set down the laptop case and fluff my pillow a couple of times before arranging it on the bed, trying to avoid her gaze.

"Well. I'll go put the kettle on, Mare-bear, okay? Take your time."

"It's Marianne, please, Aunt Jen." But she's already out the door.

I sink down on the bed, which creaks under me. The rest of my life is unrecognizable, but everything here is the same. It's like I've stepped into some parallel universe. Like any second I'll hear my parents laughing downstairs as Jen pours glasses of wine, and none of this will have happened.

There is one thing that's different. Usually there's a picture of me and my parents on the wall beside the mirror. Now a much smaller frame hangs a little crookedly in its place, holding a snapshot from some distant summer: just me, striking a *ta-da* pose beside a leaning sandcastle. I remember that red swimsuit.

The photo must be from the beach right down the street from here, so close that we used to go there all the time. I remember those trips in flashes: Mom's smile as she glanced back at me from the front seat, strings of hair whipping around her face in the gale from the open window. Dad's hand on her bare knee. My sandaled toes tipping up toward the jewel blue of the sky at the apex of a swing. Dad diving for a volleyball and sprawling in the sand, making me laugh so hard my sides ached. The sparkle of the water, its delicious chill when I waded in. Swimming out as far as I dared, diving as deep as I could, reaching for the murky bottom.

I took yoga classes with Mom after I quit dance. To help me calm down, she said. Like she thought it would fix me. The studio must have been nice during the day, with sunshine pouring in through the wall of windows at the front. At night the fluorescent lights made everyone look tired and cold. At the beginning of each class, as we lay on our thin, hard mats, the instructor asked us to picture a place where we'd found tranquility, and every time that's what I called up: the water, cold and green. It's second nature now, the one useful thing I learned in those six weeks. I can summon it easily, lower myself into chilly weightlessness, the absence of sound, and hang suspended between worlds for a few long breaths until I'm cool and reasonable again. Lately I've frosted the surface over with a layer of ice, a shield keeping me submerged.

I close my eyes. The memory of silence, an empty horizon, rises around me, but I push it aside, force it down into the depths where dark water belongs. I'm not letting a bad dream spoil this for me, the one place where I'm truly safe. Around me I summon sunlight filtering down through the waves, a translucent, icy ceiling inches thick. Perfect, thoughtless peace closes over my head.

And then a noise like a firecracker, like a gunshot, yanks me back to reality. I leap to my feet, fear splashing through my chest.

It was the mirror above the dresser. Breaking. From a smashed, spiderwebbed epicenter, it's split side to side, slicing my reflection in two with a thread of silver, frozen lightning. The two halves of my dislocated image slide past each other as the frame trembles into stillness.

"Marianne?" Aunt Jen appears in the doorway, frowning. "Is everything—"

Her words disappear into an indrawn breath. I follow her stare back to the mirror, and then to the floor, where the wooden cat from the bedside table is lying on the linoleum next to the dresser.

"Oh, sweetheart," she says. The words are gentle; horrified. I shrink away from them. What just happened? She thinks I threw it. I open my mouth to protest—*but I didn't!*—but the words wither, half-formed.

Did I throw it?

Aunt Jen looks at me for another long moment, her lips pursed in consternation, then comes over to wrap an arm around my shoulders. She ushers me downstairs, leads me to the couch like I might break, pours me a steaming cup of some herbal tea that smells like flowers. The orange lilies stand in a vase on the dining room table, brassy and loud as trumpets.

I wrap my hands around the warmth glowing from the teacup to stop them from shaking. My heart is made of moths, fluttering against my ribs, in my throat.

"Are you going to tell Dad?" I blurt out as she sits down next to me. "About the mirror?"

"I don't know, Mare-bear." She eyes me over the rim of her own cup. "Do I need to?"

I shake my head, obviously. But I can't remember picking up the figurine, much less throwing it. It's a hairline crack in the day, a thread of blank space. Just like last night.

"Well. Listen, sweetie. I'm not mad. Honestly. I know this is hard. It's awful, and I just want you to know you can talk to me if you need to. Okay?"

"Okay."

Silence descends while she waits for me to continue. Eventually she gives up and clears her throat.

"So," Aunt Jen says in a sprightly, let's-talk-about-something-else way. "You'll need to take the bus to school tomorrow. Just exams left after that, eh?"

"Yeah." Just two weeks. Just forever.

The radio chimes to announce the news. More rain in the forecast; they're piling sandbags in the East End.

"Well, I took some vacation days to look after things, so I'll have all the time in the world. You just let me know what you want to do. Or maybe you'd rather get together with some friends, you know… That's fine too."

I shake my head. Ingrid's the only one I want to spend time with. But San Francisco might as well be the moon. I slurp my still-too-hot tea and burn my tongue.

There's not really anywhere left for the conversation to go.

Aunt Jen watches me for a while and finally sighs, perches her glasses on her nose, and picks up her crochet needle. I sip my tea a couple more times and then murmur an excuse about checking my email before escaping back to my room.

No notifications, of course, when I pull out my phone. I start a text to Ingrid for the hundredth time, and for the hundredth time I sit motionless, my fingers hovering over the screen until it goes dark. The words won't condense, somehow, from the formless worry and grief. Music drifts up from downstairs: Aunt Jen's flying through the twinkling notes of a Chopin waltz on the piano. I think she means it to be comforting.

I used to dance to this when I visited, twirling around the tiny living room on the tips of my toes, my hair swinging out behind me, my arms swept over my head, fingers poised to pluck butterflies from the air, just like they'd taught us. Mom always applauded earnestly. I was her star. Dad would be watching us both, smiling.

Water can stop bullets if it's deep enough. The memory can't touch me. I just have to breathe, breathe, and let it sink. Like everything else.

Like my silent phone.

Call me, I want to type, but how many ways can you tell somebody you miss them before you end up sounding hopelessly needy? If I could talk to Ingrid about all this awfulness, it would lose its weight, disappear. If I confided in her, maybe I wouldn't feel so alone. But maybe—probably—it would just be oversharing. And I can't think of a way to tell her about the things that scare me most. Strange things.

Like the mirror. Its broken face keeps twinkling in the pale afternoon light, catching my eye, drawing it back. Eventually I grab the quilt folded at the end of the bed and throw it over the frame. Was it me? It must have been me. How else could that happen, glass simply breaking, out of nowhere?

2

MOM USED TO TELL ME all the time there's no such thing as perfect.

My family wasn't perfect. I knew that. But I thought it was working. It worked for me. My parents were never the hypercritical, clueless control freaks people at school always whine about. No brothers or sisters to fight with. It was quiet, but a comfortable quiet, a book-and-a-blanket quiet.

In my head I have this picture of us: Me curled up reading on the couch, not the chilly leather bench we got for the new house, but the old, olive-green corduroy one with a rip in the side Mom hid with a table. Dad in his habitual after-work spot, perched on an ergonomic stool in front of a canvas, taking advantage of the light from the north-facing window. He'd have traded his sober, anonymous tie and jacket for one of the painting shirts we got him every year for Father's Day, the louder and sillier the better. His favorite had flamingos on it. Mom, meanwhile, would be just out of sight around the corner, clinking and humming in the kitchen. She'd come in to bring Dad a cup of coffee, reminding him not to put his paintbrush in it. He'd emerge from his reverie for long enough to smile up at her, for her to kiss his cheek.

After Dad's company took off, when we moved to the new house, it was different: all the chrome accents, white and black, straight lines. Dad insisted on all this stupid art that looks deep but doesn't mean anything, even though he claimed it was "expressive." My dance friends stared like tourists when they came over, craning their necks to take it all in, the sweep of the staircase that looks like it's floating, the huge soaring windows that turn the rolling hills on the far side of the river into wallpaper. The quiet there was emptier. The whole house was flooded with north-facing light, but Dad didn't have time to paint anymore. He kept a little caddy of brushes next to his desk, called it his five-minute project station; he'd add a few brushstrokes at a time, he told me, in between emails.

At night, inside, the house is like a ship, the prow facing out into the dark of the river. The only lights would be a white strip under Dad's office door on one side of the house and on the other, the washed-out blue flicker of the television in their room as Mom graded papers in bed.

Maybe the cracks widening between them should have been obvious. But I hadn't heard them fight since those awful few days at the end of dance class, back in ninth grade. I think they must have, every once in a while. They never said anything to me about it, but Mom was like a barometer. Every now and again her anger suffused the whole house. Always unspoken, never explained, it seeped into every corner, followed me into every room. It echoed in the clanking of dishes as she stood at the sink, in the slam of the dryer door, in the whirring of the furnace filling the silence.

I asked her about it once. She said, without looking at me, that I didn't need to worry about it.

"Marriage is work, Marianne," she said. "Nobody agrees all the time. Reasonable people work out their differences."

That was her mantra. When I quit dance, that whole terrible week Dad didn't even come home, Mom had repeated it like a prayer. And it had worked, in the end. So I would wait, just like I had then: Holding my breath. Not rocking the boat. Being good. Keeping quiet.

And the clouds always passed. Mom would still make Dad his coffee. She would pad off to his office with it while I did my home-work perched on a bar stool at the chilly stone counter of the kitchen peninsula. And Dad would emerge later with the empty mug and ask me about my day. I'd breathe a sigh of relief and feel a little proud that they were such reasonable people. People who knew how to stay calm and work things out.

When I think about it now, it's like Dad had been leaving for a long time, a point on the horizon getting smaller and smaller, so slowly I didn't see it happen. I didn't want to admit it. There was always another explanation. In that cavernous glass ship it seemed only logical we would spread out a little thinner, bump into each other less. That I'd only see them by themselves, in their separate corners of the house.

It might have been work that kept Mom up past midnight. I was up studying for a test one night, and she came into my room with a plate of cookies to share and a mug of hot chocolate, saying she couldn't sleep. We had a wonderful, cozy chat about nothing much: the book I was reading, the shenanigans her first-year students tried to pull. I felt so grown up, like I was someone she could rely on, someone she could come to for company. But I heard her footsteps in the hall so many other nights. Dad didn't even get home until eight o'clock, and then he'd disappear into his office. Mom set her jaw and said you can't expect to work nine to five when you're running a tech start-up, even after the IPO. There was always a deadline, or a manager who left and took most of their employees with them, or a new client to meet with... He was busy, that was all. It didn't seem strange.

It's two days ago now that it all fell apart.

Tuesday night. The cathedral windows were going dim. The mascara streaking Mom's face was the first sign it was coming. She sat across from me, chin lifted, arms tightly folded, in the far corner of the couch. As far from Dad as she could get. She fixed her red-rimmed glare on a point on the wall.

And Dad, his elbows on his knees, spoke to the floor. Didn't meet my eyes except in the barest glances while he delivered this terrible, practiced speech about how he and Mom couldn't live together anymore, how they both loved me very much, how this wasn't anyone's fault. Mom snorted at the last statement, and he winced, letting his words trail off.

The rain hammered on the tall windows. I sat there, smooth and frozen, waiting for time to resume. Waiting to find out none of this weird, ugly drama was real.

But all that happened was that Mom stood up and stalked out of the room while Dad dropped his head into his hands.

"I was hoping it wouldn't come to this, bunny," he said as a door slammed, echoing across the house. "I'm sorry."

The blue-veined surface of the ice dimmed above me. I'd sink so deep they'd never find me. Dad shifted under my stare.

"It's okay to be angry." He sighed. "Let's just talk about things, okay?"

"Things," I echoed.

"Well, yeah. Lots of things. I need to explain."

A muffled, irregular sound crept through the silence between us. The sound of Mom crying.

I meant to say something. I meant to be reasonable and cooperative and all the things he wanted. But instead, I got to my feet and left the room. I barely saw where I was going. Around me the ice stretched out forever, a vast arctic sea.

Dad called after me. "Marianne? Come on, please?"

But he only called once.

Mom was lying on the bed, facing away from me. She didn't turn around when I came into the room.

"Mom?"

When she didn't answer I sat down on the bed, then lay down next to her, put my arms around her. And we stayed like that for a long time, listening to the rain beating on the skylights as the colors in the room dissolved into twilight.

Eventually she spoke, told me he didn't want counseling, and she couldn't make him stay. I listened in the dark as Mom sobbed about how she was sure he was seeing someone else, and where were we going to live now, and how could he do this, *how*. I tried to let it wash over me, to stay in the depths untouched, but I could feel the bottom dropping away beneath me, the directions melting, the compass meaningless, spinning in free fall.

After that broken night, after waking up alone in my parents' bed, nothing seemed real anymore. Going to school was unthinkable. Dad's absence was nothing unusual, but it screamed at me from every side, from every piece of furniture he'd picked out, every fixture they'd debated over. The spare tidiness of the house made no sense. The windows should have been smashed all over the floor, the rain blowing through the house. Mom couldn't sit still, pacing from room to room, raging. I trailed helplessly in her wake, wishing I could hide from the storm, unable to abandon her. If you stayed calm and waited long enough, Hurricane Laura would eventually blow herself out.

"I told him," she seethed. She stood in the middle of the living room, hands on her hips. I was perched on the edge of one of the weird, hard decorative chairs that no one sits in, hands folded in my lap. I'd been watching her stalk around the living room in a prowling circle, all explosive energy, a wild thing in a cage. "I told him if he was going to do this to us, if he was going to do this *again*, he was going to be the one to tell you. Do you know the real reason why he missed your show in Montreal?"

That show was a blur of lights and anxiety in my head. Mom was a waiting shadow, a fierce backstage whisper, an even hand wielding lip liner when mine shook too badly. She'd stayed in the wings long past the end of her volunteer shift, earning flutters of admiring protest from the others. She was the queen of the dance moms, sticking on false eyelashes, organizing garment bags, threading safety pins together, applying hairspray to running nylons.

"Well, let's just say it sure as hell wasn't a business trip. And I *forgave* him. I took him back! And now he just walks out the door. Did he think I'd let him just sneak off without a word to you?" She tossed her hair, not needing an answer. "He thought he could dump everything in my lap. Like he *always* does. Well, it's different this time. He's not coming crawling back to us again. I hope he *has* found someone else. Maybe she can clean up after him and his fucking executive job—she can—"

Her words dissolved into a cry of fury and disgust, and she stormed from the room, leaving me to sink forward till my forehead touched my knees, too wrung out from listening to her to even cry.

When she came marching back into the room she had a knife in her hand. One of Dad's fancy kitchen knives.

"Mom!"

She climbed up on the couch, her feet barely sinking into the gleaming black leather, and buried the point of the knife in the painting that filled the wall there. She sawed at it, but the canvas refused to slice, so she reached up to yank at the hole she'd punched through it, hauling on the cloth until it ripped, a long, ragged slash, leaving it curling down like peeling skin.

She stood there, panting, and I waded forward. Didn't come too close.

"Mom. You should give me the knife."

She looked around at me, her eyes widening, like she'd just remembered I was there. Cold, luminous water, I thought, looking steadily at her. A shield of ice. Beyond depth, beyond waves, beyond fear.

"I'm sorry, sweetie," she whispered. "I'm just... I'm so angry. You didn't think—I didn't mean to—"

"Mom." I was so calm. I would make this disappear like everything else. "Please."

Her mouth twisted up; she put a hand over her face, turned

away from me. I took her wrist in one hand, pulled the knife from her slack fingers with the other. Her muffled sobs followed me as I carried it back to the kitchen. I didn't run. My feet in their fuzzy socks were silent on the hardwood.

This was it. This was the bottom, the lightless sandy floor beneath the ocean, too cold and too heavy for anything to live. If I could make it through this, I thought, I could make it through anything.

Finally, thankfully, she left for a meeting with a lawyer. I fled to my room and immersed myself in cool, green silence until my heartbeat stopped hammering in my ears. Eventually the car purred back into the driveway. I ignored it, but then there were noises from the yard: a scrape and clatter.

When I reluctantly pushed the front door open, I found Mom kneeling in the mud in her nice faculty interview slacks in the middle of one of the garden beds, yanking long threads of quack grass and seedy dandelions from a matted tangle of some ground-hugging plant. Strings of black hair hung wet down her neck. The rain plastered her blouse to her back, water dripping from the tip of her nose, her forehead.

Maybe she wasn't crying. Maybe it was just the rain.

"Mom?" She didn't answer at first, just sniffed and wiped a hand across her face, leaving a streak of mud. I almost asked her if she was okay, but thought better of it. "What are you doing?"

"What does it look like?" She was crying. It left her voice

broken and gluey. A dandelion stalk snapped in her hand. She threw it to the ground. "We're going to have to sell this place now. I can't afford to pay for it by myself. So it has to be presentable."

"Mom, it's pouring, can't it wait until—"

"Until what?" she shouted, finally looking up at me through her dripping hair. "Until your father shows up to help?"

I stared back at her, frozen, still leaning against the open door. I stood my ground. I didn't back away.

"This place will take forever to sell." She snatched a dandelion digger from the path, renewing her attack. "The architect told us that when we were building it. He *warned* us. Three bedrooms in a place this size. And I said it didn't matter. I said we'd be here forever."

She sobbed once and stabbed the ground with the digger. Again, and again, and then she hit a rock and hurled the tool aside. It hit the side of the house with a bang, and she slumped over with her hands over her face. Crying like I'd never heard her cry, in noisy hacking sounds that echoed down the street.

I stepped gingerly over to her, put an arm around her shoulders, almost afraid to touch her. But she sagged into me, heavy and shaking, her forehead a weight on my shoulder. The rain prickled down around us, and the mud soaked slowly into my knees.

My phone was ringing when I finally managed to coax her back inside. The insistent chime echoed through the house as she disappeared down the hall, saying dully she was going to take a shower. Four, five, six times. Pause. And again.

I'd left it in the kitchen; it rang again as I trudged into the room. It kept ringing as I set the kettle on the stove to boil, fished the last few cookies from the cupboard, ate them mechanically. Finally I gave up and picked it up from the counter. I didn't recognize the number.

"Hello?"

"Marianne?"

Dad. For a long beat I didn't speak. My thoughts were a roaring blank.

"Marianne? Is that you, bunny?"

"Hi." I heard the word come out of my mouth. I had to say something.

"You weren't picking up. I thought if I kept calling... Is everything... How are you doing?"

I was talking to a stranger. My dad wouldn't have left us. He would have calmed Mom down, worked things out. Why did he still sound like my dad? His concern was warm as a hug.

"Fine." I took a deep breath, tried again. Was it going to be my job to tell him about the knife in Mom's hand? Would he use that against her? "Well. Not so good."

"I...I see." Dad's turn to pause. The silence stretched. A hiss of static skirled over the phone line. "Listen, we really need to talk. I need to tell you what's going on with me."

I didn't want to talk. I didn't want to know. Whatever he was trying to tell me, whatever I was going to have to accept, it loomed over me like a mountain, too heavy to carry, too huge to drown. I was choking on Mom's fury already. I couldn't do it. The phone crackled and whispered in my hand.

"Marianne?" His words faded in and out of the rising tide of white noise, like rocks in the river. "...there, bun? Listen, please, this doesn't change anyth...figure something...for coffee or..."

And after that—what? I might have closed my eyes. The rush of static on the phone washed over me between one breath and the next, an endless wave of sound, a vast, underwater gulf. Or was that part of the dream?

Because it's all I can remember after that. The dream. The sand cold between my bare toes. Stepping out of the shadow of the trees, silence smothering even the sound of my breath. The crescent of the beach stretched out to rocky points, barely visible. The faint orange glow of the city spilled over my shoulders, staining the ragged, pale boundary of a crust of ice. But out there, beyond the light, even that disappeared. There was no horizon. The surface stretching out before me was a cool breath on my face, an extension of the starless sky.

I couldn't look away from it. I couldn't stop walking. My feet carried me forward like they didn't belong to me. The water sliced into my feet, over my knees, panic climbing with it. Something pressed me forward, invisible hands forcing me down, irresistible as gravity. There was no fighting it, whatever it was—whoever it was. And if I couldn't break their grip I would drown. That's what they wanted. I knew it like I knew my heart was beating.

But it must have been a dream. When I woke up in bed it was morning, so I must have slept. When I opened my eyes in the faint gray light, Mom was sitting on the edge of my bed, hunched over, hands clasped between her knees, not looking at me.

"You should stay in your room for now, sweetie," she said hoarsely.

"Mom?" I pushed myself up on my elbow, blinking, trying to figure out what she was talking about.

"Just—please!" I recoiled from her sudden shout. She put her hands over her face, and then after a moment spoke through them. "Please listen, Marianne. I need you to stay in your room. Okay? Until I come and get you."

"Okay," I whispered. She pushed herself to her feet and left the room without ever meeting my eyes, closing the door with exaggerated care behind her. Maybe I should have gone after her, tried to help, offered a hug. But as I sat up I realized I was still dressed under the covers. When I swung my feet to the ground I found them bare, just like in the dream: no socks to hide the calluses scabbing my toes, the lizard-scale patches where the skin had blistered away and healed and blistered again under the friction of pointe shoes. My jeans were stiff and gray with mud from kneeling next to Mom in the garden while she sobbed. And my hair spilled loose over my shoulders. It's just like Mom's, long and stick-straight and easily tangled, so I always braid it at night. I'd left it that way all day. Hadn't I?

Even now, hours later, I'm trying to think back to last night for an explanation and there's nothing there; the silence and the water have engulfed the whole evening, like a sinkhole. Did I go to bed that early? Without changing out of my mud-caked jeans? Why can't I remember?

But the questions only lead me back to the dream, to the weight of the water, the pit of the sky. Of the feelings that bubble up through the icy lake, it's not bewilderment or hurt or worry that stay with me. It's dread. I don't want to know what happened. I'm afraid to think about it for very long, but it hangs over me anyway.

Like the silence did, in my dream. Like the dark.

3

GETTING TO SCHOOL FROM AUNT Jen's just means another transfer. I'm still stuck taking the 66 Special—the 666 Special, as it's aptly known. I wedge myself into a seat next to somebody's backpack. They don't bother to move it. Last day before exams means all the idiots are in high spirits, talking about how awesome this weekend's party is going to be and how drunk they're going to get. I can usually absorb their braying without a ripple, but this morning I'm all jagged pieces inside, sharp edges grinding against each other.

I'm lucky, I suppose; I'm invisible. Like magic, light bends around me, and I vanish into the seats. Mom jeans and high-necked, long-sleeved shirts are too boring for them to bother with. And it's amazing what comes out of their mouths when they don't notice you're there, when they don't think anyone important is there to judge. What they'll admit to really thinking, the golden girls and boys, the ones who get handed the community service awards, the ones who volunteer to help with the special ed classes. I hear everything that's really going on. The stuff they won't even put on Snapchat.

When Luke Schafer and Farrell Melnik got suspended, after the solemn assembly where the principal told us we would all be taking half-day workshops about tolerance and online bullying, the bus ride home explained everything. They went on about it for days, in the hushed, serious, delighted tones they reserve for the juiciest stories. It was Jeremy who told, they said. You'd think he was some whiny little ninth grader instead of a senior. But it only made sense, others argued, since he was one of those special snowflakes in the so-called gay–straight alliance. Why did they have to be so in-your-face anyway, it was like nobody was allowed to have an opinion anymore. That was Jeremy all over, he took everything so *seriously*. No sense of humor. It's not like they actually would have hurt him or anything, they protested, and why did they have to share a locker room with him anyway; it wasn't like they'd let guys use the same changing room as girls. And guys like that, what they were into? That was just gross. No offense or anything.

Another year stuck in a box with these losers. It's like a life sentence.

I wrap myself in icy water and swim through the day until

there's only one period left to get through. Math. Miss Kendrick is new this year, so I guess she still feels obligated to give preexam algebra review her best shot, even though her smile has been looking brighter and more fixed for the last few months. I'm stuck sitting right in front of Luke—youth group counselor, a regular at leadership camp—and his lieutenants.

They're models of boys-will-be-boys charm for the teachers they know they have to toe the line with, but they've long since left off even pretending to listen to Miss Kendrick. They lounge in the back of the class, texting each other and sniggering. Besides me, the only person in the room who's not talking is Rhiannon, a few rows over, sprawled over her desk with her chin on her hand, staring out the window. The gray light glints from the spiky collar around her neck and the strings of silver jewelry layered over her black clothes.

Miss Kendrick hasn't called on Rhiannon since that one time she put up her hand to point out a mistake in a question on a test, so of course I'm the one who gets summoned to the blackboard to solve a sample equation. I scrape my way out of my chair as slowly as possible. Josh Nguyen splutters with laughter as I walk by. I try to think of sunlight sifting through cold, still water. And of math. But there's a roaring in my ears, and my fingers are numb when I pick up the chalk. I stare at the equation on the board, willing it to make sense, trying to marshal some focus.

Another smothered burst of snickering erupts behind me, arrows landing between my shoulder blades. I make the mistake of twisting around to look over my shoulder. Farrell is doubled over his desk, laughing helplessly. Luke finishes saying something, smirking, and then looks up. Catches my eye. Winks.

I turn back to the board, lift the chalk. Calm down. They're not talking about me. They never are. I close my eyes, trying to quiet the moths jumping to life in my chest. Ice. I am ice, set adrift. I'm sinking out of reach. I'm breathing water.

Breathe in. Breathe out. It fills my head, a muffled roaring silence. The inside of a seashell. The blood in my ears.

And when I open my eyes the room is dark.

I blink, scrub the back of my hand across my eyes. But the light doesn't return. My arm is pale against the chalkboard. The classroom door stands ajar into darkness. The window admits a hazy orange glow.

Streetlights.

And Miss Kendrick's desk is empty.

All the desks are empty.

The seashell roar fills my ears, the only sound, even when the chalk slips from my fingers. I press the heels of my hands to my eyes, take a stumbling step back. The metal ledge of the chalkboard jabs into my back.

"Marianne!"

Miss Kendrick's voice snaps me back to daylight. To reality. I stagger, put a hand out to clutch the cool metal of the chalk tray. Something crunches and rolls under my shoe, almost overbalances me: the chalk is scattered in broken pieces over the floor, not just the one I dropped but a whole assortment of white and yellow and rose, spinning away from my feet in all directions. The tray is empty. Like someone tipped all its contents onto the ground.

And a hush has fallen over the classroom. In one sudden stroke, I'm no longer invisible; everyone is staring at me.

"A simple 'I don't know' would have been plenty," Miss Kendrick huffs. She looks betrayed. Like she might cry. "That really wasn't necessary. For the last time, take your seat."

All the questions are impossible. What just happened? What did I do?

"Take your seat!" Miss Kendrick repeats with a shrill. I duck my head and scurry back to my desk. She declares the rest of the class to be dedicated to pages 215 to 230 in the textbook and stalks from the room, closing the door with a bang behind her. I sit motionless as the class comes back to life around me, a flurry of murmurs and giggles and speculative, incredulous glances cast my way. Every now and again even Rhiannon is looking at me sidelong, her black-lined eyes wide.

Aunt Jen doesn't get around to offering dinner until late, but I'm not hungry anyway. The rain starts again, on the edge of hearing, as the light seeps from the room. I wish there was somewhere I could go, a new book to disappear into, some way to shake off the circles I keep pacing through in my head: all those weird little mysteries, the chalk, the mirror, the missing evening, the dream. Are they related somehow? How could they be? The questions cinch tight around me, numbing my hands, stealing my breath. I have to calm down. I have to stop thinking about it.

I don't want to know.

The computer screen offers no answers, no relief. Downstairs, Aunt Jen launches into something languid and dreamy on the piano.

My breath catches at the chirp of a new notification. And yes, there's *Ingrid Snow* in the corner of the screen. Finally. She's tagged me in something. A Harry Potter joke about Ravenclaws—my house, we decided. She's a Hufflepuff through and through. Her comment says: Miss you! :)

Miss you. A shock wave travels through the icy lake. I wait it out, measuring every breath. It's ridiculous, that lurch of…of whatever that is. I won't let it trick me into getting clingy. Those two words are the sort of thing you'd say to anybody. They don't mean anything.

Except that she's online.

I scramble for my phone, type out a text.

hey

Hey! How's it going??

ugh not so good

:(

how's sf

OMG it's amazing. Our house has an ocean view!!

> pix?
>
> Posted on insta!

There's a long pause; like so many times before I sit with my fingers poised over the phone. Is this weird? Is this TMI?

> so my parents are splitting up
>
> OMG!! That is horrible! Are you ok?
>
> not really
>
> :(:(
>
> dad took off and mom is freaking out.
>
> staying w my aunt.

I decide I don't care how it sounds.

> can you call me?? just need someone to talk to.
>
> things have been really weird.

But her message pops onto the screen at the same time as mine.

> Listen I have to go, going out for dinner.
>
> Call you later tonight tho OK??

It lands like a punch, scattering all those moths back into flight. I shouldn't have said anything. She thinks I'm a freak. I try to tell myself that it's not a brush-off, that she must have been typing at the same time, that she can't drop everything just for me. It doesn't help. I could cry.

ok sure

In desperation, I scroll through Ingrid's Instagram feed. I'm looking for her house pictures, but the first set she's posted looks like selfies. Ingrid wants to be an actress someday, and she totally will be. What better career could there be for a chameleon? And she's got the looks for it, the style, the perfect burnished blond curls.

It's always kind of amazed me that she even spoke to me. I don't really know how it happened. We were in a science camp together last summer. I'd heard she'd be going to Pearson too, that her family moved around a lot, but that was about it. I'd kept myself submerged in books during breaks, the twistiest, most intricate, most absorbing fantasies I could find. It was safer and easier than talking to people. But suddenly Ingrid was sunnily asking what I was reading, insisting I *had* to check out this amazing thing she'd read about a girl who discovers she's part dragon, inviting me to eat lunch with her. It was like she'd just decided I was her friend. That's what she does, and I accepted it, bemused and grateful. No one could resist her.

A few photos in, she's not alone in the pictures anymore. Another girl is mugging for the camera with her. I flip past pictures of them pouting, laughing, making stupid grimaces, their faces pressed close together to fit into the frame.

No wonder I haven't heard from her. She's forgotten all about me. I try to shake off the thought—what am I now, her jilted girlfriend?—but it clings to me and won't be dismissed. Pathetically, I tap the photos to "like" them. Every one.

And then: *ping!* New email. From my dad. "What's going on" is the subject. Great. Like I want to know. I hug my pillow close like a shield and open it.

> Hi Bunny,
>
> There was a lot of static on the phone when I called yesterday, and I wasn't sure if you could hear me. I haven't been able to reach you since.
>
> Anyway, I just wanted you to know that I'm still your dad and I love you. Nothing will ever change that, no matter what happens between me and your mom.
>
> We were really young when we got married, and I don't think either of us knew what we really wanted. I'm still trying to process everything, but the one thing I know for sure is that I need to give us all the chance to be truly happy.
>
> I'm sure you have a lot of questions. Please, please call me so we can talk.
>
> > Love,
> > Dad

I stare at the Delete button, listening to my rattling breath. I don't touch it. Instead I look back through the message, scrolling up and down. Words jump out at me again and again, like stones clattering down a well. Truly happy. Seriously? Could he be any more clueless?

I set the phone carefully down on the nightstand. I don't care. I am glacial, bottomless. But my gaze jumps from the quilt-draped mirror to the suitcase by the bed, and they propel me to my feet, down the stairs.

Aunt Jen glances up from the piano keys as I come into the living room, smiles at me, goes on playing. Mom used to play piano too, once upon a time. She used to tell me about it whenever she was after me to stretch or practice, how she'd given it up because she knew she'd never play as well as her sister, how she'd regretted it ever since. But whenever Jen urges her to take it up again, she always demurs with a self-conscious smile. It's too late, she always says. Too late for her to be any good.

I slide onto the bench next to my aunt as she leans into the music. I remember this piece, though I don't know its name. It's warm and sweet and sad, designed to draw tears. I swallow and resist it. I'm underwater, where there's no sound.

"That was nice," I manage when Aunt Jen finally glides to a stop, because I feel like I should say something. "What was it?"

"Beethoven. Sonata Pathetique." She peers at me. "Are you all right?"

"Fine," I say. "I'm fine. I'm... I think I'm going to go for a walk."

She hesitates a long moment, as if trying to find a reason to say no.

"I just need to think." I need to not think.

"Well, okay, I guess. Don't be too long."

Outside the air hangs thick and wet, somewhere between mist and rain. Tree branches slice the streetlight's glow into long, soft bars. Not a breath of wind. At first I think the noise suffusing the night is traffic, maybe from the busy street at the top of the hill; but it's the river, a far-off, full-throated, rain-swollen voice. I glance toward the seawall. Beyond it there's only a twinkling line of lights scattered across the far side of the water to interrupt the dark.

I jam my hands into my coat pockets and turn away without really picking a direction, striding down the closest street, past a few stately houses and a row of towering brick town homes. The street-lights stretch out ahead of me in a string of floating orange globes, the occasional porch light casting a dim, foggy halo. My footsteps, ghostly on the asphalt, are dwarfed by the rush of the water.

The formless churning in my head pushes me forward, past the pine trees towering over the entrance to the park, from one island of orange light to the next. The park's broad lawn is studded with them, buoys in a dark sea, turning the trees into long witchy shadows, mark-ing the path that winds past the beach.

Dread rises up around me, colder than the fog, nagging at

me. Trying to remind me of something I don't want to remember. Something awful and familiar.

I walk faster to outpace it. I refuse to freak myself out. Am I afraid of the dark now? I have to calm down. But the fear creeps over me anyway. Like the realization that you're cold. Like water stealing past your knees. I try to focus on my breath, like they taught us in yoga, listening to it as it rasps in and out—and in—and—why can't I hear it anymore?

Why can't I hear anything?

Even when it's quiet, there should still be sound: the slap of my feet against the pavement, the rasp of fabric as my jacket sleeve brushes my side, the whisper of my jeans. But it's all gone. All that remains is an unceasing, oddly muted roar. The rush of the river presses close against me, stuffing my ears.

And I'm still walking. Turning off the path.

Stepping between the trees, onto the sand.

No. It should be a whimper. I feel the breath leave my lips. But there's no sound. There's nothing. Panic screams through my head: something has changed, some fundamentally stable, unmovable thing has slipped off its foundations. It was a dream, that dark, silent beach. Am I dreaming now?

My feet aren't mine. They drag me forward. Fighting them, I slip and shamble, kicking sand. But still, I lurch onward. It's as irresistible as falling. And the water looms out of the blank, orange-tinged wall of fog: glassy, silent, fringed with a distant crust of ice.

Ice.

It's June.

When my feet meet the water they don't splash. My steps are soundless. Water soaks into my shoes, seeps up through my jeans. The world is a shoulder leaning into my back, unseen hands pushing me forward into the dark. I can't stop.

I finally manage to fling myself backward, sit down hard in an inch of water, dig my fingers into the sand. All I can think to do is get away, get back to safety, a block and a half behind me. A world away. I creep back up the beach on my hands and knees, away from the water, inch by inch. It's like leaning into a strong wind, though the air is heavy and still. Like climbing a cliff face.

And then, as suddenly as it started, it passes, the seashell roar draining from my ears. The sound of the river recedes to its proper dimension, waves rushing up onto the beach behind me, and ordinary small noises rise up around me again: the passage of a car on the next street, a door slamming. I collapse, gasping, on the sand. I can hardly see. Beyond the beach, the park is swathed in darkness, the trees that line the path dim silhouettes against the orange-lit clouds. Where have the streetlights gone?

The first time I try to get up I almost fall, leaning against resistance that's no longer there. And the second time I push myself into a run. The street is a dark corridor, the houses barely visible except for their rooflines against the sky. At its end, the pale twin stars of the lights on Aunt Jen's building beckon me back toward normalcy.

I half fall through the patio door, pull it closed, lean against it. Aunt Jen, sitting in the armchair in the corner, looks up from her crocheting in surprise.

"That was quick," she says. "I wasn't *that* worried, Mare-bear, you didn't have to—"

"Marianne," I correct her automatically, but my voice is shaky, barely there, and she talks over me, frowning as she takes in my soaking jeans, the look on my face.

"Good heavens, Mare-bear, look at you. Are you okay? What happened?"

"It's Marianne. Please." The dread comes trickling back through my relief, gathering in pools. Another thing I can't explain. Add it to the list. What's happening to me? "I-I fell. That's all."

She looks doubtful, but doesn't question me further. I decline her offer of tea—Aunt Jen's answer to everything—and hurry up the stairs. In the room that's not mine, I leave my clothes in a sodden heap, yank on pajamas, and pull a dry pair of fuzzy socks on, hiding the knobby callused joints with the little toes bent too far in. Hardworking feet, Mom used to call them. More like monster feet. The ugly truth under the pretty slippers.

I check my phone, but Ingrid hasn't called; I turn the volume to max and set it down again. I can't bring myself to turn off the bedside light. I turn away from the quilt-shrouded dresser, pull the blanket up around my ears. I stare at my shadow on the wall, my thoughts reeling in dizzy circles, a nightmare merry-go-round of half-formed questions.

Aunt Jen, singing off-key in the kitchen, wakes me up the next morning. The fear has burned itself out for now, leaving my head thick with ashy exhaustion and my whole body sore. My joints crack in protest as I point and flex my feet, rotate my ankles.

I redo my braid and pull a fleece sweater on over my T-shirt. It's ridiculous to still be wearing a sweater at the end of June, but the rain hasn't stopped, and the damp chill has settled into me, a heavy stiffness I can't shake.

I stretch my arms over my head and sink down into a side split, then flatten myself onto the ground, my nose against the cold floor, my fingers colliding with the edge of the dresser. The stretches are the one thing I've kept. I tried to leave them behind with the pointe shoes and the mirrored walls, but after a few days without them my body was a coat of armor weighing me down.

I close my eyes. Hesitantly, like I'm feeling for a wound, I think back over last night's walk.

Was I dreaming? Again?

I can't have been. The clothes I wore are still sitting in a heap near the door.

I nudge them with one foot on my way out of the room; icy wetness seeps through to my toes. I dump the clothes into the laundry basket and throw a towel on top so I won't have to look at them again.

"Marianne," Aunt Jen calls from downstairs. "Breakfast!"

"Coming." I sound almost normal. I *feel* almost normal. The bare spaces among the pictures on the wall stare down at me. The smell of bacon cooking drifts up the stairs from the kitchen. Whatever it was that dragged me toward the water—if it was even real—it must be gone.

Right?

I've always loved Aunt Jen's kitchen. Between the butter yellow walls, the white cupboards with leafy vines trailing over their tops, the comfortable mishmash of cookbooks, it's impossible not to feel like the day is promising sunshine, despite the leaden sky in the window. When Aunt Jen smiles at me, I manage a real one in return.

The sound of construction drifts in from out front as I slide into a seat at the table: the grumbling of an engine, the shrill beep of something backing up. Beyond the hedge, some huge yellow vehicle lumbers by.

"Are they working on the road?"

Aunt Jen doesn't hear me at first; she's still humming as she scoops the bacon out of a frying pan. I have to ask again.

"Hm? Oh, no, actually. Kind of strange. You know the street right out front, that goes down to the park? Ellen, from across the hall, she says they're working on the streetlights all along there."

I put my fork down.

"Right out front?"

"Yep. She always walks PJ right at the crack of dawn, and she says all the lights are blown right out. Glass all over the road. She called the city right away. Pretty impressive they got to it so fast."

Are we talking about the same street? Outside, a worker on a little platform is being lifted at the end of a long mechanical arm. I think of the rooflines looming black against the sky.

"Just on that street?" I ask. The words are tinny in my ears.

"In the park too, I guess. Weird, isn't it?"

Weird. I stare out the window, testing the idea that this didn't have something to do with whatever happened to me last night, finding that it doesn't bear weight.

"Maybe it was some kind of electrical problem. A power surge or something."

I nod, a puppet on strings. The chasm opens, momentarily, deep and wide under my feet. What am I forgetting? What belongs in that strange, dark blank where I can summon only a shadow of a dream?

What happened?

4

THE SCHOOL HALLS FEEL EVEN more dismal than usual with the downpour rattling against the windows. It's weird to be here so unencumbered. I've already returned my textbooks, so all I need is my pencil case and a water bottle. I meant to put the bottle in the freezer last night so it would stay cold all morning, but it doesn't matter. There's one exam today; just three hours. I scuff my way through the English wing toward the gym, willing my apprehension away. It's chemistry. Beyond mundane. Safe.

Rhiannon is rummaging for something in her locker. She's dressed in her customary black, her hair an improbable, spiky halo. It's black as well, fading to fire-engine red at the tips. "It's like she *wants* people to stare at her," Ingrid muttered once. And Ingrid never talks about people behind their backs.

My footsteps slow as I draw closer, and I find myself drifting to a stop across the hall from her. Nobody knows much about her, except for her grudging responses to Mr. Williams's stupid icebreaker interview at the beginning of the year. She said her mom's a psychic. Luke and Farrell and their lackeys had a field day with that for a while.

I wonder if she was making it up. I wonder if she could tell me what's going on. I wonder if there's a universe where I have the guts to talk to her.

They dubbed her "Emo Rhiannon" when she first showed up at the beginning of the year. A genuine goth at Pearson! What was she pretending to be, some kind of satanist? Maybe she'd gotten kicked out of her old school for sacrificing small animals. They tracked her hair color in gleeful indignation as it shifted from pink to green to purple. And what did she think she was doing with her makeup? So many fashion crimes to dissect!

But one lunch hour, back in October, Farrell came bolting past me down the hall, looking half pleased with himself and half terrified, and after him came Rhiannon, running like a machine, her hands knifing through the air at her sides, her black lace skirt flying behind her. And when she caught up with him she *launched* herself at him, catching him with her shoulder and slamming him into the lockers with a bang that got the whole hall's attention. He hit the floor with a squawk and before he could get up, she slung herself over his chest and straddled him with her fist cocked.

"I'm sorry!" Farrell bleated. Not laughing anymore. "What the *hell*, it was just a—"

"Don't touch me!" Rhiannon shouted over him. "Don't you ever touch me again!"

By that time the teachers had caught up and Mr. Ellis was pulling her away, a little gingerly, and when she shook him off and stalked back down the hall, he didn't pursue her. Instead it was Farrell who got hauled off to the principal's office. Farrell tried to grumble about the unfairness of it all, but that only won him laughing jibes about how he'd gotten served by a girl, so after some obligatory snide remarks about how gigantic she was, he shut right up about it.

Nobody bothers Rhiannon anymore.

She snaps her lock closed and looks around at me. Catches me watching her. I clutch my stuff to my chest. Now or never. I have to say something, anyway, or she'll think… I don't know what she'll think.

"How do you get your hair to stay like that?" I stammer.

"Egg whites." She's not nearly as foreboding when she smiles. I return it, just a little. "Seriously. You could probably use them to spike your hair, even."

Small talk concluded, she turns to go, and I blurt out, "Rhiannon?"

She makes a face at me.

"Ugh. Nobody calls me that. It's just Ron."

"Ron," I repeat, startled.

Her eyebrows go up. "What, is that not girly enough or something?"

"No, no, of course not! I didn't mean… It's just so…plain. And you're…" I didn't think this through. I flounder for an adjective while she cocks her head, waiting. "I don't know. Fancy. I guess."

And now I'm blushing. God. This is what I get for opening my mouth. She looks at me sideways, like she's trying to decide what to make of me.

"Well. Okay. That's a new one."

I twist the water bottle in my hands, making the plastic crinkle. "Listen. Can I…ask you kind of a weird question?"

Her expression turns guarded. "You can ask." Her tone isn't inviting.

I hunch my shoulders, quailing inside. No. No, I can't. I don't even know her. This is the stupidest idea I've ever had. I should just make an excuse and leave before I say something I can't take back. But the words well up anyway.

"I was hoping… I mean, since your mom's…you know…you said your mom is psychic, right?"

She folds her arms.

"That's what she calls it."

Too late to back out now. "It's just that…there's been something kind of strange going on with me lately. And I was hoping I could maybe…go see her or something. You know. Professionally."

"Professionally," she echoes. I close my eyes, actually tempted to turn and run, plunge myself into the icy lake and never resurface, never. But it's Rhiannon who breaks the long silence first.

"You know, I'd probably think you were fucking with me. But you don't go around with the kind of people who would put you up to it."

"I'm sorry. I shouldn't have—" I hate the quiver in my voice, but I can't swallow it. "I know people have been... I'm just...these things keep happening. Things I don't remember doing. Like with the chalk. I—what did I do?"

"What did you do?" She stares at me. "Are you serious?"

"I'm serious. I don't remember." I don't know how to explain those few seconds where the classroom stood dark and empty. "I was at the blackboard. And then all of a sudden Miss Kendrick was telling me something wasn't necessary. And the chalk was all over the floor."

"Wow," she says slowly. "Okay. Well. For a minute you just stood there. Miss Kendrick tried to, you know, kind of prod you along. Get you started. And you just...looked at her. She told you to sit down, but you didn't. You held up the chalk, really slowly, and you broke it"—she mimes snapping it in half—"and dropped it on the floor. And then you picked up another one and broke that too. You went through every piece on the tray, and you were staring at her the whole time. It was a little freaky, actually. You seriously don't remember this?"

I shake my head. "There's...other stuff too. I broke a mirror. Threw something at it. I must have, there was no one else there. How could I throw something without knowing it?"

She studies me, her face unreadable, a mask of black lipstick and swirling eyeliner. I'm sure she's about to back away, or make some excuse, but instead when she moves it's to take a step closer.

"Listen." She puts a hand on my arm before I can draw back, startling me into meeting her gaze. Her eyes are the color of black coffee, dark and warm, her voice quiet but earnest. "Here's my totally unsolicited advice. You don't want to see my mom. Save yourself eighty bucks and go to a real doctor. Honestly. I mean, what if something's really wrong?"

I nod automatically, my throat closing. Right. That's probably the reasonable thing to say when someone tells you something like this. The sane answer. What was I expecting? For her to name the current of fear that's been rising in my mind, fear that there's more to it than that?

"Yeah," I manage faintly as she drops her hand again. I resist the urge to put my hand to the spot where the pressure of her touch still lingers. "Thanks."

"Take it for what it's worth." She heads off down the hall, sparing me a last worried look over her shoulder. "Good luck, okay?"

I stand there watching her go, fragments of the conversation replaying in my mind all out of order, a tangle of barbs sharp enough to cut. I can't believe I did that. Talk about desperate. I feel sick. Exposed.

I feel *visible*.

Whatever. It doesn't matter. I have to keep it together for two weeks, that's all, and then the holidays will be here. By the time school starts again she probably won't even remember me. I close my eyes, drawing the hiss of the rain on the windows around me like a blanket, trying to summon indifference, a surface cold and smooth.

Bang! Bang!

I jump but can't identify the rapid succession of noises until— *bang!*—the door to the classroom across the hall slams shut. I twist around, not sure what I expect to see, but the hallway is empty. There's no other sound, although down the hall Mrs. Ahmadi opens her door to lean out, frowning.

It's almost 9:00 a.m. I force my feet into motion again. Calm down, calm down. Maybe the windows were open; maybe they all caught the same gust of wind. There's nothing unusual about doors closing. But the water bottle hits my thigh with a heavy, painful thump as I swing my hand. I pause to frown at it.

It's full of ice.

The exam passes in a blur. Chemistry should be tidy, soothing. It's like math: absolutes, right and wrong answers. No room for worry. But today my hands are cold and shaking, my heartbeat an urgent throb. I close my eyes and try to sit still, but after my dream springing up around me on the beach, after looking out at that dim fringe of ice in the dark, I can't bring myself to call up the water to wash away the fear. It coils around my chest, around my throat, and squeezes. The formulas I knew so well last week scatter like gleaming fish. Equations that should fall into neat balance end in tangles that make no sense, and I

have to go back to redo them. The hands of the clock sweep merci-
lessly forward, and panic tightens its grip. I'm losing time. I can't do it.

I do finish in the end, but barely. I spend a long time fussing
with my pencil case, letting everyone else stream out of the gym before
me, trying to soothe the screaming in my head. They're not looking at
me. They're not. I'm invisible. I'm underwater. By the time I get on
the bus I'm calmer, but I'm still drained and rattled. Jittery. Like I've
spent the morning fighting with someone.

What if something's really wrong? She's right. Of course she's
right. I have to tell my aunt. Or my dad. That's the rational thing
to do; that's what I should have done right away. It's chemical, or
medical, or something. That's the only explanation that makes sense.

I pause with my hand on the gate in the hedge and look back
over my shoulder, down the street that leads to the park. It's empty,
the wind ruffling the surface of the wide puddles filling the ditches on
either side. The road crews are gone. Whatever happened last night,
the broken streetlights weren't just in my head. Unless I imagined the
conversation with Aunt Jen this morning too. Unless I imagined the
yellow trucks outside the window.

It's like the emptiness of that missing night is spilling out into
the rest of my life, leaving everything murky and suspect, leaving me
floundering. Like the dark water slipping over my knees.

I won't pursue that thought any further. I'm not my mother. I
will stay cold and rational. I won't panic. I fumble for the latch on the
gate, push through it.

Aunt Jen won't be home until this evening. I roam the internet for a while, but the connection is twitchy, hanging annoyingly on a loading screen every few clicks. The sound of the rain on the roof fills the house. I keep unlocking my phone, but of course there's nothing there from Ingrid, and that message to her has only gotten harder to write. The furthest I get is a sentence, but after letting the phone go dark three times while I hesitate over what to say next, I end up deleting it.

No voicemail either. My heart jumps when the phone twitches to announce a text, but it's from my dad.

Did you get my email? Please call.

One line. Like a little punch to the stomach. *Please call.* And say what?

I'm still staring at it when the phone buzzes again in my hand. *Mom,* says the caller ID.

I have to answer it, but swiping the green bar to accept the call feels like picking up a grenade with a missing pin.

"Mom?"

"Hi, sweetie." I can still hear the tears in her voice. Not outright, but not far from the surface. I swallow. In the background there's a faint pop and hiss, like an old record playing. "How was your exam?"

"Fine." It's the only possible answer, but the truth settles across my shoulders, weighing me down. "Where are you?"

"I just got home."

From where? "Does that mean I can come home too?"

There's a long silence.

"Not…not just yet, okay?"

"But—"

"Sweetie, you have to understand. I went to the hospital." With an effort I can hear, she adds, "I was seeing things, Marianne."

I don't say anything. The silence whispers between us. Seeing things. I've made it through Hurricane Laura before, but this… I don't have a name for this.

And yet an awful recognition is stealing over me. Was I seeing things last night, on the beach? *What if something's really wrong?*

"I didn't know what to do. I was afraid I would hurt you." Her voice breaks. "You're my whole world. You're all I've got now. I was afraid I would hurt you."

"Mom, listen," I begin, but she forges on.

"So. I went to the hospital. And they kept me overnight, and they gave me some medicine to take, and I'm supposed to go see this therapist today." Good. Is it too much to hope that if she has someone else to talk to about it, I won't have to stand in the howling gale of her grief anymore? "I'm okay now, so far. I think I'm okay. But I can't risk having you here until I know for sure that it's working. I can't." A pause. "Marianne? Are you okay, sweetie?"

It's a long moment before I can answer, and I'm fighting to keep my own voice steady.

"I really want to come home."

"I know. Just a few more days. I have to be sure. Please."

"Mom?" I don't want to know. I have to ask. "What did you see?"

"I…I really don't want to talk about it. It doesn't matter."

I clutch the phone in silence. It matters to me, I want to tell her. I'm afraid I'm the one who's seeing things. I'm even more afraid that it's neither of us. That something really happened. That it's still happening.

"I should go. My appointment's in half an hour, and I want to make sure I don't get lost." I laugh dutifully. "I love you. So, so much."

"Love you too."

"Tell Jen to call me, okay? When she gets home."

"Sure."

"And, Marianne—" Mom's voice wavers, almost disappears. When she continues I can barely hear her. "Ask your aunt about it. If you really want to know."

When Aunt Jen finally shoulders through the front door with an armload of grocery bags, I'm coiled tense as a spring in a corner of the couch, waiting for her.

"Don't worry about that," she protests as I take one of the bags, "I've got it. Really. How was—"

"Mom called," I interrupt. Aunt Jen's smile slips.

"Oh," she says cautiously, setting the groceries down. I clench my fists around the plastic handles.

"She was in the hospital." I won't yell. I won't betray a ripple. "Why didn't you tell me?"

"I thought you knew, Mare-bear." I'm not sure I believe her. "She didn't tell you?"

"No. She wouldn't tell me what happened, even on the phone. She said to ask you."

"Well…are you sure you want to know? It's okay if you don't."

When I nod she sighs, takes the bag from me to put it with the rest, and leads me to sit down on the couch. She spends a long moment looking away, as if searching for a place to begin.

"Well. On Wednesday, she had that meeting with her lawyer. You know. This thing with your dad…it's going to cost an awful lot of money, and it's going to be pretty ugly. She was upset."

That's one word for it, I guess. I wonder if she told Aunt Jen about ripping the painting. I wonder if Dad's seen it yet, the long gash in the canvas.

"She said when she got out of the shower she couldn't find you at first. You were on the terrace. On the roof. You had kind of a discussion about things." She glances at me, watching for my reaction, and I nudge the coffee table with my toes, trying to keep my bewilderment from showing. I don't remember a conversation on the roof. Shouldn't I remember that? "She said that it got very dark and that you were floating. In thin air, over the garden."

When I don't answer she says, very gently, "You see why she went to the hospital, don't you?"

But if it wasn't real—it's on the tip of my tongue to say it—why don't I remember what really happened? What about the streetlights? If I close my eyes I can almost feel the cool black water from my dream stretching out in front of me, the silence roaring in my ears. I lean into Aunt Jen, afraid the world will slip out from underneath me again, afraid to find myself back there, stumbling helplessly forward in the grip of something I can't see.

"Are you okay, Mare-bear?" I nod, not looking at her. "This seems like a lot to burden you with. You know it isn't your fault, right? This isn't the first time your mom's had trouble. She's always been sensitive, and when you were born, she…well, she had a really rough time for a while. Right after your grandmother died."

"I know, I know." She was afraid to let me out of her sight, even for the night; crying all the time, not sleeping, barely eating. They ended up admitting her for a couple of weeks. "Hurricane Laura."

"Now that's unkind." Aunt Jen frowns at me. "Would she call you that? If it was you?"

"I just—" The words come out high; I have to stop and swallow them, change tack. "I don't understand how he could just leave me alone with her. He knew she'd blow up like this. He *knew* it."

Aunt Jen shakes her head.

"I think you have to ask your dad about that one. But this is not your fault. He did not leave because of you." When I don't respond, she cups my face in her hands, waits until I meet her eyes. The lily-of-the-valley smell of her hand lotion wafts around me.

"Seriously. You didn't do anything wrong. File that under G. For garbage. Okay?"

"Yeah." But there's still the chalk. There's still the mirror. The streetlights. It's like pieces of a dream. What's happening to me, what's happened to Mom—I know they're connected, it's a certainty I can't shake, visceral as nausea. But like a dream it makes no sense when I try to string it together in my mind. I don't understand.

"Have you talked to your dad yet?" The question is gentle. Cautious. "He said he'd been trying to reach you." I set my jaw and pull away, shaking my head.

"Well. That's fine. You decide when you're ready. But we've been talking, and we were thinking it…might be a good idea for you to be seeing someone. Your dad said he's been asking around. He's got a referral for you."

I sink forward a little, wishing I'd left my hair loose so it would hide my face. That's the opening I needed, a step taken for me already. I don't even have to say anything to my aunt. Not yet. But the dread flutters against my ribs, cramping my breath. Whatever's happening to me, I've made it real, somehow, by talking about it. Like it's pulling me forward, more implacable than any current. Out of control.

"There's nothing wrong with it. Really. It'd give you, you know, a neutral third party. To help you get through all this."

"It's not that big a deal," I mutter. I need to be alone. I need to calm down.

"It hurts to see you trying to deal with this all by yourself, Mare-bear. Won't you give it a try? Just to see?"

A shrug is all I can manage in response to that, but it seems to be enough.

"Come give me a hand with the groceries," she says, squeezing my shoulder. "I don't know about you, but I'm famished."

There's one bright spot in my evening, at least. The next time I poke at my phone, two notifications are waiting for me. Not from Ingrid, though.

Rhiannon Alexander followed you

Found you! 💀 Hang in there ok??

She looked me up.

She saw me.

Her feed is a stew of snarky memes, steampunk costumes, makeup tutorials, and arguments about *Dr. Who*. And selfies, dramatically posed. Filtered so her lips shine in vivid technicolor, parted in a pout or a snarl.

I hit "like" on the mention after a long hesitation and sit there for a while, clutching the phone close to my chest. Clinging to a gleam of hope.

Still, I go to bed with the light on again, chasing my thoughts in endless spirals, listening to the shushing of the rain. It's falling like it will never stop.

5

DR. FORTIN IS A TALL, spare man with dark skin, a neatly trimmed beard, and close-cropped, tightly curled black hair peppered with gray. His smile is wide and even, his grip firm and warm when he shakes my hand.

The office, at the top of a teetering, narrow staircase, is surprisingly inviting. The floorboards are creaky wooden planks the color of honey, and stained glass glows in the highest panes of a bank of windows. Everything else is white, from the moldings that border the high ceiling to the plushy rug in the middle of the room, where a couch and two armchairs sit in a cozy circle.

"Have a seat," Dr. Fortin suggests.

"On the couch?" How's that for a cliché.

"Wherever you're comfortable."

He settles into one of the armchairs; the couch is farthest away. I sink into the corner of it and pull my feet up into a defensive half curl, folding and refolding my hands in my lap. On the mantle of an old fireplace is a collection of cards and two framed paintings. One shows a girl huddled in a stark, coffin-like box too small for her, the background a wash of gray; the next shows the same girl flying through a rainbow sky, streamers of color falling like wings from her outstretched arms. Gifts from some grateful patient, I guess. Must be nice to be her, whoever she is. I wonder what secrets she had to spill to get there.

Dr. Fortin recites the ground rules, a practiced script: This is a safe space, he tells me, and what I say in here stays in here. He can't make me talk; he can't make me stay; he can't make me come back. He won't talk to my parents unless I ask him to. Or unless I say something to make him think I'm a danger to myself, or to someone else. I nod my way through it, studying my hands. His voice is warm, professional, a little hypnotic, with the faintest lilt of an accent. Like light shining through amber, dark gold, unhurried. He should be on the radio.

"So today," he finishes, "we're just going to start by talking about what's brought you here, okay? You got the questionnaire, right?"

I hand it to him, three pages that I pressed into a tight little square in the waiting room. I close my eyes and wait as he unfolds and unfolds them.

"So," he says after a moment, "you've checked a lot of boxes here."

Boxes like *nightmares*. *Gaps in memory*. *Intrusive thoughts*. *Auditory hallucinations*. I'd almost gone back and erased that last one, but what else was I going to call the terrible smothering roar that filled my ears in the park?

Dr. Fortin watches me, waiting. Say it, I tell myself. Come on.

"I think something might be wrong with me." The words come out a whisper.

His eyebrows go up, but all he says is "Why don't you tell me about that."

I stumble through the evidence. The missing night. The mirror I didn't break. My nightmare rising around me in the park, the sound I can't describe drowning out everything else. Rhiannon's story about what happened to the chalk. The water bottle I could swear I hadn't put in the freezer.

He sits back when I fall silent, tapping his pen against his lips. I breathe in; I breathe out.

"Thank you for trusting me with that," he says eventually. "It must have been very frightening."

I am not going to cry in front of a stranger. I turn away, leaning into my palm, and watch the fat crystal sun-catcher in the window twist gently back and forth.

"You're going through a huge amount of stress right now," he says. "Let's not minimize how hard that is. It's perfectly understandable that you'd be dealing with some anxiety and sleep disruptions.

This is an incredibly difficult time for your family. It's okay to be affected by that."

The sun-catcher gleams in the dull gray light, casts no rainbows. When I don't speak, he continues.

"I think what I'm most concerned about here is the missing time. That sounds to me like it might be neurological." He levels the pen at me, gives it an emphatic jab. "We need to get that checked out as soon as possible."

"Neurological?" I echo faintly.

"I don't want to speculate too much here. Not my specialty. But we definitely want to rule out something physical to make sure we don't miss something like a stroke or an aneurysm." He leans back. "So our first stop is probably a CAT scan. If that comes back clean, we'll try some medication and see if it gives you some relief."

"But you don't think anything happened?" I manage.

He cocks his head. "Like what?"

"Like…what my mom saw."

"Which was what, exactly?"

"Me. Floating in midair." The silence stretches. "I just thought… what if she's not…what if something weird really happened?"

"Let's look for the simple explanation first," he says firmly. "Right?"

"I guess."

"So you haven't told your parents about this. Or your aunt."

I shake my head.

"Why is that?"

"I don't know. How could I? With Mom and everything. They'd think… I don't know." I lean into the cushions. "I didn't want to be seeing things too."

"You must have been very worried."

I could wrap myself up in the warmth of his voice. It's almost like he cares. I'm not going to cry. I'm not going to meet his gaze.

"I can't stop thinking about it." I drag the words out one by one, forcing them into the light. "That dream I had. It's like it's always there waiting. I barely made it through my chemistry exam. I…haven't really been sleeping."

"And when you're thinking about that dream," Dr. Fortin prompts, "what does that feel like?"

"Like it's happening all over again." I smooth down the micros-uede fabric of the couch; my fingers leave a trail. "Like I'm drowning."

He makes a sympathetic noise. "I see. Have you ever felt like that before?"

"It…hasn't been this bad in a long time."

"When was the last time, then? When you quit dance, maybe?"

I do look up at him, at that, my heart stuttering.

"I gather that was a rough time for you," he says when I don't speak.

Right. They had Dad fill out one of those questionnaires too. I close my hands into fists around the cuffs of my sweater. That's not something I would have offered up for analysis.

"That was before."

"What brought it on then?"

"What's that got to do with anything?"

He blinks. "You don't want to talk about it."

I inhale carefully, moderate my tone. "I just don't see how it's relevant."

"I don't want to push you," he says gently, like I'm a kid balking at a needle. "I'm just trying to understand what's going on. Sometimes previous experiences can shine some light on that."

There's no reason for the tightness in my shoulders, my chest. I force myself to sit up straight. Be rational. Talk things out.

"I wanted to quit dance. Drop out of the conservatory." I speak to my hands, clasped whitely in my lap. "Mom wouldn't let me."

"What made you want to quit?"

"I don't know. I wasn't very good."

"The conservatory's pretty prestigious, isn't it?"

"So I wasn't good *enough*," I snap. "Do we have to talk about this? It was years ago!"

He raises his hands in surrender. "Okay," he says equably, "we don't have to." But he jots something down as he says it. My teeth are clenched. I have to relax.

"Let's talk about how you coped, then," he says. "How did you deal with these feelings? Is there anything there that might help you now?"

"There's...a yoga thing I learned in a class with Mom." He ought to like that.

"Oh?"

"Yeah. It helps me relax."

"Okay," he says, nodding, "that's a great start. Are you into yoga, then?"

"Not really. It was just the few classes with Mom."

"Maybe you could try it again. Since you found it helpful. Physical activity can be really important, it's a good way to kick your brain out of a spiral."

"Maybe."

"Do you find your appetite changes? When you get anxious?"

I nod after a moment. That seems like an innocent enough question.

"Try to make sure you're getting some protein in. Nice, balanced meals. I know it sounds obvious, but low blood sugar never helps anything. And you'll find it helps with the medication. It can be a little hard on the stomach."

Eat well and exercise? Seriously? But I nod again instead of saying anything.

"Well. Listen." He reaches for a notepad, scrawls something across it. "I'm going to give you this. Something to put the brakes on the ruminant thoughts. You know, the hamster wheel of anxiety. Just hold onto it for now, until after the scan. If there's nothing organic going on, you can start with that. Try to do some of those relaxation exercises, and some of the yoga stuff too if you can. Whatever gets you moving. And let's make another appointment for next week."

I take the paper he hands me, bemused. He makes it sound so easy. So normal.

"Now," he continues, "the hospital will be in touch to set things up. Do you want to take care of this yourself? You can if you want. Or you might like to have someone with you. You know, someone on your side. You might want to think about letting your dad know."

"Do I have to? I'd rather go with my aunt." Panic clamps down on me at the prospect of trying to explain. "Can't you tell her?"

He smiles kindly at me. "Why don't we invite her up for a minute," he suggests. "And we'll do it together."

Neurological. That should be scary, shouldn't it? Like maybe-you-have-cancer levels of scary. But if it's neurological, at least it's real. Reasonable. Just a thing that happens, a thing that could happen to anyone. Not something looking specifically for me. Waiting for the chance to pull me under dark water, hold me down.

Dad, all up to date thanks to Aunt Jen, texts me to say he's scheduled an appointment for the scan, offers to take me to it. But I text back that I've made other arrangements.

After fumbling through another exam—thank God computer science turned out to be such a bird course—I spend the next afternoon at the hospital, lying on a table with my head in a space-age looking machine, holding perfectly, obediently still for the cheerful voice piping through the microphone. And Dr. Fortin calls the morning after to report there's no evidence of lesions, tumors, or clots.

"So it's totally clean," I say numbly. Aunt Jen, hovering at my side, squeezes my shoulder, misty-eyed with relief I can't share. What if there's no simple explanation?

"Go ahead and fill the prescription," Dr. Fortin tells me over a crackle of static. "But remember that this kind of medication can take a while to kick in. It won't hit its full strength until four to six weeks in."

"Four to six *weeks?*" I echo.

"I know it seems like forever. Hang on to your hope, okay? And you might notice some side effects. Some people find they're a little dizzy or nauseated at first, but that should pass. See how it goes and we'll check in next week."

The label on the bottle says escitalopram. The name sounds like it belongs in a magic spell. Obediently, I swallow down one little pill in the morning, one at night.

And amazingly, I feel...better. Lighter. Am I imagining it? Dr. Fortin said it would take weeks. But as I coast through the weekend toward my math exam, all the little puzzles that have been nagging me seem to lose their power. Though I still have to ride out a pang of unease when the memory rises into my thoughts, it's a single wave instead of a storm. It doesn't stick, doesn't drag me into a spiral of panic.

Hang on to your hope, Dr. Fortin said. It's easier to be hopeful than I expected. Maybe I'm off the hamster wheel of anxiety. Maybe now I can make it through the rest of my exams.

And sure enough, in the chilly humidity of the gym, where even the paper is limp and damp, my breath stays easy, unhurried. I'm light, distant, remote as a cloud. Like part of me is floating up in the emptiness under the high ceiling, with the coughs and shuffles, the click of Miss Kendrick's shoes all echoing up to me. It's a little weird, but I can handle it.

This time the cool linearity of the numbers embraces me, a welcome relief, and I slice neatly through the problems on the first couple of photocopied pages. The floaty disorientation lingers, turns my stomach, and I pause for a moment to rest the heels of my hands against my eyes, willing the world to stop spinning. But even now, fear doesn't wrap itself around me. Nothing flutters in my chest. This is okay. This is what Dr. Fortin was talking about. It'll pass.

Seashell silence steals over me, drowning out the sounds of the gym. It's soothing at first, hypnotic, before I remember why it's familiar. I sit upright with a jerk of alarm. In the split second before I open my eyes a certainty flashes through me that I'll find the gym dark and silent.

But the windows, set high above us, are still little rectangles of cool, gray light right below the ceiling. Distantly, if I listen for it, I can hear the murmur of the rain.

I turn my attention back to my desk to find my calculator has stopped working. It's stuck on a handful of lines and dashes scattered across the screen like some sort of hieroglyphics.

And my paper—the whole page—is covered in three words I didn't write:

THIS IS MINE

I recoil a little bit, but I can't look away. The gym lurches dizzily around me, turned unreal and sluggish like one of those nightmares where you're trying to run from something. For a moment I wonder if I'm really awake. But the lines on the page are real: heavy, a little wobbly, peppered with tiny grains of graphite that smudge my fingers when I touch them. In one spot it's actually ripped right through the paper. Like someone bore down on the pencil with their whole weight. My lead, carefully sharpened a second ago, is worn and blunted. When I snatch the paper up from the desk, I can see the words etched into the next page.

My sudden movements, the shuffling and rattling they're causing, earn me covert stares. Miss Kendrick frowns at me, looking like she's about to head over. I look down at the sheet in my hand for another second, then crush it into a ball, as small as I can make it, and lurch to my feet. I manage not to run until I'm out of the gym, but then I bolt for the nearest set of double doors, down the hall, and out into the rain.

I've come out next to the field, empty even of seagulls. The bleachers are skeletal, soggy, uninviting. I sink down on the first one and drop my forehead to my knees, panting. The rain sends little cold fingers running through my hair.

"Hey," says a voice from above and behind me. I jump and crane around to see who's there: Rhiannon—Ron—with a big black umbrella leaning on her shoulder and a cigarette dangling from her other hand. I can't think what she's doing there at first, but then it occurs to me she's probably finished. She was always the first one to finish every test in that class.

"Are you okay?" she asks.

I give half a laugh and mop my sleeves over my face, trying to think of a sane answer. "I just totally failed that exam."

She makes a sympathetic grimace and, after a moment, extends the cigarette toward me, raising her eyebrows inquiringly.

"Oh. No, thanks. I don't smoke."

She shrugs and puts it to her own lips instead, sitting back to blow a plume of smoke at the sky. She's like a lion sitting on a rock, casually slouched and yet somehow utterly self-possessed.

"I saw when you tackled Farrell in the hall," I find myself saying. "That was amazing."

She looks at me, leaning back on her elbows, and a smile creeps across her face, as if she's trying to keep it down. She shrugs again and flicks ash down the bleachers.

"I played rugby in junior high. I guess I kind of miss it."

"Seriously?"

She snorts. "Yeah, seriously. What? Knocking down jocks is fun." Her smile fades. "Besides, he *grabbed* me. That shit is not acceptable. Maybe he'll think twice next time. Or once, even."

"Don't count on it."

She rolls her eyes in disgusted agreement, then grinds her cigarette into the wet bleacher. To my surprise, she stands up and carefully steps over a few rows to come and sit next to me, dropping her bag between our feet. "Here," she says, and her arm brushes mine as she holds the umbrella over us both.

"Oh. Thanks." She's bigger than me—taller too, as regal and imposing as a stone statue. The layers of black clothes and elaborate curlicues painted in eyeliner on her cheeks only add to that effect. I'm as insubstantial as a shadow sitting next to her. The water dripping from the points of her umbrella soaks into my sleeve, but I'm not quite brave enough to shift closer to her to escape it.

"I don't get it," she sighs. "I switched schools to get away from losers like that, and here they are. Again. They're like a virus or something. The human version of the common cold, with a million different mutations."

"More like an STI," I mutter, surprising myself. Ron's smile flickers again, more open this time.

"Or cockroaches," she suggests. "An infestation of them. If there's ever a nuclear holocaust or a zombie apocalypse they'll probably be what survives."

"Yeah. Not like zombies would bother with them anyway."

"Exactly. Ha! No brains to be had there." She looks at me curiously. "You used to hang out with Ingrid Snow sometimes, didn't you? Where did she end up?"

"She moved to San Francisco."

"Oh. I wondered if maybe she'd done something to piss off the viruses. Like that poor guy from the GSA."

"Jeremy. No, it wasn't anything like that. Her dad just got a job out there. Anyway, I don't think anyone would have bothered her. She has this way of blending in."

"Hm." She opens her mouth to say more, but hesitates, looking out across the sodden field, hiding her free hand in her pocket and shivering. "Look. I've been thinking. About what you said the other day. You...haven't seen anybody about that yet, have you?"

My momentary glow of satisfaction at managing a sort-of conversation with her curdles abruptly into mortification, and I study the dripping bleacher in front of us. So that's why she's talking to me.

"I'm sorry," she says hurriedly. "That was a really personal question. I didn't—"

"I did, though," I say. "See someone, I mean. Actually."

"Oh. Okay. Great. Is everything, you know... Are you okay?"

"They thought it might be something neurological at first."

"That's kind of scary."

"I guess. But they did this scan and it didn't come up with anything." The words tumble out, drawn up by her steady gaze. "So I'm taking some medicine. But I can't tell if it's working. I mean, I feel better. I thought I was feeling better. But…something kind of freaky happened just now. During the exam. It's supposed to take a while to start working for real, I just… I don't know how I'm going to wait that long. You know?"

She studies me. "I've been thinking," she says. "I wonder if I might have given you the wrong advice."

"What do you mean?"

"I don't know. Maybe not the *wrong* advice. I mean, it only makes sense to check for that, right?" She leans forward a little, frowning. "I just thought…what if, you know? What if that wasn't really you? With the chalk?"

I don't answer. I can hardly breathe; sudden hope is crushing me. Wordlessly, Rhiannon hands me a crumpled tissue. It takes me a long minute to get my expression back under control.

"I'm sorry," I croak, scrubbing at my eyes. "I didn't think you believed me. I don't know if *I* believe me."

"I suspend my disbelief. Will that do?"

I huff a laugh and blow my nose. "I'll take it."

"So I guess there's more to the story than Miss Kendrick's class the other day," she ventures after a moment.

"Well, yeah. Just…more of the same. The weirdest things keep happening to me." Haltingly, I tell her about what happened on the beach, the streetlights, the writing on my exam paper. The wind picks up, sheeting rain into our faces. Ron winces and tilts the umbrella.

"What did it say? The writing, I mean?"

"'This is mine.'" Speaking the words aloud doesn't make them make any more sense. But I'm colder having said them, all the same.

"Does that mean anything?"

"I don't know. But that's not the worst part, even." I stop, hug my arms around myself. "You must think I'm some kind of freak."

"Nah. I've heard worse, promise."

I make a face at that, unconvinced, but I'm heartened in spite of myself. "Well. There's this whole evening I can't remember. I've been trying to figure out what I could have been doing, but there's just nothing there. Except for this...dream I had."

"What was the dream?"

"It's hard to explain." I don't really want to talk about it, but she's watching me expectantly. "I was by the water. In the dark. It looked kind of like the river, but it can't have been, there was...ice. Way out on the water. And I was walking toward it, into the water, and I couldn't stop. Something was dragging me down. It wanted me to drown." I shake my head, trying to shake off the memory. It feels as if it's gathering weight, darkening the gray day, ready to sink through into reality. "It's like if I think about it for too long, it might come true. It almost did, the other night."

"And you can't, you know, ask somebody who was around to see what they remember? Like your parents, maybe."

"That's just it. My parents just split up."

She winces. "That sucks. Sorry."

"I'm staying at my aunt's right now. Because my mom checked herself into the hospital." I can't look at her. I don't want to see her reaction. "Nobody would tell me what happened at first, but she says...she says I was floating. I'm afraid I'm—I don't know. I think maybe I'm possessed or something."

Possessed. I meant it as a joke. I think. But the word comes out flat and awkward and not at all funny.

"Do you have any idea what it might be? I mean, if you're possessed." God, it sounds so stupid when someone else says it. Even stupider than when I said it. But Ron peers at me, intent, frowning a little. "Possessed by what?" she prompts.

"I don't know. Maybe that's not the right word. It's mostly just a feeling. It's not like there are any voices or anything."

"Except for the writing. You know, 'this is mine.' Whose?"

I shake my head wordlessly, without an answer, afraid to answer. The rain whispers down around us.

"What do I do?"

Rhiannon returns my pleading look with a helpless one.

"God, I don't know. I mean, I don't think they do exorcisms anymore."

I smile weakly.

"I was thinking," she continues, not looking at me as she peels splinters from the bench with her black-painted nails, "that maybe you're right about talking to my mom. It couldn't hurt, right? Just in case. I mean, I could find out."

"You don't have to. I shouldn't have asked." But her obvious reluctance sharpens into amusement.

"What, just because jackasses keep asking me if I see dead people? I wouldn't have offered unless I meant it. It's just that I wouldn't trust her to know her supernatural ass from her elbow, personally. Open your mind too far and your brain falls out." She makes a flip-top gesture at her temple and rolls her eyes. "Still, you never know."

"She wouldn't think I was faking it? Or on drugs or something?"

"Seriously, you should hear how she gets. Especially if she's had a couple of drinks. I got stuck for like an hour last night listening to her blather about how she was reviving this plant with Reiki. Personally, I think it was watering it for once that did the trick."

"It's just...the hospital only kept my mom overnight. But she *knew* she was seeing things, you know? If I start saying I'm possessed, they'll think—"

"You're taking your meds," Ron points out. "You're talking to the doctors. You're doing all the right things. Right? You're just keeping an open mind." She makes the flip-top gesture again and gives me a lopsided grin, and somehow I feel better than I have in days. I'm sitting here talking to probably the coolest person at this stupid school. She knows the whole ludicrous story. And she's on my side.

"Have you tried going down to the river?" she asks. I fold my arms against a shiver, shake my head. "That's what my mom does, when she's doing the whole paranormal investigator thing. Visit the scene of the crime, or whatever. And it kind of sounds like something wants you there."

"Does she do that a lot? The paranormal investigator thing?"

"You'd be amazed. Not that the police have her on speed dial or anything. But word gets around, apparently."

"So she's good at it, then." Is it ridiculous that the weight hanging over me seems to lift a little further? Ron makes a teetering gesture with one hand.

"I guess so. As long as she sticks to, you know, psychotherapy for hopeless flakes. She can sure read people, I'll give her that." She frowns. "Most people."

"I'm just scared." I pull my braid over my shoulder, twisting it. "I know it's stupid, but…what if I go down there, and it's like it was in my dream?" Like it was on the beach, the other night. "What if it comes true?"

"With it pulling you down, you mean." She pauses, like she's actually considering the possibility. "You said it was dark, though, in your dream. Right? And it was dark when you went for that walk. You'd think it might be safer in the daytime. There might even be people around." She pulls her coat tighter. "Well, maybe not in this weather. Still."

"Maybe. I don't know. It was the middle of the afternoon, though, that first time I dreamed about it. Or I thought it was."

"I could come with you," she offers, in an offhand way that says it's no big deal. Like we're talking about going to the mall. "If you want."

"Thank you," I stammer out. "Really. But you don't have to do that."

"It's okay," she says, and smiles a little, leaning her shoulder into mine in a comradely way. "Really. This is obviously some scary shit. Whatever it is. I wouldn't want to do it alone either."

"When did you have in mind?" It's absurdly formal, but it's comforting, helps me clear the tightness from my throat. Ron's smile widens; she's laughing at me, probably.

"Well, I'm not doing anything. How's now?"

I open my mouth, then close it again. Now she's definitely laughing at me as she slings her backpack over her shoulder. There's a TARDIS button on the back pocket that says *Bigger on the Inside*.

"It's not going to get less scary if you wait. Come on, let's go."

I follow her down the bleachers; she holds the umbrella over us both as we hurry across the parking lot. Despite the exam, despite the writing that wasn't mine, despite my parents, it's not just me anymore. The thought is as warm as sunshine.

6

BY THE TIME THE BUS deposits us at the brick pile of the Lakeside Center, it's stopped raining, but the river is still rising. Yellow caution tape, strung from fence to tree to lamppost, walls off the lawn where I once played badminton with Dad: the river has swallowed it up, its border of pine trees the only interruption in a long swath of gray water. Waves chase each other over the surface in a sharp wind that finds every gap in the weave of my sweater. Some intrepid soul in hip waders sloshes through the flood with a fishing rod.

"Wow," Ron says.

"Yeah. I've never seen it like this."

Waves spill over the path that leads down to the farthest

point of the beach. Undaunted, Ron climbs up on the raised strip of green that usually runs alongside it. The grass squelches under her feet.

"Come on," she calls over her shoulder. I waver on the pavement. Reflexive, animal fear tugs at me, the kind that's impossible to argue down. But there was no hesitating in the dream, no stopping. That's something. And there was no one with me. I look over my shoulder at the fisherman, who's casting a line out toward the open water. It's not the same.

We follow our grassy path to the pines that mark the far end of the beach. Usually they border a gravelly shore and three long fingers of tumbled rocks reaching out into the water. But those rocky peninsulas are nowhere to be seen; they've been devoured, leaving nothing behind but churning white foam. All that's left of the benches that look out over the bay toward the sunset are their very tops, two thin lines of wood sticking out of the waves. It's hard to tell the crash of the waves from the wind in the trees; they blur together into a constant, voiceless roar. The water reaches for us, slapping at the concrete, rushing past trees and lampposts standing in the river like we're in a surrealist painting. A soggy drift of little sticks and bits of plastic accumulates at our feet.

"Well," Ron says, "I guess this is close enough."

She settles down to perch at the end of the grass, looking out across the water, and I reluctantly follow suit. The bend of the river leaves a brief gap where water and sky meet in an undistinguished haze, like the world is half-made, insubstantial. About to come undone. I rub my eyes, trying to scrub away the feeling.

"You okay?" Ron asks.

"I think so." I wrap my arms around my knees, shivering, blinking. "I've been feeling kind of weird all day. I think it's the medicine."

"Sounds plausible, yeah. But no flashes of psychic insight or anything?"

"Not so far."

She sits back, like she's settling in for a wait. I pull my hands inside my sleeves, trying to think of something else to say.

"So is it, like, a family business? The paranormal investigator thing?"

"Hardly. Not for lack of trying on Mom's part. I'm just missing the psychic gene or something." Her expression darkens and she turns away, looking out toward the horizon. I have a feeling I've said something wrong, but before I can think of a way to apologize without being awkward, she speaks again, breezily, like nothing happened. "I bet I could bullshit my way through it if I wanted to. All you need is a little, you know, dramatic flair."

"Yeah, clearly you have none of that," I say, and she smirks.

"That was one thing you could say for Lebreton. You know, my old school. They had a kick-ass drama program. With a real stage, even. Not one of those crappy cafeteria ones. It had lights and everything. I was totally going to play Ophelia before I left. I would have been an amazing Ophelia."

"How come you left, then?"

"Mm." She gives her hand a vague wave, brushing off the question. "Long story. Got in trouble."

"We went to see this play they put on at the School of Speech and Drama one time in sixth grade. They were all our age, but it looked amazing. Really professional. Maybe you could take their classes instead."

"Not on a psychic's salary," Ron says wryly.

I wince. "Oh. Right."

"Well, it's not like we're destitute. My dad's not a total deadbeat."

"They're divorced?"

"Never married." She shrugs, her expression unruffled. "He left when I was little. Moved out West. I sort of remember visiting him once or twice, but mostly he just sends cards. When he remembers."

I look out over the water, swallowing the ridiculous impulse to open the floodgates and confess how awful it's been, this past week. It wasn't like this for her; she wouldn't want to hear about it. Ingrid doesn't either, and who could blame her?

"Anyway," she's saying, "classes outside of school were never really a thing. If we had the money, I'd have taken ballet. I always wanted to try it." She lifts her feet, encased in tall black boots, and points her toes, laughing. "Just as well. It's not my style. And I didn't exactly end up with a ballerina body."

"I used to take ballet." I clench my teeth belatedly. Idiot. What, like I'm trying to be impressive?

Ron just nods. "Yeah, I might've guessed that."

I blink. "I thought you said you weren't psychic."

"Ha. No, but you're tiny enough. And I don't know, you can just tell. You hold yourself just so, you know?"

I do? "I wasn't very good."

Ron raises a skeptical eyebrow. "Well, you don't have to be good at something to enjoy it."

"In my house, you kind of do."

"What," she says indignantly, "did you quit because your parents said you're no good?"

"No, no," I hurry to correct her, "it wasn't like that at all. My mom was all about me doing dance. She used to have this whole wall of pictures from all my recitals. Since I was, like, four." She'd made me pose for a professional photographer for the last few. My stomach does a familiar, awful little flip at the memory. I can't believe I'm talking about this.

"So why, then?"

"It was like…" I wave my hands, trying to pull an explanation from the air. "You know that fairy tale, about the girl with the red shoes? The one who danced herself to death? That's what it was like. It just got…out of control. This thing that just kept going and going, faster and faster, and I couldn't stop it."

"Well, at least you didn't have to chop your feet off."

That response is so bizarre it actually makes me laugh. "Okay, what?"

"Have you read the story? The original?" When I shake my head Ron crosses her legs, sits forward, bizarrely intent. "It's Hans Christian Andersen. That guy was fucked up. The story goes that this girl likes her nice red shoes so much that she wants to wear them to church, and because she's thinking about looking nice instead of about God, some random guy she meets on the way—of *course* it's a guy—he curses her shoes."

"And the shoes start dancing," I supply reluctantly, "and she can't stop them." I wish I hadn't made the comparison. The dream feels close behind it, the memory of my feet pushing forward, step by step, against my will.

"Right. And so eventually she's so exhausted that—get this— she asks the local executioner to chop off her feet. Like, begs him. And he does. And even then the shoes keep dancing. With her severed feet *still in them*. And they keep coming back to haunt her. The guy that cursed her shows up again too, I think, but all he ever says to her is 'oh, what pretty dancing shoes.' I mean, how creepy is that? Eventually she repents of her vanity, so she's *allowed* to die. And go to heaven. Yay."

"That's horrible."

"Right? He had a real thing about dancing. It's in 'The Little Mermaid' too."

That one I remember. "Yeah. With the dancing on knives."

"Exactly. And she dances anyway. To make the prince happy." She rests her chin on her hand, studying me. "Do you miss it?"

My smile feels false, not my own. "Maybe. Not really. I mostly try not to think about it."

Ron gives me an inquiring look, so I fumble for an explanation. "Well. I quit in about the messiest, least dignified way possible."

"Somehow I have trouble believing that. You're, like, unshakeable. If Farrell tried his shit on you, you'd brush him off like a bug."

"Not likely." Is that what she sees, looking at me? The thought leaves me disoriented, like the world has just picked me up and swung me around. "I'm invisible. You can't harass a ghost."

"That's one way to deal with that brand of assholery, I guess. It's a pretty convincing disguise."

"Disguise," I echo. "For what?"

"I don't know. Hidden depths? Superpowers?"

I don't really know either. Dance was the whole world for so long, the end of every road. What am I if I'm not a dancer? What's left? After I quit, it was like some deafening soundtrack had been silenced. Like a heartbeat had ceased. I've been drifting cool and empty ever since. It's easier. Peaceful.

"So now you have to tell me what you did that was so awful," Ron declares, and then quickly adds, "Or, you know, tell me to butt out if you want. Sorry. I just can't resist a mystery."

I watch the water washing over the asphalt at our feet. I haven't told anyone about this. Not Julie and Shayna, who I used to be so close with at my old studio. Definitely not Ingrid. But I brought it up. It's my own stupid fault. Am I that desperate to seem interesting, to have something in common with this girl so outrageously visible everyone's afraid of her?

"I'd been...trying to quit for a while. Anytime I talked to my mom about it I'd just get these...ragey pep talks. You know, commitment this, excellence that. If I pushed it she'd pretend to give in and tell me that if I could live with wasting all that time and talent after she'd worked so hard to support me, then I could go right ahead. And I couldn't, obviously. I mean, we even had a barre in the basement. They built this whole room in the new house just so I could dance."

"That's pretty intense."

I shrug uncomfortably. "It sounds worse than it was. Really. My grandmother was this total perfectionist, so she was always too scared to do stuff like that as a kid, and...anyway. This one day I said to myself that's it, I can't do it anymore, I won't go back. So. After that, when Mom dropped me off, instead of going to rehearsal I hid in the library. For weeks. I mean, obviously she was going to find out eventually. It was the only way I could stop the red shoes. You know? It took longer than I thought it would. But finally she stopped by the studio early one day, and, well."

"I bet it really hit the fan then, huh?"

"You could say that. It was awful. But by then it was kind of too late to make me go back."

We sit in silence for a while after that. A few drops of water mist over me; I'm not sure if it's rain or spray from the waves. My fingers, knotted in the sleeves of my sweater, are going numb.

What breaks the quiet is the click of a camera. When I look around at her, Ron's pointing her phone at me.

"There." She holds it out to me. "Want me to send it to you?"

It is a good photo. I'm looking out into the distance, wisps of hair escaping around my face, framed by cool, gray sky. Instead of cold and afraid, I look pensive, mysterious. Untouchable.

"You can delete it if you want," Ron says. "Sorry. I should have asked."

"No, that's okay." I hand it back to her. "That's great. I don't selfie very well." *Not like you do.*

"I'll text it to you. What's your number?"

"You could just post it."

"Well, yeah," she says and shrugs, meeting my eyes. "But this way I get your number."

I manage to recite it for her before the pause grows too awkward, letting the waves rushing past steady my voice. It doesn't mean anything. Relax. She pokes buttons for a moment, and my own phone pings in my pocket.

"There," she declares. "Perfect." She peers at me. "So what do you think? Are you, I don't know, getting anything?"

"Nope. My feet are wet." I giggle, a little punchy from oversharing and relief. "Oh God, I don't know what's wrong with me. I'm an idiot. And I'm freezing."

"Do you feel better, though?" She stands, holds out her hand to help me up.

"Maybe. Less afraid." I meet her eyes. "Thank you."

Her searching look dissolves into a smile. A real smile, a sudden dip and flash like a bird's wing, like sunlight glancing off a wave. It transforms her whole face; it pins me to the spot. I should look away. But if my eyes linger on her too long, she doesn't notice, just leans over to grab her bag. Her phone chimes, chimes again, and she pulls it out to scan it, rolling her eyes.

"Look, I gotta go," she sighs. "But I'll see you on Friday, right? And if the weird shit isn't getting better by then…my mom does readings at a coffee shop in Chinatown. Maybe you could try one. You don't even have to tell her anything. Actually, you know what? Don't tell her about it at all. Just see if she notices anything. And if she does, maybe it'll mean she can help."

"I guess that makes sense," I say slowly. Whether it does or not, it means we'll talk again. It means I haven't driven her away. Doesn't it? "Yeah. Okay, sure. Why not?"

"Just…" She hesitates, looks at me sidelong. "Don't stop taking the meds. Seriously. Okay? Promise?"

"Oh. Sure." That seems inadequate, so I add, "Promise."

She shoulders her bag and hurries ahead of me, back over the grass toward the bus stop. Maybe she feels like she said too much too.

"I gotta go," she throws back over her shoulder. "See you. Be careful!"

I practically float back to Aunt Jen's. Not only did I talk to Emo Rhiannon, I spent almost the whole afternoon with her. I wasn't the one who suggested we see each other on Friday. And our conversation isn't hanging over me like a flock of crows either. That was okay. That was good, even. Is this thanks to the medicine? God. If it is, I should have started taking it years ago.

The lightness in my step lasts until I turn onto Aunt Jen's street, when I realize that I'm still going to have to tell Dr. Fortin about the writing on my exam.

I push my shoulders down, focus on my breath, on the lines of waves rippling out over the bay past the seawall. I'm supposed to see him on Wednesday. It can wait until then. Until then, I will forget about it. I can do that. I'll think about something else.

But that night I'm pulled from dreams of drowning—thrashing for the surface in the dark, lungs screaming, pounding on the underside of the ice, soon I'll have to inhale, I'll have to, but the surface is a solid wall, and hands snake around my ankles to pull me down, drag me deeper—by a jarring crash of notes from the piano. From my hands on the piano. I'm bent over the keys, their white bars like teeth. They're chilly under my fingers.

I jerk away and almost lose my balance, then grip the bench with both hands to steady myself. The bench. Where I'm sitting. I stare at the keys, my head thick and fuzzy, trying to force this to make sense. Am I dreaming? There's a rattling swirl of sound from the window, but it's only the rain blowing against the patio door.

I was in bed. I'm cold. How did I get here?

A light blinks on behind me, yellow light cascading over my shoulders. I look up to find Aunt Jen at the bottom of the stairs.

"Marianne? What on earth?"

I can't let go of the bench. The world reels around me. I'll fall if I let go. Aunt Jen hurries over to put an arm around my shoulders. The contact burns through my T-shirt. I'm so cold. I can't think.

"Are you awake, Mare-bear?"

"I am now." I think I am. I uncurl my fingers from the edge of the bench, one by one, and reach out with one hand to touch the keys again, to confirm they're real. "What was I doing?"

"Playing with the piano. Pounding on it, actually. It woke me up. I think you must have been sleepwalking."

Is that what it was? It's the obvious explanation. The simple explanation. But I've never walked in my sleep before. The floor is icy under my feet when I stagger upright. Under my bare feet. My crooked toes are stark against the floor, the permanent black splotches on their nail beds standing out like splashes of blood.

Aunt Jen leads me to the dining room, making noises about some tea she always makes when she's having trouble sleeping, but we stop short when she flicks on the light. The lilies in the middle of the table have been shredded, orange petals scattered all over the table.

She stares at them for a moment, then looks back at me, her eyes wide.

"I think you'd better tell Dr. Fortin about this," she says.

7

"IT'S NOT WORKING."

Dr. Fortin studies me, tapping his pen against his lips.

"What makes you say that?"

I should find his radio voice soothing; today it makes me bristle, makes me want to interrupt, to yell, to shake him. But that's not me. I'm rational. Calm. I smooth the fabric of the couch down with my fingers, letting waves wash over me in my mind.

"It's still happening. Even when I'm awake. I think I was awake. There were…things on my exam that I don't remember writing. But it must have been me. Right?" The words spill out, faster now. "And I was sleepwalking, a few nights ago. I went to bed and woke up in the living room. That's never happened before. And I...tore up some flowers, I guess. In my sleep. How could I do that in my sleep?"

Dr. Fortin frowns, but doesn't interrupt.

"It's not working," I repeat. I won't be shrill. I'm in control. This is a reasonable request. "It's getting *worse*. You have to give me something else."

"I can see why you're concerned," he says slowly. "Was there anything else you noticed?"

"I don't know. I've been feeling weird. Kind of...spacey? Dizzy, maybe? I thought the medication was helping at first. Things don't... stick to me the same way. It's easier to talk to people. But you said it's not supposed to work that fast anyway."

"Well, it's certainly possible to notice an effect from SSRIs right away. Usually I'd prefer to give them time to reach full strength. You've only been on them for a few days. But still...it sounds like the most worrying symptoms here are escalating. And more quickly than I'd like."

I trace lines on the arm of the couch while he watches me, his brow furrowed.

"This is a significant step," he says at last, "especially at your age. But I think I'm going to give you another prescription."

He jots something down on a notepad, hands it to me. Quetiapine is the next magic word.

"Given your mom's symptoms and everything you went through with...well, a couple years ago, I think it's worth getting out the big guns. If what we're seeing here is early indicators of something run-ning in your family, there's research showing it can make a big differ-ence to get on top of it early."

"What if it's not enough?" I ask him, staring at the looping blue lines of the word on the paper. "What if it keeps happening?"

"It's scary, not knowing," he says in his gentle amber voice. "Isn't it?"

I nod, not looking at him.

"Give it some time. I know it's hard, but this is some serious medicine, and we don't want to rush to conclusions. And if it turns out it doesn't help, it's not the end of the world. We've got a few other things we can try. Medication's not a silver bullet, unfortunately. Give it time."

The quetiapine hits me like a fist. *May cause drowsiness*, it says on the bottle. They're not kidding. Exhaustion descends in a leaden curtain. It's not even seven o'clock when I collapse into bed, but sleep rolls over me right away, heavy and sticky.

I'm startled awake by a butterfly touch on my shoulder, the faintest brush of cold fingers, light and hesitant. I open my eyes in the dark. I left the light on, didn't I? My head swims. It's hard to think. An awful, familiar roar fills my ears. The wall is washed faintly orange, my hand a strange inanimate thing on the pillow beside me. At first I can't remember how to move. Am I awake?

When I roll over, it leaves the room swinging dizzily around me. And there's someone there. A shadow in the dark, bending over me, a pale familiar face with hollows for eyes, framed by long trailing wings of dark hair. At first what gleams through my murky thoughts is hope. Relief.

"Mom?"

But the word is soundless. And the face above me contorts, goes ugly with rage before hands slam into me with an impact that knocks the breath from my lungs, cracks the ice beneath me, plunges us both into bottomless, drowning darkness while something screams its wordless fury at me, not needing to breathe, a howl that goes on and on.

When I flounder out of sleep, gasping, the light is back on, a reassuring yellow glow flooding the room. But I can't catch my breath. I can't shake the fear. Fear is what makes a nightmare, and it hammers through my head, unreasoning, refusing to ebb.

Am I awake? Am I really awake this time? My thoughts feel mushy, sluggish, a beat behind everything.

There's sound, though. At least there's sound: the creak of Aunt Jen's bed in the next room as she rolls over and the faint, ever-present drumming on the roof.

I grab the phone, desperate to put as much distance as possible between me and the figure that wasn't my mom. The clock reads 2:45 a.m.

Ingrid just posted something two minutes ago.

I let my breath out, sagging against the pillow. Right. She's three hours behind me. But I can't text her about this, especially in the middle of the night. It would be weird. I hesitate over the screen for an agonizing minute before snapping a horror-movie selfie and tapping out a post for the world at large, all three of my followers. Well, three if you count the bot.

> my whole life is upside down rn and i just woke
> up from the most intense nightmare. too scared
> to sleep.

A friend would at least send an emoji if they saw that, wouldn't they? It's a sad little private test, a message in a bottle. She loves me, she loves me not.

But while I wait, hugging the phone, sleep sneaks up on me, a tide creeping in to suck me down again. The next time I open my eyes the room is bright with morning, and the phone has slipped from my hand to lie facedown on the floor.

There aren't any notifications when I pick it up.

I've never been so tired. The world creeps by in slow motion. I zombie my way through my last exams, English and history, past caring about my marks. If my parents are disappointed, they can blame themselves. I'm still trying to drag myself through the essay question on the causes of World War I when they declare our three hours up.

Ron falls into step next to me as I trudge from the gym. Her hair's tied up in a dozen little knots today. Between glossy, eggplant-colored lipstick and a swishy little black skirt paired with her tall boots, she looks like something out of a cartoon.

"How're you doing?" she asks. The words are tinged with caution, but I don't really care. She's talking to me. Our conversation at the beginning of the week seems so impossible that half of me thinks I dreamed it; I was bracing myself for her to breeze past me like we'd never spoken. "Are things still, you know, weird? I saw your post from the other night."

"I was sleepwalking," I say, so quietly she has to lean in to hear me. "That's never happened before. So I'm on this new medicine, and I'm supposed to give it time to work, but the dreams…they're awful. And they haven't stopped. They're *supposed* to stop."

Around us, people cast furtive looks at her, keep their distance. She draws stares as if she glows in the dark, leaving a wake of whispers. I'm torn between a faint, smug glow of satisfaction and alarm. Invisibility compromised.

"Do you still want to talk to my mom today? It's okay if you don't." The question is casual, but she's watching me, and when I don't respond right away she drops her gaze, fiddling with the unraveling edges of her fishnet gloves. "Look, I know I said she's the flakiest flake that ever flaked, but—"

"Yes," I interrupt. "Please. Let's...see what happens."

She looks up again and nods, crimps her violet lips into a tiny smile. But she still looks worried.

My turn to say something. I cast around for a normal topic of conversation. "How did your exams go?"

"Eh. I predict a C in English. It's like they pick the reading list for maximum boredom. And I was mostly making stuff up for history."

"Join the club. I barely studied."

"Well, obviously. You should talk to the guidance counselors."

I frown at her. "Very funny."

"God, not about *that*. The exams. You should talk to them. Claim extenuating circumstances, with your parents and everything. Maybe they can get you a rewrite, or extra credit, or whatever. They must be good for something."

"Oh." I hadn't thought of that. "Yeah. Maybe."

Ron hesitates. "Listen, I brought something for you."

She pulls a necklace over her head, a long, pointed obsidian pendant strung from a black ribbon.

"It's for protection." She holds it out to me, sounding embarrassed. "It's not much, but maybe it'll help. You can keep it."

The pendant's warm from resting against her body. I slip the ribbon over my head.

"Thanks," I manage.

"Don't thank me yet. Let me go get my coat, and then we can head out, okay? I'll meet you by the front doors."

She ducks around me and hurries off down the hall, ignoring the losers who turn to watch her pass, nudging each other and smirking. I clutch the pendant in one hand, its glassy edges biting into my palm. Its warmth is already fading.

"Just remember that ninety percent of this is just reading people," Ron mutters as the bus roars away from us, leaving us under the gilded red-and-blue arch that stands over the street, its Chinese letters gleaming in a scrap of sunlight. "Don't let her lead you into telling her what's going on. And don't let her weird you out or anything. Okay?"

"Weird is my life right now." I sound less apprehensive than I feel. Good. "Don't worry."

Wind chimes clink and jingle as we step inside. The café is furnished in a mismatched vintage chic, with an assortment of Formica-topped, metal-banded tables in different sizes scattered around the room. A couple of people work studiously away on laptops on the threadbare couches in the back. At a little table by the window sits a woman with a riotous cloud of curly gray-blond hair and half-moon glasses perched low on her nose. She bends over a coffee cup in earnest, low-voiced conversation with a paunchy man in a business jacket. Colorful cards are arrayed over the table between them; as I watch, the woman points to one of them and taps it a couple of times in an emphatic sort of way.

A moment later, the conversation is wrapping up. They stand, exchange a hug, and the man presses some folded cash into her hands, thanking her over and over again. Beside me, Ron sighs.

"Rhiannon!" she calls, sitting down again as her customer ducks past us out the door. "And you must be Marianne, right? Rhiannon mentioned you might be coming by. I wish I could say I've heard a lot about you, but she's been very secretive. Infuriating, really."

"Marianne, this is my mom," Ron mutters. "Mom, Marianne."

"Niobe." She gives me a showman's smile as she sweeps the cards on the table into a pile, shuffling them together with an expert snap of her thumbs. "Usually Rhiannon finds all this a little high on the 'woo' scale for her tastes, so I was surprised she asked me to read for you."

"What," Ron says, saving me from having to reply, "you hadn't predicted that?"

Niobe gives her a look over the rims of her glasses but otherwise doesn't respond.

"It's a joke," Ron mutters, folding her arms and looking away. Niobe turns to me instead.

"Come sit down."

I slide into the seat across from her. Ron pulls another chair up to the table and straddles it, draping her arms over the back and resting her chin on them. Niobe shoots her another glance. Ron sets her jaw, but doesn't meet her eye. They didn't look much alike to me at first, but somehow in irritation their gestures speak the same language: the downturn at the corners of their mouths, the way their eyebrows draw together.

"All right." She taps the cards against the table to settle them into a neat stack before presenting them with a ceremonious little flourish. "Shuffle, please."

The cards are worn to a soft, almost fabric-like texture, their backs printed with a plain, faded plaid. The smell of incense clings to them, coils up around me. They're bigger than playing cards, awkward to hold in one hand. I cut them clumsily a few times and then hold them out to Niobe. Instead of taking them, she clasps both her hands around my outstretched one, cards and all. She closes her eyes, takes a deep breath. Ron rolls her eyes and drops her forehead silently onto her arms.

"Knock it off," Niobe growls, without opening her eyes. "You asked, remember?"

"Yeah, yeah," Ron mutters.

"Don't 'yeah yeah' me! You're going to throw me off. Go for a walk or something."

Ron shoves her chair back from the table. The wind chimes at the door jangle as she stalks outside, yanking a box of cigarettes from her coat pocket on the way.

"Honestly." Niobe rolls her shoulders, shakes out her hands. "Let's try this again."

This time, after clasping my hand for a moment, she takes the cards from me and turns the first one over onto the table. In washed-out primary colors, a bolt of lightning strikes a flaming tower, people tumbling from the fiery windows, their mouths open in dismay. *The Tower*, I read upside down.

"Mm." Niobe studies me over the rims of her glasses. "Rough go of it lately, I take it."

Ron told her as much.

"Kind of."

"This tells me the whole world has come crashing down around your ears. Like a house of cards." She narrows her eyes. "A bad breakup, I think. Messy. The kind that blows up and leaves you picking shrapnel from the wounds. It wasn't mutual."

She pauses. I drop my gaze to the gold-speckled table.

"Here's the thing," she tells me, businesslike, draining her coffee cup. "And this is going to be hard to hear, so bear with me. It wasn't real. It's like building your house on sand, or the San Andreas fault. It could never have lasted. Of course it hurts when it comes tumbling down, but it was inevitable. You have to clear all that away and start over. With the truth. Whoever this was, you're better off without them. Okay?"

I fold my arms. She thinks this is about some stupid teenaged romance. I guess it might be accurate enough if it was my mom sitting here.

"Maybe," I say eventually, because she seems to expect me to respond. She gives me a dry look, but flips over the next card: a woman standing bound and blindfolded, swords piercing the ground all around her, their hilts standing as high as her shoulder. Water twisting at her feet. A roman numeral takes me a moment to decipher upside-down: VIII.

"Helpless, is how this feels," Niobe says softly. "Like you're all alone. And trapped."

Ninety percent of this is just reading people, Ron said. I keep my face impassive.

"Part of what this card has to tell you, though, is that there *is* a way out. You just aren't letting yourself see it. When you get right down to it, this is self-inflicted, this trap you're in. You made your bed and now you're ready to swoon into it and wait for some prince to come and kiss you awake." Her tone grows stern; she points a warning finger at me. "Well, that's bullshit. Don't fall for it. Just because you made your bed doesn't mean you can't choose to walk away from it. You need to stop thinking of yourself as the victim here and take some action."

I blink at this assessment, baffled, a little indignant. How could any of this possibly be my fault? Isn't that the exact opposite of what you're supposed to say in this situation? It doesn't even seem to apply to my mom, to Dad leaving. What could she have done?

"Make sense?"

"Not really."

Niobe sighs.

"It will. Trust me. This is plain as the nose on your face from where I sit. Keep it in mind, all right?"

On the next card—*Page of Wands*—a man in an embroidered tunic stands in the desert, holding a long wooden staff that sprouts a few shy springtime leaves.

"Ah," Niobe says in satisfaction, "this is good news. You don't have to go it alone. Now, this isn't a prince, right? Nobody's riding to the rescue. But you do have a friend here. Someone who will to go to hell and back for you. Someone who's new in your life, or will be soon."

I can't help a sigh at that. Niobe makes an inquiring sound.

"That just...seems like a lot to hope for." There's been exactly one new person in my life lately. She's leaning against the wall outside with her cigarette, slouched over her phone under the dripping awning, looking surly. Downright intimidating, actually.

Niobe watches me, her brows climbing.

"Not at all," she muses. "In fact, maybe this is more than a friend."

It's a frozen heartbeat before I can swallow. I study the card, refusing to let a glance betray me. It doesn't mean anything. It doesn't matter. She's just telling a heartbroken kid that there's a new prospect on the horizon.

"I doubt it," I mutter. Niobe, thankfully, turns the next card without commenting further.

The caption reads *The Moon*. It's a weird image. A frowning face, set into the curve of a radiant orb, hangs in an empty sky. Two dogs bay at it from the ground, and a lobster crawls from the waves at the bottom of the picture. Something about the lobster's scaly, black body, the way the sky bleeds into the landscape below it, reminds me of my dream.

"Now, this," Niobe says and stops, frowning, to peer at me. I wait for her to continue, trying not to let my sudden tension show.

"Something…isn't what it seems here." She pokes at the card with one finger. "Only I get the feeling that's a warning to me as much as it is to you."

She slides the cards over the table, rearranging them so the woman with the swords is next to the moon, studies the two of them together. Her frown deepens.

"What is it?" I ask anxiously.

"Hang on," she says. "This was so clear a second ago. But something… There's something about the water here. Someone else who's trapped. I don't understand."

She glances up at me. Her eyes are lighter than Ron's, a bright cinnamon color. I hold my breath, wondering what she's looking for. Wondering what she'll see.

She inhales sharply, once, and the frown disappears into a look of ashy shock that makes me think of my mom. *Nothing happened. Nothing. Nothing. Nothing.* Slowly, she sits back and puts a hand to her mouth.

"I'm sorry," she says at length, her brisk business voice gone thin and strained. "I don't think I should do this here."

"What?" I fight down a wave of panic. "Why? Did I do something wrong?"

She shakes her head, watching me. Like she can't look away.

"No. But it's not safe. Something's following you. It's not far off. I can feel it." She hugs herself, leans away from me. "I'm not going to risk attracting its attention. Not here."

"What do you mean? What is it?"

"I don't know yet. I didn't think this would be… I don't know." She shakes her hands out again and gathers the cards together, but she drops a few of them on the floor and has to bend to retrieve them.

"I don't understand," I plead. "Please. I've been so scared."

"It's complicated," Niobe says shortly. "You need to come and see me at home. So we can deal with this properly."

"But—"

"I'm sorry, but I mean it. This is a question of safety. For both of us. And for Rhiannon." She looks at me, unreadable. "I'm going to have to ask you to stay away from her."

"What?" I cry. The students at the back of the room look up at us. "I thought you said—"

"Here's my business card." Niobe pushes it at me, cutting me off. "Call me so we can set something up. I don't think I have to tell you how important this is. Right?"

I open my mouth; she nods curtly.

"Right. Go on, now. I'll talk to you soon."

I cram the card into my pocket and stand up, feeling every eye in the café on me. Rhiannon looks up, grinding out the butt of her cigarette with her heel, as I push my way outside.

"So," she says. "Was that useful?"

"I should go," I grate and turn blindly toward the bus stop.

"Wait!" She comes jogging up behind me, catching my elbow. "Marianne, what the hell? What did she say to you?"

"She said this was my own fault, basically. That I brought it on myself."

Ron stares at me. "Seriously?"

"She seemed kind of upset. I don't know what I did. She said I should see her at home." I can't meet her eyes. "She said I should stay away from you."

"What? You're fucking kidding me!"

"She said there's something after me," I say tightly, pulling my arm from her grip. "She said it was dangerous. I should go."

"That's bullshit! She can't just—what am I, five?" She's practically vibrating with outrage. Seeing me retreat from her by a step, she subsides a bit, shoving her hands in her coat pockets and kicking at the pavement with her booted toes. "Look. Don't let her go all *Exorcist* on you. She's just jerking you around. Some things you're supposed to banish with medicine, not magic."

"But what if this isn't one of them?" I plead. "What if she's right?"

"You're letting her get to you. Don't buy into it. Seriously. Jesus, I should never have let her near you." She looks around at me, her mouth set in a grim line. "Did she tell you how much it was going to cost?"

"No."

"Right. She's probably saving that for when you call." She gives the sidewalk another kick, her lips twisting. "Fucking *hell*."

"But what she said. That's exactly how it feels. Like there's something following me. And whatever it is…Ron, she was scared of it."

"Look," she sighs, "if you're really worried, we can always try it ourselves."

"Try what?"

"Talking to it." She shrugs, then folds her arms, like she's embarrassed by the suggestion. "Whatever it's supposed to be. And if something talks back, *then* you can try her schtick."

"Do you think that would work?" I don't ask whether it's a good idea.

"I think it's bullshit. But if it'll make you feel better, I'm in."

The wind picks up, tugging at my hair, scattering a few pinpricks of cold rain across my face.

"Okay," I say.

"Yeah?"

"Yeah. Sure. Let's try it."

She draws a long breath, gives me an edged smile. "Right. All right. Perfect. Let me look some stuff up. I'll text you, okay?"

The concrete walls of the bus station slide past as the bus pulls away. I turn Niobe's reading over and over in my head. It doesn't make any sense, but I can't dismiss it.

Maybe I'm just clinging to that one card, the man with the leafy staff. Someone who will go to hell and back for me. Someone in my corner. *You don't have to go it alone.* I close my hand around my phone in my pocket. The concrete gives way to the banks of the river as we turn onto the parkway. Is it possible? This isn't a prince, Niobe said. There's no one riding to the rescue. But Ron's smile flashes through my mind.

She didn't have to come to the river with me. She didn't have to meet me today. She looked *me* up. She asked for my number.

God. I refuse to pursue that train of thought any further. *Get a grip.* She probably just feels sorry for me. And now that exams are over, she has the perfect opportunity if she wants to quietly disappear.

I'm too tired to think about this anymore. I slouch in the hard seat, lean my head back. Closing my eyes is all it takes for sleep to pull me under. The roar of the bus drifts and fades around me.

I struggle back to the surface. I'll miss my stop. But when I open my eyes the light has vanished from the sky, from the water, leaving empty darkness stretching out forever beyond a crust of broken ice. I could fall into it.

I jerk back from the window, jostling the person sitting next to me. But reality and daylight have reasserted themselves. Low clouds scud through the sky. The river is flinty with white-crested waves, the hills on the far side a gray haze. It's June again and nowhere near cold enough for ice. I blink and blink, but the darkness doesn't return.

"Sorry," I mutter to my seatmate, a woman wearing a long

black coat and a floral-print hijab; she gives me a polite smile in response and goes back to her book. She didn't see anything.

Fear beats through my veins, pushing the clinging fatigue aside. I keep my eyes fixed on my hands, twisted together in my lap, until the bus rounds the corner, away from the water, leaving it behind.

8

BY SUNDAY AFTERNOON, THERE'S STILL no word from Ron. I take my pills, which leave me light-headed and my stomach hot and roiling. I keep my phone in my pocket, the volume at max, willing it to chime, hoping I don't sleep through it. I am not going to call her first. *Soon.* What does that mean? Soon like this month? Soon like tomorrow? Outside the water creeps higher; sandbags are piled on top of the seawall, around the drains.

Maybe she's not going to call. I can still feel Niobe's stare boring into me when I close my eyes. I wonder what it was she saw. What she's told Ron. Maybe it was enough to change Ron's mind. Wouldn't she have called by now, if she was going to? The memory of her expression turning closed and angry blurs into Niobe's sudden wariness and leaves me feeling a little sick, wondering what I did, wondering whether Ron will turn that glare on me next time I see her. Telling myself I'm being ridiculous doesn't help. I should never have opened my mouth.

I keep the necklace on under my sweater, a heavy and unfamiliar weight against my chest. For protection, she said. The nights have passed dreamlessly—fourteen hours, fifteen hours in a leaden blink. Sleep. What a concept. Is it the medication working? Or the necklace?

When the phone finally rings, I'm huddled in a corner of my bed with it, playing a mindless game. If I don't keep busy, sleep steals over me and time slips through my fingers. I haven't walked in my sleep again, I don't think, but I wake up from those unintentional naps disoriented and afraid. Wondering what might have happened this time. The bedside light is already on against the gathering twilight, and the wind whistles around the eaves of the building.

But it's not Ron calling. I don't know the area code; my phone says it's in California. Telemarketing?

No. Ingrid.

She's actually calling. I let my breath out in a long, steadying stream, let the water rise around me, cool and calm. I can do this.

"Hey," she says when I answer, and the worry in her voice makes my throat close up. "How's it going? Are you okay?"

"I don't even know where to start." My voice quavers. *Keep it together*. The phone stutters, fizzing static at me. "I'm…really glad you called."

"No problem. Sorry it took me so long."

There's a pause. I clear my throat.

"So how's San Francisco?"

That keeps us going for a while. She has a funny story about a chemistry period where some guys managed to sneak a dozen beakers and three stools out the window while the teacher's back was turned before they finally got caught. The ringleader was a snarky hipster with dorky glasses, wiry arms, a killer smile. He's painted murals in the cafeteria, wrote the school play.

"That sounds kind of like a crush." I barely know this script, but I can guess I'm supposed to tease her, or press her for gossipy details. I'm not sure how. It's like a play where everyone got their parts somewhere around seventh grade, leaving me faking my way through mine.

"Maybe crushing a little bit." She giggles. I'm silent, glad she can't see my face. "Don't sound so worried. It's not like he knows I exist. Georgia's been asking around for me."

Oh God, do I sound worried? I have to keep my voice light. I close my eyes, imagine sun sparkling on the water.

"Georgia?"

"Yeah, she's the one in the pictures I posted. You'd like her."

"Mm." I don't know what to say. There's a pause, like Ingrid doesn't know what to say either.

"Sorry," I come out with. "I'm not very good company lately. I just…" *I just wanted to hear your voice.* "Things are…kind of messed up, you know?"

"Yeah. I get that."

Another pause. Words crowd my mouth, but I can't speak. *My mom went to the hospital. She saw me floating in midair. I think I might be possessed. I think something might be after me.* I remember Ron's first advice. *Save yourself eighty bucks and go see a real doctor.* With Ron, it had seemed just possible enough to blurt it out. But with Ingrid? I can't imagine it, I can't even think what she would say to me. The world where we sat in the sun talking about books is a bright bubble, impossibly distant. If I let the words fall they'll vaporize it on impact. Matter and antimatter.

"Marianne?"

"Listen, I have to go." The words are mostly natural, only a little rough around the edges. I don't think she notices. "I…can I call you later?"

"Sure," Ingrid says easily. Relieved? "Whenever. Hang in there, okay?"

I hang up and let the phone thump down onto the bed.

I've never known how to tell Ingrid anything, really. She seems so serene, so far above all the frantic churning that fills my head. I couldn't tell her about what had happened with dance. She never would have freaked out like I did; she never would have quit. If there was worry simmering under her relentless good cheer, it never showed. I was in awe of her. A little jealous.

What am I to her? I still don't know. Someone who needs her, maybe. She called, didn't she? She said I could call her later. It might have been out of kindness. Out of obligation. I've been so careful not to let her see how desperately I've clung to her. How badly I craved a friendly face. My dance friends from my old studio fell away after I joined the conservatory. Our competitive class had been a tight little circle. They all celebrated with me when I got the letter inviting me to attend, but when I actually left, the circle just closed up and went on without me. When I quit, I never told them. I couldn't bear the idea of them talking about it, low-voiced, while they stitched ribbons onto their shoes: what a fake I'd turned out to be, how I'd never deserved the spot in the first place.

But Ingrid didn't need to know about my dance meltdown. And she had it so together. If she could do it, so could I. I needed to know it was possible.

In the picture of her in my head, she's firelit and smiling. Our science camp went on one overnight trip. They took us on a tour of a mine where they used to dig for mica. The lake nearby was full of it, glittering, golden flakes suspended in the weedy water, sparkling in the sand. Ingrid and I spent a hot, hazy three days stomping through the woods, lagging behind the rest of our group on the winding trails through cathedrals of leaves, and later, talking in whispers as the August night breathed through the wide-open cabin windows. It was what I'd always imagined having a best friend would be like.

We spent the second night on the beach watching a meteor

shower. It was cloudless, moonless, the sky alive and infinite. Looking up into it made gravity seem precarious, like you could lose your grip on the world and tumble into the air. Ingrid and I lay side by side. She was cold, asked to share my blanket. We stared into the sky with sand in our hair, counting the meteors as they fell: flickering needles of light slicing down toward us. The laughing voices of the other camp-ers fell away. We could have been the only ones there. It could have been just the two of us.

That was the only time I ever heard her falter, the only time her armor showed any cracks. She spoke into a long silence.

"Are you ever afraid—" She hesitated, started over. "Sometimes I think I'm not a very good person. You know? Sometimes it's like any minute someone's going to read my mind and find out how awful I am inside. Do you ever worry about that?"

All the time, I didn't say. *I've never stopped.*

"I think you're the best person I know," I told her instead.

Her fingers laced through mine under the blanket, her bare arm warm and smooth against my skin. She was a silhouette beside me, an outline against the sky. A star streaked down past her lips, burning.

And I had this thought, this absurd, impossible idea. What would happen if I moved closer? What would happen if I touched her face, tipped it toward mine?

But I knew the answer: it would ruin everything. And then I'd have no one at all.

So I turned away, back to the sky, and drew the sound of the lapping waves over me. With her hand in mine, I let the murmur of the water pull me down until my heartbeat slowed, until I could remember that between us and those falling stars was an ocean of lifeless cold. Above us they burned themselves into nothing without ever making a sound.

We weren't in the same classes at school; I didn't see her often. She was so much more outgoing than I was. She floated from clique to clique, and all they ever talked about was how *nice* she was. She tried to draw me in too, but I shrank from them. It wasn't her fault I was too quiet, too awkward to fit in comfortably.

Still, she never abandoned me. Sometimes we'd eat lunch together, cross paths in the library. We'd trade texts. I was okay with that. I savored those rare, luminous moments. I was so careful. I meted out every message, every smile, carefully spaced, determined not to stumble. Trying to inch closer to her without being obvious.

I found out she was leaving through social media. On December first she made this chirpy, flippant post about how she'd get to skip winter. I sat at the kitchen table, my fingers ice cold on the keyboard, and watched the comments pop up: how lucky she was, how much they'd miss her. I had to add my own, to make her remember me. But I couldn't think of anything that would stand out without being weird.

My restless pacing carried me up to the terrace on the roof, the moth wings a blizzard in my chest, a storm of all the things I couldn't say. I stood at the railing and hurled every possibility out into the icy expanse of the river, the cold wind whipping my hair back from my face.

I should let her drift away if that's what she wants. That's what you're supposed to do if you love something, isn't it? What is it I'm even hoping for? That moment on the beach didn't mean anything. It was just a thought. You're allowed to think stupid, impossible things if you keep them to yourself. Nobody's going to read my mind. I have to forget about it. Let it go.

Still, even when I close my eyes, suspend myself between the light filtering through the ice and the endless depths, the fact stubbornly refuses to sink.

She called. She did call.

I keep chewing over the rest of Niobe's reading, hoping to figure out some way it's relevant, shake loose hidden answers. Don't be a victim. Take action. By doing what? I don't even know what to google. When I hesitantly tap *I think I'm possessed* into the search bar—and refresh the page five times, trying to get it to load—the result is an avalanche of religious weirdness. *Suspend your disbelief,* I tell myself sternly, and sift through it anyway. The internet connection stutters and hiccups, and I smack the track pad in frustration.

If you can't stand the word of God, I read, that's a definite red flag. I drag myself through an hour reading the Bible online, fighting to keep my eyes open. The King James version, to be extra authentic.

But nothing unusual happens. Does boredom count, I wonder, scrolling irritably through endless lists of who begat whom.

The rite of exorcism also turns up in the search results, but it
likewise goes on approximately forever without saying anything helpful. Other sites warn me to throw out my tarot cards and Ouija board.
Right. If that was the problem, shouldn't all this have started after I
talked to Niobe?

There's a prayer that comes up a few times. Experimentally, I
read it aloud, first under my breath, and then again, louder. Does it
make a difference how many times you say it?

*Saint Michael the Archangel, defend us in battle. Be our protection
against the wickedness and snares of the devil. May God rebuke him, we
humbly pray; and do thou, O prince of the heavenly host, by the divine
power of God, cast into hell Satan and all evil spirits who wander now
throughout your world seeking the ruin of souls.*

Aunt Jen pokes her head into my room and frowns at me.

"I thought maybe you were on the phone," she says.

"Just reading something," I mutter, shrinking down a little to
hide behind the screen. She accepts this with a shrug and closes the
door. I sit there listening to the silence. Has anything changed? I
can't tell.

But when I finally set the computer aside and open the door to
leave the room, something tumbles inward with a scrape and clatter,
smacking painfully into my shins. I've jumped backward with a little
scream before I realize what it is: one of the dining room chairs.

"Marianne?" Aunt Jen calls.

"I'm fine," I say, my voice high. I give the chair a shove with one foot; it's inert, ordinary. It must have been leaning against the door. Why would Aunt Jen put it there? I'm about to call down the stairs and ask, but cold doubt seeps in, rising in my throat. Am I missing time again? Was it me somehow? How could I have done that?

And then my phone chimes, signaling a text message.

Can you meet tonight? Ron writes.

I run downstairs to where Aunt Jen is singing along—badly—with '80s show tunes as she chops up ingredients for the slow cooker. She looks up, startled, at my thumping approach.

"Aunt Jen"—I try to stay casual, but it comes out breathless—"is it okay if I go out? My friend just texted me."

Aunt Jen's eyebrows go up in an amused *oh, really* kind of way.

"My friend Ron." The look deepens, and I rake my hands through my hair, disarranging pieces of it from my braid. "*Rhiannon.* Okay? Can I go?"

"It's getting pretty late," she says cautiously. "Do you think she could come here?" I roll my eyes, but turn away to tap out a return message to Ron, asking if she can come and meet me.

Sure, comes the reply, and I feel a smile stealing onto my face as I tap out the address.

"She'll be here in twenty minutes," I report in satisfaction. Aunt Jen tips some sliced mushrooms into the pot without comment, and I dash back up the stairs without waiting for one.

9

AUNT JEN DOESN'T EXACTLY STARE at Ron when she shows up, but I can see her stealing little shocked glances. I hide a smile. She's not dressed that outrageously—jeans and a creaky leather jacket that's too big for her, albeit all in black—but it's probably the makeup that does it, the black spirals around her eyes, the violently red lipstick. The front of her hair is slicked down into neat, red-tipped points on either side of her face, the rest of it caught up in a skull-and-crossbones clip, little bits of red sticking out like flames.

I close the bedroom door behind us; Ron slings her backpack to the floor, drops onto the bed.

"So," she says briskly, "if we assume that my mother is *not* a hopeless fraud, our first task is to find out what it is that's after you."

"Well, it's not a demon, according to Google."

"The Necronomicon of the modern age. What makes you say that?"

"Well, that's the sort of thing that comes up for 'possession.' And none of it fits." Stumbling a little over the words, heat creeping into my face, I explain the tests I tried.

"What was the prayer?" she asks. I pull it up on the computer and turn it toward her. "No, no, read it out loud. I'm curious."

I roll my eyes, but read it through.

"Huh." She sits back thoughtfully. "I'd never heard that before. It's pretty cool, actually."

"I guess. It didn't work."

"Go figure. Mom would probably say you're supposed to speak with authority."

I make my voice deep, hold my hand out in a mock dramatic gesture. "'Saint Michael the Archangel—'"

Ron snorts.

"No, no. Like, if you really believed in Saint Michael as your protector, and casting demons into hell, and all that. I'm guessing you don't, though."

I shake my head.

"Well. Stuff is getting thrown around, right? Like...assuming it's real...what if the thing that's after you is some sort of poltergeist?"

"What, like a ghost?"

"Kind of. A ghost that's haunting a person instead of a place. This all started at your parents' place, right? Not here? So it can't be about the house, then. Or it would have started here. Or got better once you left. Right? Plus you fit the profile. Poltergeist victims are usually youngish. And they're attracted to tension in the home."

"Because of my parents?" I say blankly. "That doesn't make any sense. People get divorced all the time."

"It makes about as much sense as this stuff ever does. I don't know, maybe you're special."

My turn to scoff. "Right."

"Come on, what kind of paranormal investigator are you? We'll ask. Here, see, we can use that." She gestures at me and it takes me a second to figure out that she's talking about the necklace. "Give it here for a sec."

I hand it to her. "I thought you said this was for protection."

"Well, yes, but we can use it for this too." She holds the necklace by the ribbon in one extended hand. It swings slowly back and forth. "See, it'll always move a little bit, even if you're holding your hand still. If it moves side to side this way, that means no. If it moves side to side *this* way, that means yes. And if it just goes around in circles, it's not sure."

"I guess," I say dubiously. Ron grins.

"Here, you hold it." She draws a breath, straightens up, and says in a commanding voice, "*Are you there?*"

The pendant drifts slowly to a stop. It seems heavier. Is it my imagination? I keep my hand as still as possible, but my fingers tremble.

"Are you there?" Ron repeats, a little louder. My hand is definitely shaking now, but the pendant doesn't move, except to turn very slightly on its axis. And to sink a little lower as it drags my hand down.

And then it's pulled out of my fingers, like I've lost my grip on a huge weight, and the little clink it makes as it hits the floor seems out of all proportion to the relief in my arm. Ron and I both stare at it.

"Well," she says, letting out her breath, "that was weird. *Ouch!*"

She had gone to pick it up, but lets it fall with a clatter, cradling her hand to her chest.

"It's cold." She gives me a stricken look, all her wry irony vanished. "*Really* cold. Like, liquid nitrogen cold."

The wind mutters at the window. My voice is almost steady when I speak.

"Maybe this isn't such a good idea."

Ron scowls at the pendant and snatches it up by the ribbon, dropping it on the bed, where it bounces a little and lies glittering in the light of the lamp.

"Bullshit. I mean, that could have been you. Right?"

"It wasn't me," I say faintly. Ron waves this off.

"That's the problem with this stuff. I thought about bringing a Ouija board. That'd be a lot more specific than a pendulum. But it's the same problem, it's way too easy to manipulate. What we need is something objective. Something you couldn't do by yourself."

"Like what?" I pull my shaky hands inside my sleeves; I'm freezing.

"I don't really know. We could go for the most dramatic option and try to summon it directly. But it might not listen to us if we don't know what it is. I don't think poltergeist is specific enough. You've never seen it, right?"

I shake my head.

"Dreamed about it, maybe?"

"I don't think so. Maybe once." There was that figure standing over me in the dark. But it looked like my mom, and that doesn't make any sense. "It's the water I keep dreaming about."

"Aha!" Ron exclaims, and sits forward a little. "So maybe it's something from the water, then. Something that latched onto you somehow."

"D'you think? Why me?"

"I don't know. Do you spend a lot of time by the river?"

"Well, you can see it from our house." And from here, I guess. "But so can lots of people."

"And you haven't had any, I don't know, special affinity for water, or dramatic near-death experiences in it, or anything?"

"I used to go to the beach here sometimes with my parents, but I don't think that counts."

Ron taps her fingers pensively against her lips.

"I don't know why it didn't use the pendulum, though. If it's really there. I mean, why would it be making all this fuss, if not to get attention and be heard? What does it *want*? There's something, obviously. 'This is mine,' right?"

She's talking about this like she's diagnosing a cold or solving a puzzle. Nothing unusual, nothing uncanny. Nothing that should turn the world dizzy and unreal or make my insides crawl. Is she simply humoring me? Playing along?

But the necklace... She wasn't faking that.

"Do you think there is something there?" The question comes out timid. Shaky.

"I suspend my disbelief, remember?"

"You just...seem to know a lot about this."

"Hey, if I'm going to be a paranormal investigator, I need cred, don't I?" Her teasing smile becomes a pensive look. "It's osmosis, mostly. I used to think my mom was the real thing, when I was little. Like, I don't know, like Gandalf." She scowls. "You can imagine how well that went over at school. I held out for a long time, but there's only so long you can insist there's a Santa Claus when everyone's laughing at you, you know? And I...well, I had a really bad year last year. And she never figured it out. She barely *noticed*. She says it's harder to read people you're close to." Ron hugs her knees, her shoulders hunched. "I told her I was meeting my friend Tristan tonight. And she huffed and puffed a little because she doesn't like him. I guess she figured out he was getting me the cigarettes. But she didn't catch on that I was lying. I should probably be glad. I mean, it'd be pretty inconvenient if she was the real deal."

"So…disbelief."

"Damn straight. It's a cheat. Just stupid theatrics. And seriously flaky people. Do you know how she signs forms and stuff? Like, for school? Niobe. No last name or anything. I mean, for God's sake. That's not even her real name. I guess Joan is just too mundane. And she *has* to put 'psychic' down as her occupation, she can't just write 'self-employed.' I don't know how people don't see right through her. She's such a *fake*." She hesitates, glances my way. "But you're not. And now I don't know what to think."

"Is that why you're helping me?" I ask, and then I'm afraid I've insulted her, but her smile returns, wry and crooked.

"Maybe a little bit. But mostly you just seemed so shell-shocked, the other day. I felt bad for you." Of course she did. I knew it. "And you hate Farrell. That was definitely a point in your favor." Her smile broadens momentarily, then fades. "If it's real, I just want to know, I guess. That's all."

"Her reading was pretty hit and miss," I offer. "She said I brought this on myself."

Ron's scowl returns. "Exactly. See? She's full of shit. Who says that to someone?"

"It didn't make any sense to me," I concede, but I'm more relieved by her reaction than I want to let on.

"Right? I mean, what could you have done to make this happen, buy a cursed antique? Although come to think of it… You haven't bought any antiques lately, have you?"

"Seriously?"

"C'mon, why not? While we're entertaining the idea. These stories have to come from somewhere, right? Seriously, though, no antiques, nothing you inherited?" I shake my head. Her eyes narrow thoughtfully. "Well, there's plenty of ghost stories around Ottawa. Maybe you picked something up somewhere." She reaches for my laptop. "Here, look."

We spend a few minutes bent over the computer, Ron's shoulder a comfortable weight against mine, looking through local hauntings. But they're all downtown or out in the boonies, places that are either hopelessly ordinary—the nature museum, for instance, which I've been to on class trips—or that I've never visited. I've never even heard of the Bytown Museum.

"That doesn't really make sense anyway," Ron says eventually, sitting back on her heels. "I mean, otherwise you'd think everyone who went on that haunted walk tour would have this problem. Somehow I don't think that would be good for business."

"I hate this," I burst out. "I'm so sick of it. What if it hurts somebody? What if I hurt somebody?" I stumble to a stop at that and drop my head down onto my outstretched knees, hugging my legs. Mom's words, almost the same ones, seem to whisper in my ears. "I don't know. Maybe this is ridiculous. The simple explanation is that I'm hallucinating. Maybe we should just go with that."

She's silent; when I look up at her, she's watching me, her eyebrows up, and I sit up, suddenly self-conscious.

"What?"

"Nothing. It's just…flexible much? Holy crap."

"What, this?" I fold myself down again and grab my feet. She nods. I shrug, heat prickling in my cheeks. "Not really."

"Are you kidding? Here, watch." She stretches her legs out and reaches for her feet, but she's barely past vertical before she stops, wiggling her fingers uselessly at her toes.

"Now you're just making fun of me."

"I'm dead serious! This is as far as I go. I promise."

I roll over onto hands and knees and sink down into a frog stretch, knees sliding out to point to either side, toes touching, hips and stomach flat against the floor. "Try this one."

Ron obeys, grimacing, but only manages to sink an inch or two toward the ground before she collapses awkwardly out of the stretch, sprawling on the floor. And now we're both laughing.

"Not fair. You've probably been doing that since you were, like, three years old."

"That's why I picked it," I protest. "It's what you do when you're a little kid. You know, basic stuff."

"Oh my God, that's basic? Show me something hard."

I shouldn't. I'm showing off. She's going to think I'm something I'm not. But it's been so long since anyone was impressed by me. She grins and makes a gesture that says *well?*

So I get up, lift one leg behind me through arabesque into a back split, reach up to clasp my calf in both hands, point my toes toward the ceiling. Then I stretch up, pushing roots down into the ground. Steady. Steady.

Her gaze meets mine; the silence stretches. Isn't she going to look away? Should I close my eyes? Something tightly coiled lurches in my chest, and I tip out of balance, stumble back to the ground.

"I thought you said you weren't very good."

I lower myself onto the edge of the bed, avoiding her gaze. "That's nothing. Seriously."

She clears her throat. "Well. Anyway. Ghosts."

"Yeah. Ghosts." I twist my fingers together. "Or delusions."

"Well, like I said, you're taking the meds. We're just, you know, doing due diligence."

"I guess. Only…if I can't trust what I remember, how do I tell the difference? How do I even know what's real?"

"Well, you know I'm real, at least, because I kicked Farrell's ass. Right?"

I can't help smiling at that. "Right."

"So that makes me a witness. If something happens, I'm right here to see it too. And if I don't see it…well." She looks at me, considering. "You were just going for a walk, the other night, when all that weirdness happened. Maybe we should try that. You know, together."

I hunch my shoulders.

"But what if…what if we can't get back this time?"

"What do you mean? Get back from where?"

I have to think about that for a second; I'm a little taken aback by my own words. "I don't know, that just came out. It just felt like a different place. I didn't really look around."

Ron considers this, and then slaps her hands on the floor, all decisive.

"We should," she declares. "We totally should. Come on, let's go."

"But—"

"It's a fact-finding mission. Reconnaissance." She softens a little bit, seeing my expression. "I'll be with you the whole time, I promise. And look, see, I brought some provisions."

She rummages in her backpack and pulls out what looks like a little bundle of gray-green twigs, tied up with purple string, and a cardboard box, which she hands to me.

"Salt?"

"Yep. And sage. Let's take all the protection we can get, right? Good paranormal investigators come prepared. Put this back on." She hands me the necklace by the ribbon. Gingerly, I obey, trying to avoid touching the stone. "And here, take your sweater off." She takes it from me and reaches into the sleeves, pulls them inside-out. "Put it on like this. It makes you invisible to spooky things."

I make a face. "Maybe you're just on a secret campaign to make me look like an idiot."

Ron wrestles with her own sweater, pulls it back over her head with the pilling fuzzy lining facing out, black seams running down her arms. She stuffs the sage and salt back into her bag, zips it up.

"Only because I love company," she smirks. "C'mon, let's go hunt some ghosts."

10

AUNT JEN RAISES HER EYEBROWS when she sees us trooping down the stairs, but doesn't ask about the inside-out clothes.

"Are you going out, Mare-bear?" she inquires mildly.

"Aunt *Jen*," I groan. "Please."

"That's right. I'm sorry, I keep forgetting." She flashes an apologetic smile at Ron. "She's been Mare-bear to me since she was about two. There was a song I used to sing to her, you know the one about the teddy bears' picnic?"

I drag my hands down my face, but Ron grins at me.

"Don't worry," she says, "Mare-bear is kind of cute."

"*Anyway*. I'll be back in a bit." It takes an attempt to shove my shoes on for me to realize I'm still in my fuzzy house socks. Hurriedly, I strip them off and cram the sneakers on without them. I don't want Ron to see my monster feet.

But Ron's occupied with the laces on her own boots, and when she straightens, it's to wave to my aunt. "Nice to meet you."

Outside the clouds fly low, ragged gray swaths edged in orange from the lights of the city. The trees bend and sigh, the pine branches lift and wave. Beyond them, the bay is crested with little white waves, churned by the wind. Even with the new sandbags, sloshes of water crash over the seawall every now and again, splashing into a wide puddle that almost covers the whole width of the road.

Ron cups her hands in front of her face, struggling to light a cigarette; the shivering flame makes her face a Halloween mask of light and shadow. The wind whips the smoke away as she exhales.

"So which way did you go the other night?"

I point, not trusting my voice. The streetlights are working again, fortunately, and the street leading to the park is a corridor of little orange-lit islands leading into the night.

"Here." Ron digs the sage out of her bag and pushes it into my hands. She tries to hold the lighter to it, but the flame gutters out in the wind. We have to stand close, making a shield with our bodies, before she finally succeeds in lighting the tip of the bundle. She lets the flame billow up for a moment before waving it so that the wind puffs it out again, releasing a thick column of smoke that shreds apart in the wind. It smells acrid and sick-sweet at the same time, in the same way I associate with the stoners who smoke behind the tech wing at school. Ron wafts it all around me, ignoring my coughing and grimacing, and finally holds it out to me again.

"You carry it," she says.

"Ugh. It smells like pot."

"So? Maybe it'll make the ghost mellow or something."

Reluctantly, I accept the smoking bundle, and at Ron's gesture I step slowly out onto the street.

Fear coils around me, pinching my ribs, making my breath shallow and my head swimmy. I clutch the twiggy bunch of sage before me. The wind steals all but the occasional whiff of the smoke. But I keep moving, pushing myself forward step by step, and Ron walks beside me, and nothing strange happens. Someone hurries past us down the street, sparing us a curious glance.

"Does it feel different at all?" Ron asks. "From last time?"

"I don't think so. I'm not sure." There's still that same tide of sound in the background, augmented now by the lift and gust of the wind, but it stays where it belongs. If something's out there, it hasn't noticed me.

Not yet.

We follow the streetlights to the corner, to the stand of shifting, sighing pines that borders the path into the park. The street's orange glow lights their trunks, but their tops are shadows against the clouds. Ron stamps out the end of her cigarette and looks up at them and then into the darkness beyond, the little islands of lampposts scattered over the grassy slope of the park. I take an inadvertent step back.

"What?" Ron says, instantly alert. I shake my head.

"Nothing. Nothing. I just don't want to go this way." Which is stupid, it's *Britannia Beach*, for God's sake.

"Then this is definitely the way we should go," she says. I stare up at the shadows of the trees so I won't have to look at the water. The sage crackles in my hands as my grip tightens. Ron's touch startles me; she pulls one of my hands away, her fingers twining through mine. I could map each point on my palm that touches hers. Warmth steals into my blood from every one of them. Her voice is gentler when she continues. "Reconnaissance, remember?"

Niobe's words flicker through my mind as I let her lead me onto the path. *Maybe this is more than a friend.*

Which is ridiculous. Thank God Ron's missing the psychic gene. It's holding hands. Just like with Ingrid. It means nothing. Relax already.

Gravel crunches under our feet. We skirt around a long arm of water that reaches way past where it should, stretching across the path and into the grass. Wide puddles reflect the streetlights. On my right, out of the shadow of the houses and the trees, the river roars, the faintest shadow of white waves visible at the edge of the beach. The faint orange shadows of a few lonely trees stick out of the water. Orange-gray light stains the clouds, but out over the water, where the distant twinkling lights trail off, it bleeds into a dark so deep I can't make out the shape of the river or where it meets the sky.

I pull my hand from Ron's so I can walk faster, lengthening my steps, until I'm almost running to the next lamppost. It stands before a row of towering poplars that line the edge of the sand and gives off a faint electric whine.

"Marianne, wait up! What is it?"

"The water," I manage. "It's the water. In my dream—can we please get away from the water?"

"It was dragging you into the water, wasn't it? In your dream, I mean."

I nod, folding my arms against shivers my sweater can't ward off. Ron slings her backpack to the ground, pulls out the box of salt.

"What are you doing?"

"If there's any place it'll talk to us, it's here."

"Ron, I don't—"

"We need some evidence, right? So here, I'm hitting record." She pokes at her phone, pockets it again. "And check out what my mom still had." She brandishes something I can't see clearly in the dim glow of the streetlight. A little oblong box, silver maybe. "Tape recorder. For backup, in case it catches something the phone doesn't."

She hands it to me. It's smooth plastic; I can feel buttons along one side.

"Very vintage," I manage.

"An artifact from the dawn of time," Ron intones, reclaiming it and grinning as she presses a button.

"Seriously, Ron, can we go? Please?"

But Ron holds up a hand for silence. She's shaking the salt onto the soggy ground, pacing around me in a circle. When the orange light catches her expression it's fierce, frowning. When the circle is complete, she sets down the box, pushes her hair out of her eyes.

"I think I'm supposed to say something." She folds her arms, glances furtively up and down the path, and makes a face at me. "Brace yourself. This is going to sound stupid."

"Ron, I really don't think—"

"Just hang on, okay? Due diligence. This'll only take a second, and then we can go."

She rolls her shoulders, heaves a deep breath, stretches her hand up to the sky. Then like a fencer issuing a challenge, she swings her hand down to point at me, and her voice is like a bell:

"By my will I bind you and charge you: speak!"

For a second it seems as if it's the wind that will answer her, swelling and voiceless. But it goes clotted and muffled, settling into my ears in a horribly familiar way. It's happening—it's happening again. I throw my arms over my head and cry out Ron's name, but I can't make any sound. I try again, put my hands to my face, feel my lips moving, my breath on my palms. But everything is lost in that same silent roar, that endless, susurrating unsound. Like I'm underwater. But when I gasp for breath, I can feel the air rushing in.

When I can finally bring myself to lift my head, the wind has vanished. Around me the trees are immobile, uncannily so, their leaves sharply outlined in the glow of the lamp, innumerable overlapping orange coins. Nothing moves.

I'm alone.

Ron! I try to shout, but I can't make a sound. And again. I feel it shred apart into a scream, and only then can I hear a pale echo, distant, leached of all meaning.

But maybe silence would have been smarter. Suddenly I feel exposed, standing in the middle of the path in the orange and black shadows. If something's following me…does it know I'm here? Did it hear me?

"Saint Michael the Archangel," I whisper. "Saint Michael the Archangel—"

But the words are as soundless as my screams. And I can't remember the rest of them.

I let my breath out in a long, shivering sigh, and in the space between exhaling and inhaling I become aware of the water at my back: its flat, black face stretching out behind me beyond the trees. The chill green smell of it fills my nostrils. I don't turn around to look at it, though, because an awful certainty is flickering through my chest, a familiar weight dragging at me—subdued, a current around my ankles—and I can barely breathe.

If I turn around, if I step out there, past the trees and onto the sand, I'll find the water smooth as glass, breathing damp chill into my face, a shelf of ice barely visible at the edge of the light. If I turn around I won't be able to stop walking. I'll be stepping back into my dream.

Only I'm awake.

Aren't I?

I don't turn around. I take a step away from the river, and another step, another. The not-quite-noise won't drain from my ears, there's no sound to mark my footfalls. It's not as hard, this time, moving away from the water. Soon I'm running, pelting across the grass, the scattered immobile trees of the park whipping past me. I run, run away from the water, against the pressure tugging at my legs. I cross the bike path, the grassy slope surrounding it, the rocks livid with graffiti, and I'm out under the streetlights again.

But the houses are all dark and silent, and I run. I run down the street that should take me up the hill, but it's not the same, it's not right. I can't hear traffic, can't hear dogs barking, there's no sound and nothing moves. The orange light outlines each blade of grass, each pebble in the street. I can't outrun the roaring in my ears. And in the space of a blink the street has changed direction on me, sloping *down*, back toward the dark sea of the park. A weight has sprung up at my back like a tidal wave, pressing me forward, and I can't stop, I can't slow down. The slow, cold smell of the river rises around me. My feet connect not with pavement, but with sand.

And in that moment, a voice I know and don't know rips through the silent noise that stuffs my ears, livid with terror, making the world shiver and blur around me.

"*Marianne! MARIANNE!*"

I whip around to find its source, and for a bottomless instant, I stand face to face with someone—with something—all black staring eyes and floating hair, and the whole world shrinks away from it, even the darkness flees from the hate beating out of it in smothering waves.

But then the sound crashes back in: I'm screaming, my own voice filling my ears, the echoes ringing away into the trees, the wind roaring in the branches above me, and when I force my eyes open I know the pale, painted face I see in the lamplight, startlingly close: it's Ron, it's only Ron, lowering her arms as if she'd been trying to fend something off. I gulp her name and she flinches a little.

"Where were you?" I sob out. "Where did you go?"

She stares at me, retreats a few steps.

"Where did you go?" I wail. "There was something—oh my God—where did you go?"

"I didn't," she begins, but it comes out hoarse and she stops, shakes her head, folds her arms. Her eyes never leave my face.

"Ron—"

"I have to go." She makes a fumbling snatch for her backpack. "I didn't think it would... I have to go."

"Ron, wait!"

She shoves the tape recorder into my hands and turns away.

"Ron! Ron, *what happened?*"

But she's already running, leaving me a shadow under the trees, running away into the light.

I turn to go and let out a yelp at the bite of wet sand and sharp bits of gravel against my skin. I stare down at my feet, pale, black-scarred shapes against the asphalt of the path. Where are my shoes? It takes me a long minute, fumbling in the dark, to find them; one is lying on the wet grass, the other in an inch-deep puddle. My hair falls around my face, blowing into my eyes, as I crouch to retrieve them. It's loose down my back, my braid completely undone.

I stumble back toward Aunt Jen's, keeping my head down, clutching the recorder. I can't stop shaking, a rattling tremor that goes bone-deep. But the noises of the world stay with me: the ordinary sound of a bus coming down the next street, the squelch and slap of my wet shoes on the pavement, the clatter of a garbage can rolling down a driveway in the wind. The wind swirls around me, indifferent and ordinary, not the weird current that pressed me toward the water.

It's over. It has to be over. Whatever it was.

I count the steps up to my room, grateful for the faint sound of the TV coming from Aunt Jen's room, and wash my pills down with a glass of water that trembles in my hand. Gingerly, I set the tape recorder on the dresser. It's a strange, clunky alien among the little china animals. I crawl fully dressed into bed and roll over, facing away from it. But I can feel it sitting there anyway, a silent accusation.

11

I WAKE TO THE SOUND of crows cawing outside. The clock says 11:22 a.m. I lie there, cool and empty, like after a fever or a bad dream. It must have been a dream. Again, just a dream, disappearing into the light like any other. Maybe I won't even remember it later.

But if it was a dream…

I roll over, burying my face in the pillow, trying to escape the thought, but it follows me. If it was a dream, when did I fall asleep? Would I remember falling asleep? Ron was here, wasn't she?

I stare up at the ceiling, the dread settling back into place, cold and viscous. If I close my eyes, what swims into my mind is the empty street, the blind faces of the houses leaning over it, the street running the wrong way, not up into the city but down, down toward the sand and the water.

I should stop thinking about it. My thoughts are like the street, leading toward something I don't want to remember.

I start to do my stretches but can't relax into them properly. The black splotches on my toes keep drawing my eye. I pull my book from my backpack, but I just end up reading the same two pages over and over again without tracking a single sentence, jumping at every sound: wind rattling the windows, Aunt Jen's footsteps, the bathroom door opening and closing. After a while she knocks on my door to remind me to take my pills.

"You should have some breakfast," she says as I toss them back. "They'll make you sick on an empty stomach."

Obediently, I force down a banana and a cup of milk, but it isn't enough. I spend the next couple hours huddled on the couch in a miserable knot of nausea. Aunt Jen *tsks* over me, covers me up with a blanket, brings me a PB and J.

"I had the same problem," she says, sitting at my feet. "Have some more to eat. It'll help."

I've pushed myself reluctantly onto my elbows before I realize what she said.

"Wait. You're on these too?"

"Was. The SSRIs, anyway." She doesn't return my stare; is she avoiding my eyes? "It was a long time ago. After I got divorced. Your grandma had passed away a few years earlier, and your mom's my little sister, and she was so busy with you. It was like she and your dad were off in their own little world. I got to the point where I was having trouble putting one foot in front of the other anymore, but it kind of felt like there wasn't anybody left I could go to." She does meet my gaze then, gives me a meaningful look. "It's hard when you don't feel like you have anyone to lean on. The medicine couldn't change what was going on, obviously. But it took some of the load off so I could get through it."

I sit up, sorting through this.

"You were *married?*"

Aunt Jen's lips quirk. "Not for very long. Not for the right reasons."

"I used to wonder whether you would ever get married. You never said anything." All she'd ever said was "Well, maybe someday." When I'd asked Mom, she just told me Jen didn't seem too interested.

"Oh, I've seen a few people over the years," Aunt Jen says in an offhand way. "I guess I'm still a little gun-shy. I like having my own place, without having to depend on someone else or fight about chores." She settles back into her corner of the couch and smiles at me. "And anyway, it's more fun when it's not too serious." I blink at her, and she laughs. "Oh, Mare-bear, you look so shocked. What did you think I was, a nun?"

"It's just weird," I protest, and she shakes her head, still laughing. Aunt Jen is six years older than Mom, and between that and her gray-streaked hair, her prim reserve, she always seemed ancient to me. Grandmotherly. Among the pictures on the wall above the staircase are some snapshots from the surprise party Mom threw for her on her thirtieth birthday, where I was a baby in a pink sundress. It occurs to me now she's not even fifty.

"Was it like this?" I ask. "When you got divorced?"

"No," she says gently. "We didn't own much of anything. And we didn't have kids. It was...well, it's never easy. But it's simpler, you know, when all you have to manage is your own broken heart."

How is it possible to love people so much and never know these things about them? What else haven't they told me?

I've seen a few people over the years. People. I look up at her again as she takes a long sip of tea.

She never used a pronoun. Not even about her ex. Not "he." Not once.

The questions come bubbling up, and I swallow. I will not ask. I take a determined bite of toast and force them down, rocks vanishing into the water. I will not ask. I don't need to know.

What I need to know is what happened last night.

I steel myself to call Ron, to ask her, but I only get as far as picking up my phone. In my mind I see her running through the orange-lit darkness, and I throw the phone back in my bag. She doesn't want to hear from me. And I'm afraid of what she would say.

So much for Niobe's reading. Nobody's going to hell and back for me.

But, well... There's always the tape.

I can almost feel the little silver box waiting for me upstairs, a magnet tugging at me, a weight on my chest. I have to listen to the tape. I can't listen to it.

Later. I'll do it later. Once I work up the nerve.

The afternoon crawls by. Between the gray weather and the north-facing windows, it already feels like twilight. Aunt Jen snaps on the light next to her armchair and goes on crocheting. I almost fall asleep, but before the wash of the rain can blur into underwater silence, a knock at the door jerks me back to reality.

Aunt Jen calls my name from the front hall. I steady my breathing, shaking off the incipient dream hanging over me.

"Coming," I manage.

I stand, feeling wobbly and wrung-out, then trudge around the corner. And freeze.

Dad stands just inside the door, his hands in his coat pockets, looking back at me.

"Hi, bunny," he says. His smile is hopeful, uncertain.

I blink at him and struggle for my voice.

"Hi."

"I've been hoping you would call."

"I know."

"Listen. I know it's hard right now, but…can we please talk?"

I cross my arms, look away. Aunt Jen catches my gaze and gives a minute, encouraging nod.

"We can go out for some hot chocolate, maybe," Dad offers, watching us. "What do you think? Please?"

Out of the house. Sudden hope wars with dread. Away. Do I dare? What if something happens in front of Dad?

The tape is still waiting for me. If I stay here, I have to listen to it.

"Okay," I whisper.

I steal glances at him as we drive. He looks tired. Dad has an artist's face; if you put him in nineteenth century clothes he'd look like a poet, with thoughtful gray eyes, a quick smile, and a pensive frown. His hair is thinning, something he's a little self-conscious about. Mom used to tell him it made him look distinguished. Gave him a "noble brow."

He's drumming his fingers on the wheel. I think of him smiling at me over his shoulder, some past summer in another world, the evening light slanting through his sunglasses as Mom dozed in the other seat, her breath rattling in and out.

"What do you think, bun," he'd asked, "should we tell her she snores?"

He pulls into the parking lot of a Starbucks a few minutes later, surprising me.

"I thought you hated it here." He always complains that everything is three times as sweet and three times as expensive as it needs to be.

"Well, maybe," he says, pocketing the keys and attempting another smile, "but you don't."

I drop into a chair, my back turned to the windows so I won't have to see my shadow reflected in the glass, while Dad heads to the counter. The rain rattles down behind me. God, I'm exhausted. I fold my arms on the table and rest my aching head on them for a minute, surrounded by the comforting, busy sound of the place: the rattle of plates, the swoosh of the cappuccino maker. But then Dad comes back to the table, carrying a big, white-and-green cup topped with a mountain of whipped cream and a brownie on a plate.

I can't even stammer out a thank you. He sits down, watching me in silence. I poke at the brownie with my fork, take a bite without tasting it.

"Are you okay, bun?" he asks eventually. I can't suppress a snort at the stupidity of the question. He looks away, fiddling with the receipt. "I wish you'd let me go with you to the hospital. I was really worried about you."

"I'm fine," I mutter. "They told me they couldn't find anything wrong."

"I know. Jen told me. I just wish you and I could talk about this, you know? Like reasonable people."

I stab another forkful of brownie. "There's nothing to talk about."

"Of course there is. You're obviously pretty angry."

I rattle a spoon around my cup, sloshing a little wave of chocolate over the edge, trying to figure out what to say. How much does he know about what's happened with Mom? Should I tell him? He might blame himself. Maybe I want him to.

When I still don't speak, he tries again. "Jen said your mom's kind of coming apart at the seams."

"What did you expect?" I demand.

"That must be hard on you."

"Yeah. Well."

"I just wanted to make sure you got a chance to have your say. You must have a lot of questions."

He's repeating himself from that stupid email. Like he's prepared a script in advance. No, not a script: talking points. I'm another crisis to be managed by staying on message. I let the silence pool between us, but he's got lots of practice at this game and waits unmoved for me to speak. Finally I look at him and flatten my voice until it's level.

"Were you going to tell me why you didn't go to my show? The one in Montreal?"

"She told you about that, did she?" He sighs. "I don't know, bunny. I guess I was running away. Trying to figure things out before I said anything. I didn't want to burden you with it until I was sure. You…had a lot going on. That's why I couldn't go through with it, in the end. I couldn't leave you."

"But you can now?" I snap. He sits back a bit, looking unhappy, and it occurs to me that this is why we're here, with people chatting comfortably all around us. So I won't make a scene. So I won't freak out. I take a long, calming breath. I am ice over deep water. "I thought you'd worked things out. Like you said people are supposed to do. I thought you were *fine*."

"I tried. I really did. I've been trying for sixteen years."

"So what happened? Are you cheating again or what?"

He gives me a pained look. "Is that what she told you?"

I take a long slurp of the hot chocolate so I won't have to answer.

"Look," he says, folding his arms on the table. "I just want us all to be happy. Your mom... She can't be happy with me. I'm glad she's finally getting some help, at least. She's always been so fragile. I can't make her happy. And neither can you. Don't put that on your plate, okay?"

"What else am I supposed to do?" I'm not yelling. I won't crack. "Just let her sink? Like you are?"

"Bunny, it's not your responsibility." He's earnest now, leaning across the table. "You can't take that on. That's what happened with dance, isn't it?"

The table shivers, making the plate clink against the surface. I put out a hand to grip its edge, panic splashing over me. That wasn't me. I know that wasn't me.

Dad, though he's watching me intently, doesn't seem to notice.

"I hated the way that ended," he says. "I know how much you loved it. She ruined it for you. She shouldn't have pushed you so hard. You haven't seemed yourself since you quit."

Like he'd know. I close my eyes. I'll wash it away. I'll make it disappear. But the only water I can summon is dark and glassy. "That wasn't about Mom."

"What was it about, then? I wish you'd talk to me. I want to have a real relationship with my daughter."

Of course he doesn't know what it was about. He didn't really want to know; he left instead of asking. He ran. Just like he's running from Mom now.

Maybe Mom's not the one who's fragile.

Under my hand the smooth stone tabletop feels colder, stealing the heat from my fingers. When I speak, the words seem to come from very far away. "You're never even here."

"I guess I tried to escape into work for a while. I thought maybe that's what I was supposed to do. Be the provider, hold everything together. But it was so lonely. I don't want that to be my life. I need to save what's left of our family."

By leaving me to hold everything together instead. A picture floats up through the icy lake: Mom sobbing in the garden. My grip tightens on the table.

"I haven't abandoned you, Marianne. I'm still here. I just need to find a place that's not a hotel room, and then you can come stay with me. Okay?"

"What if I don't want to stay with you?" The words boil out of me before I can stop them.

"You don't have to," he says after a long pause, the words reproachful. "I just wanted to make sure you had a choice."

"Maybe I don't want to leave Mom!" I cry. "What choice do I have? That's not a choice at all!"

"Bunny, please," Dad sighs, "I know you're angry, I really do. Please, just calm down and—"

The table rocks under my hand, and I jump to my feet, trying to hold it down, but it rebels, pitches on its side, and the cup and plate are catapulted to the floor, shattering the plate, sending shards of porcelain everywhere. Hot chocolate splatters on my jeans and runs in streams all over the floor.

"Marianne, what the hell?" Dad's still in his chair, his hands clapped to his forehead, his eyes wide. He speaks into a sudden hush; everyone is staring at us.

"It wasn't me." I force my numbing lips to form the words. They're barely audible.

"I know you're upset, but I thought we could at least have a conversation!"

Whispers rise around us. People turn away, eyebrows raised.

"Can we go now?" I plead. "Please?"

Dad throws his hands in the air, but before he can even get to his feet, I'm already out the door.

"Call me, okay?" Dad says wearily as he pulls up to Aunt Jen's building. "When you're ready to talk."

Whatever. I scramble out of the car without answering. I can feel him watching me as I run for the gate in the hedge.

I take the stairs two at a time, ignoring Aunt Jen's hesitant call behind me. The tape recorder is sitting where I left it, a little silver patch gleaming against the colorful quilt draped over the mirror. I stand there staring at it, the chill of the linoleum floor seeping through my socks.

At first I can't identify the source of the noise—a faint buzz, becoming a rattle, growing steadily louder—and then I see the little china animals on the dresser starting to jump and shake. It's like there's an earthquake, but the floor is cold and steady, the dusty frames on the wall don't move. And then one of the figurines catapults from its place, smashing on the floor. Another. The next one goes a little farther, spattering my feet with little ceramic shards. I fall backward onto the bed as another whips past my shoulder, crunching into the wall. Another one strikes above me, raining broken debris over me as I cower.

I stay huddled there for a long time after everything has gone silent again before I dare to lift my head. Downstairs, someone on the radio is laughing. I pick my way through the shattered remains of the china animals. If I run I'll cut my feet.

In the hall, I yank the door closed behind me and lean against it, breathing hard. I just got home. I must be awake. And that wasn't me. Am I seeing things now? Like Mom? There's no way that could have been me.

Knock knock knock.

It's like someone's tapping on the door with their knuckles, right next to my ear, quiet but emphatic. I jerk away from the sound, but then it moves, ranging all around the hallway, behind the walls, the ceiling.

"Marianne, sweetie?" Aunt Jen calls from downstairs. "Is that you?"

I wheel into the bathroom, slam the door, muttering under my breath with each step—"Go away, go away, go away!"—and the knocking dies down behind me. Downstairs I hear the front door opening, Aunt Jen calling out into the hall—"Hello?"—and then a sigh of exasperation as the door falls closed again.

She heard it, though. She *heard* it.

I collapse onto the edge of the tub, draw a trembling breath, and close my eyes, trying to steady myself. Cool, green-tinged sunlight. I'll suspend time, let it all filter down to me through the water. But that only leads me to the memory of water meeting sky on that black horizon, the street running the wrong way.

I jerk the bathtub faucet on, mostly to keep Aunt Jen from thinking she needs to check on me, and shuck my T-shirt onto the floor. The gesture produces an unexpected twinge of soreness from my shoulder, and I glance down to find the tops of my arms marked with bruises, little elongated bluish circles under my skin. They almost look like fingerprints. Carefully, I fit my fingers over the marks. They line up disturbingly well.

When I look up again at the mirror above the sink, in the glass all I can see is darkness, a window into nothing, framed by a pale crescent of sand.

I whip around with a little screech of indrawn breath, half expecting to find it stretching out behind me, but of course all that's there is the yellow tiled wall of the shower, the rush of the water, billowing steam. All around me, as if from behind the walls, comes that same quiet, insistent sound. *Knock knock knock. Knock knock knock.* Like someone testing for a weak spot, looking for a way in. Helplessly, I turn back to the mirror, and though the nighttime beach has disappeared, my face blurs and vanishes beneath a layer of gray fog blooming on the glass as if someone has breathed against it. And as I watch, lines drip through it, forming unsteady letters.

THIS IS MINE
MARIANNE

I snatch a washcloth from its hanger beside the sink and scrub the words from the glass, but I can't erase them from my mind. I can't erase the certainty sinking in my throat.

Whatever it was I saw last night—it saw me too.

12

WHEN I FINALLY THUMP BACK downstairs, Aunt Jen is in the front hall with her coat on, rummaging through her purse. Is she leaving me here alone?

"Where are you going?" I whisper.

"To check on your mom," she says, and looks up at me. "Why? Are you all right?"

I swallow.

"Don't feel so good." It's true. With the red edge of panic receding, I'm left sick and dizzy, my stomach still simmering. I cling to the handrail, not trusting myself not to fall.

"You've had a hard day," she says sympathetically, and reaches up the stairs to squeeze my hand. "I won't be gone long. I promise."

"Can't you stay?"

I see the words strike home in the tightening of her mouth, her hesitating glance toward the door. Desperation is making me selfish. I'm making her choose. I'm holding on too tight.

"I know it's bad timing, Mare-bear—"

"Never mind," I interrupt, hugging myself. "It's okay."

"I told her I'd come," she pleads, "and she's so worried about something happening to you. She made me promise I'd go alone."

"I know. I'm sorry. I'll be fine."

"I'll be back as soon as I can. I promise. You text me if you really need me, okay?"

I nod, keep nodding, until she finally shoulders her bag and reaches for the doorknob.

"I won't be long," she says firmly, and even as the door closes behind her she's still watching me, blowing me a kiss before it falls shut with an echoing bang. As her footsteps recede, silence rises around me, inch by inch, filling the apartment.

Carefully, I lower myself to sit on the stairs, fold my arms over my head. I'd be tempted to just sit here until she comes back, as small as I can make myself, but the quiet is deepening every second, making my breath loud in my ears and my arms bristly with goose bumps. I should turn on the radio. I should do something to shake off the memory of that figure I glimpsed last night: a shadow, half-seen, like a reflection in a pool.

"Go away," I whisper. The air is charged and heavy, pressing down on me. My words fall flat in front of my face, like I'm speaking into a dead phone connection. "Go away!"

Knock knock knock, comes the response. KNOCK KNOCK KNOCK. And this time it doesn't stop. It escalates into deafening crashes, like someone's pounding on the wall of the living room with a sledgehammer, but when I run into the room there's nothing there, just the leaves of the plants trembling with every relentless blow. The windows rattle in their frames.

"Stop it!" I cry. "Go away!"

The hammering continues, heedless, a wall of sound pushing me back, until I give up and flee from the room. As I pound up the stairs it drops abruptly into ringing silence, and I stumble to a halt on the landing. My breath shivers in my ears. Doors open outside in the hall; neighbors' voices drift in through the wall, raised in bewildered exclamation.

It's real, this time. It's not just me. It can't be.

The floor of my room is still littered with bits of ceramic. I snatch a T-shirt from the suitcase at the foot of the bed and use it to sweep the pieces up, pushing the whole bundle into the trash can.

Ron's tape recorder is still waiting for me on the dresser. I'm out of excuses. I have to know.

I pick it up and stare at it for a long time before hitting rewind, sinking down onto the bed.

The first thing I hear is our voices: "Seriously, Ron, can we go? Please?" Then Ron's crunching footsteps as she paces around the circle. The wind whuffles in the speaker. Ron calls out her incantation—recorded, it sounds flat and silly, theatrical. Fake.

But her last word is lost in a sudden crackle and howl of static. I barely stop myself from leaping for the Stop button. It ebbs to a faint snarl, and Ron's voice emerges again, blurred and reedy as though coming from a radio not quite tuned.

"...we tried, right? I'm not sure what the hell I would have done if it worked, honestly. But I hope it...helped..."

She falters, falls silent. There's a long pause, and then a strange sound. A long, shivery sigh. The static rises and falls with it, winding through it. As if the static is part of it.

"Okay," Ron says. Her voice has gone faint and hesitant. "You're kind of freaking me out here." Silence. And a breathless little laugh, shot through with white noise. The sound makes my scalp prickle.

"Marianne? Seriously, please say something."

"Is that her name."

Though it's not loud, the voice is clear, harsh, more solid than any other sound on the tape. It's not mine. The static pops and whines.

"Oh." Ron sounds very far away. "Oh my God."

"Listen," the voice breathes. **"Listen. The wind. It's so beautiful."**

"Stay away from me!" Ron yelps. I hear a few hurried footsteps, a scrunch of gravel. "Just—look. Tell me what you want, okay? Stay back!"

"But you're the one who brought me here." Anguish creeps into the other voice, the kindling of anger. **"I was trying to find the way for so long. And you called me. I heard you!"**

"There's something you want, isn't there?" Ron insists. "Tell me what it is!"

"I want...what's mine."

"What do you mean? I don't—no, stay away!" Another scrape and crunch. "Just...just tell me. What's yours?"

"This. This!" The voice rises to a horrible, ugly wail, full of desperation and rage. **"This is mine! This is *all* mine!"**

Ron sounds frail, inconsequential, after that sound; her response dissolves into a tide of noise. When her voice becomes audible again it's shrill.

"...whatever you are! I called you, you have to do what I...what the fuck—!"

"You think I'm just going to go?" The other voice is quiet now, but heavy, deliberate, sharp as a drawn knife. **"You called me, and now you think I'm just going to go back there and let her have all this? Because you *say so*?"**

"Tell me what you want! Who are you? Tell me!"

But the voice doesn't answer; it just laughs.

"Don't touch me!" Ron screams. "Go away! You don't belong here, go away!"

"I will *not*. She can't drown me anymore. I'll drown her instead. She can rot in the dark. This is ALL. MINE."

"It's not! It's not! You don't belong here! Marianne, where are you? Marianne! *MARIANNE!*"

I snap the tape recorder off, cutting off the beginning of my own wordless scream, and scramble away from it, staring at the little plastic box on the mattress like it might bite.

I fumble my phone from my backpack and bring up the California number from the call log, hit the button before I can think better of it.

"Come on," I whisper as it rings and rings. I hang up when it goes to voicemail, dial again. And again. Finally it goes through.

"You're lucky I'm picking this up."

The statement is flat and hard as a slap, not even softened with a hello. It scatters my thoughts into icy shards of panic and I sit blankly for a second with the phone in my hand, trying to pull them back together enough to respond.

"Ingrid?"

"Yeah, it's me."

"I don't... Is everything okay?"

There's a long pause. "I don't know if I'm interested in an apology, Marianne."

"An apology?" My heart climbs into my throat, makes my voice squeaky.

"Were you drunk or something?"

"What are you talking about?" I grip the blankets in numb fingers. "Did I do something wrong?"

"Oh my God." Her laugh is pained. "This is so awkward. Look. I'm not gay. I mean, not that I have a problem with it. But I don't like you that way, okay?"

I lurch back to my feet, clutching the phone, across the room before I even realize I'm pacing. No. No no no.

"What way? You're my friend, that's all. You're my best friend."

"You barely know me. Look, you seem nice and everything, but we've hardly even talked since last summer. I don't know what I did to give you the wrong idea."

I'm asleep. I must be. This is a nightmare. Why can't I wake up?

"I don't know what you mean! It's not like that, I—"

Ingrid sighs.

"That's not going to work, okay? You can't make a phone call like that and just pretend it didn't happen."

"But I didn't call you!"

"Come on, Marianne, seriously? It was your number. It was your voice."

I can't breathe. I'm going to throw up. I'm going to scream.

"What did I say?"

"You said enough. Let's just leave it at that."

"Ingrid. Oh my God, Ingrid, listen, that wasn't me. It wasn't." She starts to say something but I push forward, ignoring how shrill my voice has gone. "Please just listen to me. That wasn't me. I'm so scared. It must have been... There's something here, and it's throwing things and—"

"What are you talking about? If you're trying to convince me that—"

"There's something here," I wail. "Something I can't see! Some sort of ghost!"

"What? What do you mean?"

I put my free hand to my forehead, squinch my eyes closed, fighting for calm. Why did I say that? Why did I think this was a good idea?

"Listen." Calm. Coherent. Cold. "There's been really weird things happening over here. Ever since Dad left." I rattle through the list, keeping my eyes closed, knowing how unhinged I sound, pushing through it anyway.

"Holy crap," Ingrid says, after a long silence.

I laugh, helplessly.

"I know. I know. I couldn't tell whether or not it was real at first. I went to a psychiatrist and everything. But I told—you know Rhiannon? From school?"

"What," Ingrid says, in blank disbelief, "Emo Rhiannon?"

I cringe, plunge ahead. "I told her about it. She said maybe we could test it to see if there was really something there. Try to talk to it. I don't think she expected it to work, but it did. It was horrible. And now it's a million times worse, and I don't know what to do!" The phone squawks in protest as my voice rises; I knock it against the edge of the dresser, but the noise continues. "God, this stupid phone! Can you hear me? Ingrid?"

"…have some real issues." Ingrid's voice is muzzy and distant. "…shouldn't call me again, okay?"

"Ingrid, no, please, wait—"

"…sorry, but…too weird. Good…everything, okay?"

And the line goes dead in my ear.

I stand there with the phone in my hand, my knuckles going white, every desperate excuse I couldn't make howling through me. I stab at the screen, pulling up the call log. There: Last night. The California number. A fifteen-minute call at 4:21 a.m.

It wasn't me, it wasn't me, *it wasn't me*.

I lift the phone, almost throw it. But it won't help. It won't even make me feel better. I've tried that before. I will not be the hurricane. I force my arms to my sides, taking slow, desperate breaths. Calm down. Calm down. There's a way to fix this. I just have to calm down. I close my eyes, but in my mind's eye there's no more sunlight, and all I can think of is that empty horizon. The fringe of ice over the bottomless depths.

When the sound begins my first thought is that I somehow missed pressing the End button on my phone, leaving the static to hiss and simmer. But the screen is dark, and as I stare at it, the scouring metallic noise grows louder, more distinct. It's coming from behind me.

From inside the closet.

I set the phone down carefully on the dresser, my fingers gone nerveless. The sound pauses, starts up again with a rattle:

chickachickachicka. The closet door jerks and trembles, making me jump. But then silence falls, cold and mocking.

None of this can be real, none of it. Something's broken in my head. The difference between reality and a nightmare should be obvious, a sharp line, an on/off switch. I can't open that door.

I have to.

Unable to contain a whimper, I give the door a little yank, as if the handle might burn me. And a little metal box, a candy tin, tumbles off the shelf and lands at my feet with a clatter.

I shriek, spring away from it. But it rattles to a stop with the lid flopped open. Empty.

And then all around me comes a shower of little metallic pings and rattles, and I throw my arms up to shield my face against a hail of little stinging somethings raining down on me, tiny sharp bites against my scalp, through my sleeves. When it stops, it's a long, sobbing moment before I can bring myself to slowly lower my arms. They're peppered with sewing pins: slivers of silver jabbed through my shirt, stinging bright needles topped with bright little plastic globes. I pick them out with trembling fingers, run a careful hand through my hair, dislodging a few more. They ping across the linoleum. I remember just in time not to move my feet. I sink into a shaky crouch, collecting them one by one into a little pile on the dresser. After a long hesitation I collect the empty tin, sweep the pile into it, drop it into one of the empty drawers. Slam it shut.

I missed one: a last thread of silver that almost rolled away under the dresser. I pick it up, watch the light slide off it, and lean the pad of one finger against the point, feel it snag into my skin. Pricking my finger. Like Sleeping Beauty. Did she dream while she slept for a hundred years? The point is vanishingly sharp. It's real, isn't it? Isn't it?

I push my finger down against the pain, through it, until blood wells up in a bright bead. It's real, all right. God, does that mean that phone call was real too? The tape? Did I take this pin from the closet and imagine the rest? How can I trust myself?

Ron saw something. Something that sent her running from me.

She said she couldn't resist a mystery. But she's not here. And who else would ever believe it?

After that, mercifully, everything is quiet. I pull a bandage from the cupboard in the bathroom, rip the paper off with clumsy fingers. I feel hollow, as burnt out as ground zero. Though my hands shake, I'm surprised at my calm, my ability to observe my own thoughts dispassionately from across a wide gulf. Maybe it's the medicine. I suppose I should be grateful.

Aunt Jen eventually calls up the stairs to announce that she's home, but when I don't answer, she tactfully leaves me alone. Eventually the smell of cooking slides under the door.

When I finally let it lure me down the stairs, Aunt Jen is humming in the kitchen, clattering around in the cupboards. An invisible band around my chest loosens a notch or two. I sink into a chair at the table.

"Marianne, do you know where all the forks got to? I just emptied the dishwasher this morning."

Nothing spooky about this, I tell myself.

"No. Sorry."

"Well, good thing it's stew instead of steak, I guess. Spoons it is."

I can't eat more than a few bites, and even that leaves me feeling a little ill. The things I'm not talking about sit in my stomach like rocks, irrefutable. I want to jump up from the table and scream. How are we just sitting here, eating dinner? Somehow that's the most awful thing. The thing that makes it real and not a nightmare.

"You okay, Mare-bear?" Aunt Jen asks eventually.

No. I nod. She's watching me push the spoon around the bowl; I set it down.

"Anything you want to talk about?"

I almost demur, but then something occurs to me. Aunt Jen has lived here since forever.

"Aunt Jen, did anyone ever drown in the bay? Near here?"

She blinks, sits back. "That's…not quite what I had in mind, but…I guess there's always some dimwit wandering out onto the ice during the thaw. So yes, I imagine there have been a number of them, over the years."

"No one you know, though."

"Nope."

"How old is this building, anyway?"

"About fifty years? I guess there used to be other apartments here before that too. They built those on the site of an old sawmill."

Nothing helpful there. I knew it was a long shot.

"So," Aunt Jen says in a bright, final way that makes it clear she's trying to change the subject. "Where did you meet your friend with the wild makeup?"

"At school." I study the table, smooth my fingers over a faint circular scar where someone once set a mug without a coaster.

"She seemed nice," Aunt Jen offers. "Polite."

I shrug.

"Dad says he's not cheating," I come up with eventually, when the silence wears thin.

"Well," Aunt Jen sighs, "I suppose maybe he's not, Marianne. I don't know. Did you take your medicine yet this evening?"

Changing the subject again. I fold my arms.

"So you haven't," Aunt Jen prompts. I sink a little lower in my chair.

"I will," I mutter. "It's just that they make me sick to my stomach."

Her phone pings—once, twice—and she pulls it from her pocket. Her eyes dart toward me as she scans the messages.

"Is that Dad?"

She hesitates. "He's just checking on you."

"He said I didn't have to stay with him." I stick my chin out. "Can he make me?"

"I don't think so. I don't really know. I guess it's up to the lawyers."

Not up to me. I push the chair back, leaving the rest of the stew uneaten, and head for the stairs.

"Don't forget your pills, Mare-bear," Aunt Jen calls after me. I don't bother to answer.

All the way back to my room a thought dogs my steps: home, here, with Dad, it makes no difference. If something is following me—the ghost, or whatever it is—it doesn't matter where I go.

That night I dream I'm dancing. I'm in the wide, bright room in the basement, with a rightness and a sureness pouring through me down to my fingertips, bearing me up. It starts as the grand allegro from one of my conservatory classes and then spirals out beyond it: endless fouettés, grand jetés, high and strong, my arms swept out triumphant and stern. My feet are ghost-light in pointe shoes, the stiff canvas honing them into delicate blades that meet the floor with barely a whisper. I'm perfect precision. Perfect delight.

There's no music; it doesn't matter. I sweep through the house, past the huge expanse of windows, a swan on a hardwood river, my neck a long curve, stretching my wings. I could be Odette, I could be the Sugar Plum Fairy, I could be anyone. I'm unstoppable.

When I come to the kitchen, Dad's standing at the island with a gleaming knife, chopping something. The certainty falls away from me as abruptly as the harsh scratch of a record needle, and I stumble to a stop on the flats of my feet. He's standing there like nothing happened. Has he come back? Again? I don't know how to ask. The blade clacks against wood in expert rhythm.

He's always loved to be the chef; he keeps those knives carefully honed. "It's important to look after your tools," he insisted. He showed me once how he could shave the hair off his arm with one of them.

And Mom sits at the kitchen table, slouched moodily over her coffee. Her feet are gone. Her legs dangle from the chair, blood dripping into a vivid pool beneath her. She looks up at me, scowling.

"Well, what's it going to be," she says in a hurt, huffy voice. "Choose. Go ahead. Him or me."

Dad's knife goes *thock thock thock* against the cutting board. He looks up at me and smiles.

"What pretty dancing shoes," he says.

I turn and run, no elegance left, only clumsy terror. But the house has become endless, full of dark hallways, secret passages that twist and double back on themselves. When I finally find the front door and shoulder through it, I'm stepping out from under the trees onto a dim and silent beach. And somebody is standing in the water, barely visible, a shadow against the faintly luminous expanse of the ice.

I want to turn back, I want to run the other way, but my feet carry me forward, stumbling across the sand toward a figure I've glimpsed before, hollow eyes and twisting hair. It lurches through the water, coming closer, flickering into the light, all hunger and hatred.

It steps onto the shore in dance shoes, just like mine but red. Ruby red. Red as blood. Limp, shining ribbons trail over the sand behind it like seaweed. Its pale hands are claws reaching out for me. Another heartbeat and its fingers will close around my throat.

I finally manage to pitch myself back into the waking world, to the yellow glow of the bedside light spread across the ceiling, but something holds me down, pushes back against my flailing attempt to sit upright. I fight my way free of the blankets, trying not to scream. Something metallic goes clattering to the floor, making me jump.

All around me, standing upright with their tines stabbed through the quilt and into the mattress, are the forks. They're still cold to the touch when I yank them out.

13

I SPEND THE REST OF the night curled in the farthest corner of the bed, watching the room, fighting the quetiapine, waiting for something to happen. The night oozes by, and I can't tell whether I'm awake anymore. The moments flake apart into fragments, like the mirror, sharp-edged, disjointed. I'm not sure whether I've slept by the time gray morning finally thins the lamplight. Either way, it's a relief, kind of, despite the gritty feeling in my eyes and a dull headache. I scrub my hands over my face and swing my legs over the side of the bed.

My feet splash down into icy water.

I snatch them back up. My socks are soaked through, the cuffs of my pajamas clinging wet around my ankles. The crows tock and chuckle outside. A car door slams. The rainy-day light is limp, ordinary. But my feet leave soggy prints on the dry sheet.

Slowly, I lean out over the edge of the bed. My shadow looks back at me, the faintest ripply reflection. Clear water covers the linoleum, laps at the feet of the dresser. The cords of the lamp and the alarm clock are underwater; I jerk the plugs from their sockets.

I jump, cringing, at a sound from the hallway, but it's only Aunt Jen opening her door.

"Good lord!" she exclaims. She knocks on my door, but opens it before I can answer.

"Mare-bear, get up, there's—" She gasps as the door splashes through the water on the floor, and lets out a wail. "Oh, *look* at this!"

"It wasn't me!" I cry. "I don't know where it came from!"

"Well of course, of course it wasn't you! Why would I think that?" She reaches a placating hand toward me. "Don't cry, sweetie, it's okay. A pipe must have burst. Or maybe it's the roof, with all this rain. I'll call the landlord right away. It's okay, Mare-bear, it's—"

"My name is Marianne!"

My shout brings her up short, but only for a moment; she splashes across the floor, pulls me gently, insistently to my feet in the knife-cold water, wraps her arm around my shoulders to lead me from the room. I wipe my eyes, feeling guilty, feeling stupid. She may as well call me Mare-bear. Look at me, crying and needing a hug.

Behind us, the lamp on the nightstand crashes to the floor.

We sit on the couch while the maintenance guys clank around the furnace room, troop up and down the stairs. I can feel Aunt Jen looking at me, but I keep my eyes on my hands. They declare the drywall in my room shot, make noises about checking the insulation, set up huge clattering fans.

"Damnedest thing," one of them tells Aunt Jen. "I mean, the *ceiling's* dry. And there's a lake up on the roof, all right, but it's on the other side of the building. And all the pipes are fine, but they're across the hall anyway. So where the hell did it come from?"

"I guess that's what you get with an old building," Aunt Jen responds helplessly.

"Well," she sighs with half a smile once the door has finally closed behind them, "I think that's *quite* enough excitement before nine in the morning, don't you?"

I can't summon an answer to that, so I blow out my breath in something that could be interpreted as agreement. She gets up to answer the phone and disappears with it into the dining room. The sudden tone of concern as she answers and her *mm-hmm*ing with long pauses in between make me think she's probably talking to my mom; an "Oh, Laura" confirms it.

"Well, I need to talk to you about that, as it turns out," she says eventually. "We had a bit of a flood here this morning. No, not yet anyway, the city added some more sandbags the other day. No, they're not quite sure where it came from, but Marianne's room is a mess."

She leans out of the kitchen to flash me an apologetic smile. "I think that would probably be best, honestly… Laura. You'll be fine. You can always give me a call if you have any trouble, right?"

Going home? The prospect is a relief, for a split-second, before all the reasons to dread it pile back onto me. I want my mom, desperately, but what's going to happen if she sees what's been going on? Or if I end up in that other place again? Should I tell her? She thinks she was hallucinating.

Am I so sure I'm not?

What we need is something objective, Ron declared. Well, we've got it now. I could play Mom the tape. But there's no way anyone would believe Ron and I hadn't cooked that up ourselves. We could use it to audition for horror movies. I hug my knees, wondering momentarily whether going away from here might be enough to lose whatever is stalking me, but I can't summon much hope at the thought. It followed me here, after all.

"Mare-b—Marianne?" Aunt Jen is holding the phone out to me. "Your mom wants to talk to you for a second."

The static is a scouring storm in the background, making Mom's voice pale and distant.

"Marianne?" When I don't answer she says it again, anxiously. "Are you there?"

"Yeah. Yeah, sorry." I swallow. "Can you hear me?"

"Of course." She sounds puzzled. "Can you hear me?"

"There's just…a lot of noise on the line here for some reason."

"Listen, sweetie. Did you hear us talking just now?"

"Yeah."

"Do you...do you think you're ready to come home?"

I lean my forehead against the cool glass of the patio door. The phone crackles and whines.

"Yeah," I manage eventually. "I just. It's just that—"

"I know it's not the same." She speaks in a low, hurt voice that makes me wince.

"It's not that, Mom. Really. I'm just afraid that—"

I don't know how to say it. *I'm afraid you were right. I'm afraid it's real.*

"Would you feel better if Aunt Jen stayed over for a few days?"

"That's not what I mean," I cry, and take a deep, trembling breath before trying again. "Mom, what if you didn't really—what you saw, what if it was—"

But it's no good; the static escalates into a feedback howl, so long and sustained that I give up and press End to make it stop. Aunt Jen is watching me with her hand at her mouth. I slam the phone down on the table and wipe my eyes on my sleeve.

"I can stay over for a while, if you want," she offers hesitantly. "It's no trouble. You don't need to worry about your mom; she's seeing the doctor twice a week for the next while. They'll keep an eye on her."

I shake my head without looking at her. All the rational explanations, the medical explanations, hang between us.

"What if it's real?" I blurt out.

"Oh, Marianne."

"No, seriously, I know she didn't just imagine it. What about the water upstairs? I didn't break your mirror. It wasn't me. What's going to happen if I go home?"

"Mare-bear. Sweetie. Listen. All of this has a perfectly reasonable explanation. Okay? Your mom is having a really hard time just now. You are too, come to that. People believe all kinds of things when they're under that kind of stress. I shouldn't have told you about it, no matter what she said. Don't let it get to you. This is *not* your fault."

Defeated, I let myself be hugged. It doesn't matter what I say. She doesn't believe me. She won't believe me, unless she sees what Mom saw.

Or what Ron saw.

Under the pretext of packing my stuff, I hurry up the stairs to my room, perch on the stripped-down bed with the fan roaring in my ears, and dig my phone out of my backpack. Fumbling, I type a text to Ron.

plz plz plz plz call me. listened to the tape.

But when I try to send it, the little loading graphic goes around and around and around in circles and then freezes altogether. I poke the screen, hit the Power button, the Menu button. The display flickers, congeals into a weird, scrambled overlap between the app and the home screen, and goes dark.

14

WHEN MOM OPENS THE DOOR she looks thin and hollow, her eyes ringed with dark smudges. She's trembling when she hugs me. Aunt Jen lingers in the doorway as I lug my suitcase up the sweeping staircase and down the hall. Their low voices echo up to me.

"...really worried. She's afraid it was actually her. Laura, you have to..."

"...can he do this to us? He hasn't even..."

"...hasn't said anything about it, I don't know if..."

I close the door, shutting them out. My own room looks hopelessly foreign to me. Like it belongs to someone else. I used to love it: the one corner of this huge glass ship that was truly mine. I lost track of how many shopping trips Mom took me on, but I wasn't tired of them yet when we picked out the eggplant-purple curtains for the tall arched window, the sparkly light fixture, the sleek, chrome-trimmed desk. I helped Mom paint the walls in the snowy color she insisted was different from all the other whites and held the level while she adjusted the shelves.

Now we'll have to move, eventually. Would any of this have happened if we'd stayed in the town house? I walk around the room with some idea of picking out a book, but I just end up trailing a finger along their spines. I curl up on the bed and don't look at the tall standing mirror next to the closet.

A tiny creak and a whisper of slippered feet on slick hardwood betray Mom's presence outside my door. I listen tensely for the sound of her hand on the knob, but it doesn't come. Instead there's a sigh, and a door down the hall opens and closes. The furnace whirs to life. Rain spatters against the windows.

The minutes creep past, and there's no other sound. It's getting late; the light is a murky gold that says the sun is getting low behind the clouds. There's a draft sighing down from the window, and I crawl under the covers to escape it. Maybe I left all the weirdness behind at Aunt Jen's. It's like nothing has changed, like any minute Dad will come shuffling up the stairs from his office and knock on my door.

Stupid thought. Useless. I close my eyes against it, but it lingers anyway, a heaviness that won't dissolve.

"Marianne?"

I startle awake at the sound of my name. The room is almost dark. Mom sits next to me on the bed, her hand tentative on my shoulder, her hair trailing into my face.

I jerk upright, away from her touch. Mom's face falls a little.

"Sorry," I stammer. "Sorry, Mom, it's not you, I just... Is everything okay? Are you okay?"

"I just woke up," Mom says. "*I'm* sorry. I didn't mean to leave you alone all evening. This medication is killing me. I think I was awake for about four hours yesterday."

"Do you...feel better, though?"

"Maybe. I got through my last appointment without crying. I ran some errands. I guess that's an improvement. It's not...quite such an avalanche, you know?"

We sit in silence for a moment. She studies me, tucks a stray lock of hair behind my ear.

"I thought it would be nice to be home," she whispers, looking past me, out the window at the rain. "But it's not. It's awful."

I don't know what to say to that. She turns away, her hair falling over her face, hiding her expression.

"I expect you feel the same way," she says. "Don't you?"

"I wish—" I begin, but I can't find a safe way to finish the thought, one that doesn't end with me crying. I swallow and twist the edge of the blanket into a tight coil between my hands.

"Listen," she offers after a second, clearing her throat, "how about we go downstairs and watch a movie? Something funny. I'll make some popcorn. And we can forget about all this for a couple hours and try to rescue the evening. What do you think?"

I clutch the blanket. I'm afraid to leave the room. I'm afraid to be awake. I can't tell her that. She'll think it's because of her. She already thinks it's because of her; I can see it in the downturn of her lips, feel it in her weight shifting away from me. "I guess you're pretty tired," she says.

"No, it's okay," I protest. I push my way out of the covers. "That sounds great, Mom. Really."

She casts me a long, sideways look, like she's not buying it, but finally gives me a watery smile and clasps my hand.

"I'm so glad you're home," she whispers. "I really am, sweetie. I don't know what I'd do without you."

She sets off to the kitchen to make popcorn and urges me in an almost normal voice to go ahead and pick something to watch. Reluctantly, I shuffle my way to the basement, turning on every light switch as I pass. I don't look into the long, echoing room with the barre on one side. These days its only other furnishing is an elliptical trainer, dwarfed and lost in the corner.

When I flick on the lights in the den, I find the sliding doors of the built-in cabinets standing open, pictures strewn over the floor. My dance pictures. All the old recital photos.

I start back from the doorway, my hands over my mouth, but

after a first panic-soaked moment I realize this isn't the ghost's handi-work. The pictures are all intact, wiped carefully clean of dust, some of them still neatly stacked. Mom must have been going through them.

She's the one who took them down. Because she didn't want them to upset me, she said at the time. But it still felt like a message. A reminder of what I'd failed to become.

Dance is the first thing I remember. *The Nutcracker* at the National Arts Centre. Mom let me wear some of her lipstick. I can close my eyes and still see the snow maidens swirling onto the stage, one by one, spinning into the light exactly like the first dizzy flakes of a blizzard. The lights from the stage lit my parents' upturned faces, blue and violet, their heads tilted together, Mom's carefully lined lips curved in perfect happiness.

When the house lights came up, I turned and declared to her that I would be a ballerina. Someday I would be the one up there on the points of my toes, the Snow Queen, poised in effortless, sparkling perfection. It would be me.

"Do you remember the first time you got up on a stage?"

Mom has appeared in the doorway behind me, wearing a wobbly smile.

"No, but you've told me about it."

Many times, actually. But she doesn't take the hint. She sets the popcorn down on the shelf next to me, picks up one of the pictures on the floor. I was a peacock that year, with a streaming blue-green tail.

"You were only four. You were so little. I was sure you'd get

scared at the last minute, going up there without me. So I took you
to the dress rehearsal half an hour early, so you could get used to it up
there. You stood in the middle of the stage, and you twirled around,
and you *laughed*. And I just knew. You were born for it. I thought,
that's who she is. My Marianne. She's a dancer."

"Apparently not," I mutter, turning to the DVDs on the shelf.

"Sweetie—"

"Mom, I know you were trying to encourage me. I know. But I
just wasn't that good. It wasn't going to happen."

"Well, it won't happen *now*," Mom sniffs. "It's too late *now*.
You should have been off to one of the feeder schools we talked about,
not Pearson. You should have been dancing for scouts from the big
ballet companies. I don't understand why you just fell apart like that.
You could have had it all."

I lean against the shelf, close my eyes.

"I wasn't even good enough for the conservatory."

"Bullshit!" Mom says, making me flinch. She takes my hand,
pulls me toward the TV. "Look. Let me show you something."

"Mom," I protest, but she's already queuing up something on
the DVD player. On the screen a pale pink room appears, its carpet
shaggy and tired, with a few moving boxes stacked in the corner.

"*Mom*." I sigh and try to push past her, but she catches my
shoulders, holds me fast.

"Shh," she says. "Look."

"Are you recording?" an imperious voice calls out on the

screen, out of sight around a corner. Behind the camera, startlingly loud, Mom laughs.

"Yes, yes! I'm hitting Play, okay? Three, two, one…"

Carmina Burana is tinny on the recording, too quiet. Stalking through the doorway comes a girl with a black spangled skirt swirling around her thighs, fabric belling out from her outstretched arms like wings or a cape, diamonds flashing in her coiled hair. She's a storm of drama, all wicked glee and carmine lipstick.

"You loved that costume," Mom whispers tearfully.

Then-Marianne catches a toe in the stupid carpet and stumbles out of step, making me wince. But the Marianne in the video collapses gracelessly onto the floor, where she laughs and laughs. And Mom's laughing too, the camera shaking.

"Oh, that *sucked*," then-Marianne gasps. "Let me do it again."

"There won't be a rug at the conservatory," Mom says, unfazed. "And they'll be done laying the floor at the new house next week. You've got weeks to practice. You'll be great."

Then-Marianne tosses her head, beaming.

"I know," she says smugly.

The camera zooms in, blurs, focuses again on her made-up face. She bats her eyelashes, strikes a pose. Dissolves into giggles.

"So." Mom pitches her voice artificially low. "Miss Vandermere. What are you going to do next? What's in store for the youngest star of the Muse Studio of Dance?"

"Everything," Then-Marianne tosses out, giving the camera a

devilish grin and swirling her gauzy cape. "I'll be the best thing the conservatory's ever seen. I'll dance every part they've got. And the company schools will all be fighting for me. I'm unstoppable."

"That's my girl," Mom beams off camera. Then-Marianne grins back. Blows a kiss.

"Now start again," she demands, levering herself to her feet. "I'm going to do it right this time."

"See?" Mom pleads, hugging my shoulders. "Don't you see what I see? You were full of light, Marianne. You were on *fire*."

"I screwed it up," I say numbly. Though I had nailed the conservatory audition. That's what I was practicing for, in that video. It was one of those times my feet were made of light and sound, connecting with every pulse of the music, my lines scimitar-sharp. One of those times it was magic.

"But you *shone*," Mom insists, pointing at the TV with the remote as then-Marianne sweeps onto the screen again. "Look at you. I don't understand what happened. Was it that cow of a teacher?" She takes a deep breath, looks away. "Or maybe it was me. I know I was... leaning on you pretty heavily for a while."

"No, no. God, Mom, of course it wasn't you. I don't know, okay? I just didn't want to do it anymore. That's all."

The Marianne on the screen can't feel my presence, my cold-eyed evaluation as she steps and leaps her way through a footwork sequence with the music building behind her. Glissade, petit battement, pas de chat, turn, turn... She's overeager, too exaggerated, undisciplined. No control. Her lines are sloppy. She doesn't know it. She will soon.

But I can't turn away.

Once upon a time that was me. I was that effortless, that sure of everything. Focused like a laser beam, that's what my teachers at Muse said. Ready to burn through any obstacle. An arrow hurtling toward the bull's-eye of a single goal. An ambition I should have known was overinflated, ridiculous.

It was like some sort of alchemy. I got to the conservatory and felt the magic leaching away, leaving me heavy and sluggish, bowing my shoulders, pulling my arms across my chest. Some poison crept through me and planted the certainty of eyes on me. Watchers who knew I didn't belong there, from my battered secondhand shoes to my hair pulled into the highest bun I could manage to add a few more inches of height. I could almost hear their whispers about my stiff, scared face, my flat, stupid breasts, the line of underwear under my leotard.

The daily adage, slow and flowing, was the worst. I trembled and wavered and fought for every pose. Stage presence was no help there, nor quick feet. Not even focus. Only control.

Miss Giselle stopped us over and over again, offering corrections, exhorting us to move together as one, like a flock of birds or particles in a magnet, not one of us standing out. She called Jessica Ye out in front to demonstrate: she made all the slow extensions and retractions look effortless, an ebb and flow as natural as breathing, like a butterfly's wings folding and unfolding. I couldn't look away from the long swell of her extended calf, the arabesque arch of her back.

"Look what musicality she has," Miss Giselle said. "How *centered* she is. There's softness and strength here. That's what you're aiming for."

I take the remote from Mom and stab the Stop button. She doesn't object, though her lips go thin.

Jessica Ye was perfect. There were so many perfect girls at the conservatory. Rising stars, glittering snowflakes. They barely touched the ground.

I was never one of them.

Mom ends up picking the movie. *Pride and Prejudice*. Ordinarily I might have protested; Mrs. Bennet is so cringeworthy I end up anxious and embarrassed by proxy. But it's Mom's equivalent of comfort food, so I settle into the couch beside her without complaint. She snuggles me in close against her shoulder, rests her cheek on the top of my head. We sit mostly in silence, crunching mechanically through the popcorn.

"I missed you," she murmurs over Elizabeth being snippy to Mr. Darcy. I reach an arm across her lap to hug her in response, and then wriggle down into the cushions a little bit to make sure she won't see me tearing up.

When I open my eyes again the first thing I see is the glowing green numbers on the DVD player flashing 12:00.

Mom is gone. I must have fallen asleep. I drag myself out of the cushions, feel my way around the couch, reach for the doorjamb in the dark. The quiet makes me think it's still far from morning, but I can't really tell; without the clock the night feels unmoored from time, changeless.

I scurry upstairs to my room, into the cold blankets of my bed. My alarm clock blinks at me. 12:00. The windows are blank, orange-tinged oblongs. I lie there listening to my heartbeat in my ears. I can't even hear the rain anymore. The silence is so complete the fear congeals around it: I'm afraid to make a sound, afraid to find that I can't.

"Mom," I whisper, finally. The word rasps in my ears, and I let out the rest of my breath, pulling the pillow over my head. But the relief doesn't last long. I peer out from under the pillow; the numbers on the clock blink on and off. A conviction is rising in my mind like a tide.

It's here. Something has happened.

I reach out and snap the light on. Nothing's out of place. I run my hands over my braided hair, even steal a glance in the mirror. Nothing, nothing.

I hunker down in bed, watching the room. I can't keep my eyes on everything at once.

Then: movement. The door swinging open with the faintest

sound, the knob bumping gently against the wall. I scramble backward into the corner of the bed, but the door shivers into stillness, and that's all. The silence crouches, waiting.

"Mom," I croak. No sound, no response. I've never wanted anything like I want to run down the hall to her room, crawl into her bed like I did when I was little. But I can't, I can't. What will happen if it does something where she can see?

I'm not going out there. Whatever stupid game it's playing with me, I'm not rising to the bait. When I stumble across the room, it's to push the door closed again, and I slide to the floor to sit leaning against it. Barricading myself in.

I spend the rest of the night there, dozing fitfully, until morning seeps in to steal the edge from the darkness. I watch the windows brighten, willing the dread away. At first I'm resolved not to move until Mom comes to get me, but I can't let her walk into whatever's waiting out there. Whatever it left for me to see.

Its handiwork is facing me as soon as I open the door. The spare silver picture frames on the opposite wall haven't been disarranged from their usual spots, they're all intact, untouched, hanging straight and level as ever. But every one of them has been wiped blank. Empty, except for the white cardboard backing. And as I stare up at them, I notice the faint trickle of water echoing through the house.

I hurry toward it before I lose my nerve, thumping down the stairs to the kitchen. The vast ceramic square of the sink is overflowing, a steady stream of water dribbling down the face of the cabinet and pooling on the floor. I snatch a handful of dish towels from the drawer and go to mop it up.

In the sink, spiraling in a slow circle, are the pictures. A watery kaleidoscope of our three smiling faces, atop layers and layers of colorful copies of me: the recital photos.

There's no salvaging them; they've turned into a sticky, soggy mess. I try to fish one out and it shreds apart in my hands.

"Happy now?" I say under my breath, yanking the silver bar of the faucet around to shut off the water. There's no response; of course there isn't. But in one of the floating pictures, one of me and Mom— the one where I'm usually smiling over her shoulder as she clasps my hands in hers over her chest—I could swear my image is glaring back at me, its arms tightening possessively around my mother's shoulders.

Mom silences her alarm several times before I finally hear the shower running. By then I've cleaned the water from the kitchen floor, buried the sodden, shredded photographs in the trash, taken down the empty silver frames and hidden them under my bed. I even make some scrambled eggs for breakfast. One of the eggs manages to lurch from the container to splatter on the floor, and I set my jaw and mop that up too. I start out thinking I'll make coffee, but whatever's following me waits until the floor is clean again before it knocks the milk carton over, and by the time I've stemmed the river on the floor the eggs are about to burn.

"You made breakfast?" Mom arrives as I'm dividing the browned eggs onto plates. The catch in her voice snags into me like hooks. "Thank you, sweetie. Thank you. I...I really needed that today."

"It's just eggs," I mumble. She hugs me anyway, not noticing—or pretending not to—that I'm wound so tight I'm shaking. She slides into a seat at the peninsula with her plate. Instead of joining her, I eat hurriedly where I am, standing up.

She takes a few bites, pokes at the rest. I can feel her question coming like a storm, the tension prickling against my skin.

"What is it," I say, more sharply than I meant to, when she finally opens her mouth to speak.

"Did you...notice that the pictures are gone?" she says carefully. "Upstairs?"

I force down my last forkful of eggs.

"That was me." The words are small and tight. "I took them down."

"Marianne—"

"I don't want to talk about it!"

She folds her hands against her lips. Tears slide down her cheeks. I set my dishes carefully in the sink.

"I'm fine, Mom. I'm *fine*. I just didn't get much sleep last night, okay?"

She sniffs, wipes her face. Rakes her hair back, stabs a barrette through it. "So who's this doctor you're seeing?" she asks.

"His name is Dr. Fortin." I watch her warily, not sure if this is a safe subject or not.

"And you feel like you can talk to him?"

I shrug. "He has a nice voice."

She looks at me, starts to say something, then pinches her mouth shut and shakes her head.

"Mom. What is it?"

"I just hope this isn't your father trying to get information from you. Ammunition."

I lean against the sink. "I'm pretty sure it doesn't work like that."

"He'll try to get custody," she insists. "I know it."

"Mom, please—"

"Fine." She throws her hands in the air, her voice gone hurt and huffy. "Fine! It doesn't matter. It's not like I have a choice."

"I'm going to go get dressed," I mutter desperately, before she can say anything else, and hurry from the room.

In Dr. Fortin's office, after shaking my head in response to his first two questions—no more sleepwalking, no more missing time—I sit in antsy silence for a long minute. He asks me if I'm having trouble with any side effects from the quetiapine; asks me how it's going, being back at home. I keep my answers to a shrug. After that he just watches me, unhurried. Waiting for me to crack.

"Do I really have to keep coming here?" I ask finally.

"You don't want to?"

"I don't see how it's helping," I say truthfully. Talk therapy isn't going to erase what's on that tape at home. I look up at him. "Mom thinks Dad's using you to gather ammunition. For custody."

"Is that what you think?"

I look away again. "I don't know."

"Well. It's true that I can be subpoenaed in court. But actually, at your age, most of the custody decision is yours."

"It is?" Funny how nobody's told me that.

"If they really can't sort something out between them, it would be your wishes the judge would use to make a ruling."

"So if I told you I'm possessed by the devil or something," I say recklessly, "you couldn't tell my dad?"

He smiles. "Why, do you have any demonic possession to report?"

I show my teeth, hoping it looks like I'm smiling back. Like I'm joking.

"Like I said," he continues, "if you sound likely to hurt yourself, or someone else, then I have to report it. At that point, you need more help than I can give. But otherwise, anything goes."

"And if I need more help than you can give," I shoot back, "that means 'go directly to psych ward, do not pass go, do not collect two hundred dollars.' Doesn't it."

He's not fazed. "Does that scare you? The idea of being hospitalized?"

"My mom's been in the hospital before. A long time ago, when I was a baby." I study the carpet. "She said it was horrible."

"In what way?"

"She said they treat you like you're less than human. Like you're a...broken thing they're stuck with."

"Do you think that's accurate?"

I shrug.

"I'm sorry to hear she had a bad experience," he says. "But I promise you that the children's hospital is not some horror movie scenario. Okay? It's a place where you're safe. A place to get better. Until you can cope again. And inpatient treatment isn't the first step anyway. You might find their day program helpful."

I look at him warily. "What do you mean?"

"It's a more intensive course of treatment. You'd spend the morning and part of the afternoon there, do therapy in groups and one on one. But you'd still be an outpatient. You'd go home every day."

"Are you saying you're signing me up?"

He shrugs. "Your call. At this point, it's just an idea. But I think you might consider it."

I bet something like "I think I'm possessed" would have him backtracking on that pretty fast. Or "a ghost is after me." Hallucinations. Paranoia. I'd sound just like Mom must have. Except that Mom thought it wasn't real. I'd sound worse.

And what if they locked me up in there and it followed me?

"Do you believe in ghosts?"

He blinks, rests an ankle over one knee.

"That's an interesting question," he says neutrally. "Do you?"

Giving me enough room to say something incriminating. Something delusional. I chicken out.

"I just…keep thinking about what my mom saw."

"You're still looking for an explanation," he interprets. I shrug. "Your mom is someone you trust a lot, it sounds like."

I study the sun-catcher twisting slowly this way and that in the tall arched window.

"Usually. Yeah."

"Usually. This whole thing must have shaken that up pretty hard." I don't answer. "How did you feel about staying at your aunt's the last little while?"

Niobe's card flashes through my mind: the blindfolded woman in the water, the tall swords standing around her like bars.

"Trapped," I say eventually. Dr. Fortin nods, but doesn't say anything, waiting. Outside a bus roars down Bank Street. A horn honks. Someone laughs and yells something in the street below. Inside it's quiet, an old-house quiet that fills the room. Except for a tiny sound, on the edge of hearing, so quiet I'm not sure what I'm hearing at first: the faintest scratching. A slow, deliberate noise. Like fingernails on wood.

"What's wrong?" Dr. Fortin asks. I'm clutching the arm of the couch. I swallow and force myself to let go, to sit back. I don't know what to say. What if he doesn't hear it? *Auditory hallucinations*. For a dizzy, awful moment the whole week is splintering to pieces beneath me like rotten ice. What if none of it was real? Could I have imagined the tape, even? Maybe I should tell him. Maybe I'm drowning and I can't even tell.

"I thought I heard… I mean, do you hear something scratching? That little noise?"

"This is an old building," he says, unconcerned. "They keep setting traps, but the place is full of mice. I should get an office cat."

That means he hears it too. Breathe in. Breathe out. Keep it together. If that sound was anything unusual, he'd know. It doesn't have anything to do with me. Not necessarily.

"Are you angry at your parents?" Dr. Fortin asks. "I think I would be. Your dad leaves, your mom's upset—"

"Why would I be mad at Mom?" I interrupt. "This isn't her fault."

"Is it your dad's?"

"He's the one who took off."

"So you're angry with him, then. Have you talked to him about that?"

"What would be the point? It's not like he'd listen."

"You don't think you can go to him with your feelings."

"What, so I should explode at him or something? That's why he left in the first place. He said he was tired of picking up the pieces."

"Are you? Tired of picking up the pieces, I mean."

I stare at him. The scraping, scrabbling noise is still there. Steadily, without moving, without changing. I wish it would stop. I can almost feel it, like little claws at the nape of my neck.

"I guess I'm surprised that you're not mad at your mom at all, after everything that's happened in the last few weeks. You don't feel even a little bit resentful?"

"What was she supposed to do?" I demand. "Just smile and accept it? Of course I don't like picking up the pieces. But she did that for me. That's what you're supposed to do for your family, right? Support each other? And I'm the only one left."

Dr. Fortin sits forward, resting his elbows on his knees. "What would happen if you got mad at your mom, Marianne?"

"I don't know." I won't look at him. I'm not going to confess that I'm afraid she'd break, that she'd hurt herself, that she'd never forgive me. I can't be a family by myself.

"When was the last time you got good and mad at her, then?"

"I don't *know*." I pause, smooth the edge off my voice, try to explain. "We were never like that. We get along." Or we did, anyway.

"What about when you quit dance?"

"What about it?" I snap, and then press my lips together. He waits for me to speak. Eventually I come out with a passably cool sentence. "I don't want to talk about dance. Seriously. It's got nothing to do with this."

"Okay," he says mildly, "that's fine."

He'll circle back to it eventually, I bet. My one freak-out and he's determined to hear about it. I'm not giving him the satisfaction.

There's a sudden thunk and rattle right behind me, and I jump halfway to my feet, twisting around to find the source of the noise. It takes me a second to figure out what's different: the sun-catcher is gone.

"It just fell behind the couch," Dr. Fortin says. "Don't worry about it, I'll get it later. Really, it's okay, please sit down."

I obey, trying to slow my breathing without being too obvious, fixing my gaze at a point over Dr. Fortin's shoulder to keep from looking frantically around the room. *Go ahead,* I think. *Go ahead. Do something he can't explain away. Give me something objective. Make him believe me.*

But everything is still. Even the rustling, scratching sounds have fallen silent.

"You seem tense," Dr. Fortin observes. "Is something bothering you?"

I shake my head. He doesn't look convinced.

"Why don't you tell me about your morning," he suggests.

"There's nothing to tell. It was normal. Boring. I had scrambled eggs for breakfast."

He studies me. "Do you feel safe at home?"

"Safe," I snort. "Safe from what?"

"Well, physically safe, for a start."

"What, are you asking if I'm afraid of my mom? No! She's just upset. Anyone would be!"

"All right, how about psychological safety? Is home a safe space for you?"

"What does that even mean?"

"Well, what does a safe space look like for you? What are *you* safe from in a safe space?"

The answer to that is so obvious and so impossible I can't think of a more normal one.

"Think about that, maybe," he suggests when I stay silent. "About what would make you feel safe."

He changes tactics and asks me what I like to read. Asks me why. Asks about school, about my friends. I draw out a conversation about Ingrid for a little while, as close to monosyllables as I can get away with. I don't mention Ron. What's to mention? She might never speak to me again.

"I definitely get the feeling you don't want to talk to me today," Dr. Fortin remarks. Not accusingly, but with mild interest, like he's talking about philosophy or a math problem. I lift my chin and don't answer.

"Well, you don't have to," he says. "But that's what I'm here for. I might be able to help. You never know. Think about it for next week, okay? And think about the day program. Let's keep our options open."

The room recedes from me, a peaceful island, insubstantial as an image on a screen. A mirage. I close my eyes.

"Yeah," I manage. "Okay. Sure."

But even as I say it, the resolution is forming. I'm not coming back here again.

15

MOM IS DRAWN AND SILENT on the way home. At least she doesn't ask me how the appointment went. As we step through the door she mumbles something about taking a nap before her meeting with the lawyer, dropping her coat on the bench in the front hall. It slithers off onto the chilly tiles, but she disappears up the stairs without turning. I hang it up in the closet, next to Dad's winter coat. Quiet settles over the house, crowds close around me.

It's like Dad's ridiculous excuses were some kind of curse. The house might have felt empty before, but it was never lonely. Now it feels full of edges hard enough to bruise, without comfort or refuge. The farthest thing from a safe space.

Dad said he couldn't make her happy. Since when? There's a picture of them sitting on Mom's night table. Or it used to, maybe she's gotten rid of it now. It was grainy and old, a weird size so that it sat a little askew in the frame. From sometime when Dad had more hair and a goatee that looked, to my eye, kind of ridiculous on him. Mom looked just like me. Frighteningly like me. She's always said that we're twins twenty-two years apart. In the photo she's scooped up in his arms, her head thrown back, her hair a long, black fan. And Dad's looking into the camera, half smiling, like he can't believe his luck. Like he's about to tell you how he got away with it. They're standing in the middle of the patch of mud that became the front garden at the town house; the paneling above the door was the same weird teal I remember. What could have driven them apart? Was it the house?

Was it me?

I lean against the closet door. Think about what would make you feel safe, Dr. Fortin said. I'll never feel safe again. I'm so tired. My head is killing me. How am I going to make it through the rest of the day? The one after that?

I drift down to the basement with some notion of watching TV and pause outside the long, hardwood corridor of the studio. It's cool and dim, still holding a ghost of that new-house smell. Paint and varnish. In another lifetime it was filled with blaring music, the thump of shoes against the floor. Julie and Shayna used to come over to dance here. Others too, sometimes. We'd help each other stretch, chat over our phones, bound up the stairs for a snack. It was easier than trying to elbow our way into the scraps of rehearsal time available at the studio. It was more fun.

I'm glad we lost touch. They inhabit some alternate reality where I'm dancing down the road to fame, forgetting all about them. Maybe in that world I'm a better version of myself. Maybe I'll open my eyes to find the last two years were just some incoherent stress nightmare from the night before a show.

I pad inside and rest a hesitant hand on the barre. The wood is cool and smooth under my fingers. I arrange myself into first position, sweep my arm out à la seconde, extend a leg into a développé, feeling for that glow of rightness from my dream. All that's left is embarrassment, ungainly weight, joints gone stiff and sullen, refusing to form a clean line. I drop back to the floor, wishing I hadn't tried it. Mom's right, after all. It's too late. I could never go back to it.

Even if I could, there's no way. Not after that last awful week when Mom confronted me about the weeks and weeks of rehearsals I missed.

I want to hide from the memory. But I was hiding then too, a mouse down a bolt-hole. The library was where I'd discovered fantasy novels. I started with Tad Williams, almost at random; *To Green Angel Tower* caught my eye as I huddled on the floor at the very end of the stacks. It was the biggest volume on the shelf. Big enough to get lost in. All I wanted was to disappear, to escape from the impossible waiting game I'd landed myself in, the hovering question of how long I could keep it up.

It worked for a while. It worked so well that when familiar footsteps came stalking down the aisle I barely heard them. Until they were closing in. When I finally felt a lurch of premonition and looked up, Mom was standing over me, her mouth a bowstring. Drawn and waiting.

"Is this where you've been?" she asked. She didn't yell. "All this time?"

What was there to say? I stared up at her, hugging the book a little closer, until she yanked it from my hands. She hauled me to my feet, pushed me stumbling forward.

"Mom—*ow*, Mom, let go—"

"They said you haven't been to rehearsal in weeks, Marianne. Months." We drew stares as she frog-marched me past the circulation desk, out into the airy, echoing foyer. My face was hot, my hands blocks of ice. "I went to ask Miss Giselle if they needed volunteers for the recital. Do you think they were a little surprised to see me?"

She ignored my attempt at a protest, spoke over it.

"I got all the way through the form before they told me. In front of the whole office. They didn't know what to do with me. Like I was some sort of—I have never been so *humiliated*, Marianne!"

"*You* were humiliated!" I jerked my arm free from her grip as we reached the doors. The words rang from the high concrete walls; Mom flinched. "I told you I wanted to quit! I told you over and over!"

She pinched the bridge of her nose and stood there for a

moment, her shoulders rising and falling with a deep breath, like she was grasping for her last shred of patience.

"Okay. Look. It might not be too late. Here's what we're going to do. I am setting up a meeting with Miss Giselle. You will explain this to both of us."

"I won't!" Wings were beating in my head. My vision pulsed.

"Marianne, lower your voice, for heaven's sake!"

"I *won't!* You can't make me!"

"I can, and I will!"

My words ran dry. There were none left. I was choking, my ribs were splitting open, bending me double. I clapped my hands over my ears and it came raging out of me: I screamed until my breath ran out, until my throat was ragged. It filled my head, it filled the foyer, it brought people running to doorways to see what was wrong.

"Oh, for the love of God," Mom said desperately. She had to put her arms around my waist and heft me bodily through the doors, half carrying, half dragging me as I kicked and thrashed and fought.

I lay sprawled over the back seat, sobbing, as she drove home in stony silence. I think she expected me to have exhausted myself by the time we got there. But I hadn't. When we finally pulled into the garage she slammed the door and headed for the house like she didn't care whether I followed her or not. I went after her anyway. The words drove me forward, a pressure building in my chest, weapons waiting to be used.

"You don't want me!" I hurled at her as she dropped her keys on the peninsula in the kitchen. "You never did! You want a trained pony! You want a performing monkey! On a leash!"

"I'm trying to help you, Marianne! *You* were the one who wanted to do ballet! You wanted to be the best! That takes discipline and courage and, well, grit!"

"Well, maybe I don't have that! Maybe I never did!"

"Of course you do! Look how far you've come already! You can't just throw this away!"

"Why not? You did! Why is it so horrible for me to be a failure *just like my mother?*"

Her eyes pooled with tears at that. Just like I'd known they would.

"How can you say that to me?"

I didn't care. I was impervious, white hot.

"You want me to be perfect. Because you're *not*. And fuck that, Mom! Fuck it!" The words I never dared to say flew through the air, incendiary. "You're not perfect! You don't *do* anything, you don't have courage, you don't have grit, all you have is me! You're nothing! And you've made me into a nothing, too! Are you happy now? Are you satisfied?"

Mom buried her face in her hands.

"I can't have this conversation," she said in a weepy, stuffy voice designed to make me fold. "Not when you're going to speak to me like that. You can deal with your father whenever he gets home. Get out of my sight, Marianne. Go!"

But I wasn't done. I snatched the nearest breakable thing—Dad's cup, left in haste that morning on the counter—and threw it across the kitchen, splattering cold coffee everywhere. Mom's mouth fell open, but I didn't care what she was going to say.

"*Make me!*" I shrieked. "*Make me!*"

The days that followed are a sleepless haze in my head. My throat was raw and scratchy from screaming. Every conversation devolved into a spiral of rage. I can close my eyes and see my father's horrified face. He didn't know what to do with me, with this sudden explosion of messy violence. Let's talk about this, he said. Calm down. We can't discuss this when you use that tone of voice, young lady.

But I couldn't calm down. There was nothing to discuss. I was a firestorm, a volcano. I don't know what I wanted. Maybe to make them pay. And I did. Over and over. I threw everything I had at them: They didn't love me. They just wanted a doll to dress up. Every melodramatic thought I'd ever swallowed while I thumped through pirouette after jeté after sauté under Mom's watchful eye. I watched every missile find its mark. Mom cried and fled the room; Dad's shoulders sagged. And he said in this gray, strained voice, "I don't even know who you are when you're like this. Is this what it's going to be like now, Marianne?"

The last time he shut me in my room, I tore the pictures off the wall, swept everything off the shelves, wreaked as much destruction as I could. When I finally ran down and stood panting in the middle of the floor, their arguing echoed down the hall, low and fierce. They were talking about me. I knew it. When I opened the door a crack, it made every word razor sharp.

"She just needs time to calm down," Mom said tearfully. "There's no reason to pathologize this. She's just angry. Maybe she's angry at me."

"It's been days," Dad snapped. "How long is she going to keep this up? We're out of our depth here. She needs help, Laura."

"Just give her a chance," Mom pleaded. "Please. We can handle her. I just need you to back me up. I need *your* help."

"I can't deal with this right now, I have to be at the meeting with the military stakeholders tomorrow—"

"Of course. Because they *need* you."

"Laura—"

"No, go ahead! Your only daughter is falling apart and you just want to throw her in the psych ward so you can get back to what's really important!"

"Jesus, Laura, be reasonable. Yes, she's falling apart, okay? What's so terrible about getting help when you need it?"

"Don't you dare make this about me."

"This is already about you," Dad sighed. "It's *always* about you."

"How can you say that to me! After I've been dealing with this by myself all week!"

"You're not dealing with it at all! You're just... Look. Let's think about this rationally for thirty seconds, okay? Please? Let's think about Marianne. She needs help."

"Right. And you would know. Because you're paying such close attention."

"How can I not pay attention? I can hear you screaming at each other across the house! I swear to God, sometimes I think I should find somewhere else to stay just so I can hear myself think!"

"Maybe you should!" Mom shouted. Heavy footsteps thumped into the basement; a door slammed. Like a spell had broken, I pushed my door quickly, silently closed, backed away from it. But the sound of her crying seeped through anyway, little hands clinging to me, inescapable. I hid from them under the bed, like I was a little kid, staring up at the cobwebby underside of the box spring, my hands over my ears, drowning in the roar of my own heartbeat. Wishing I could disappear.

Dad came into my room later that evening with hardly a sound. Curled on the bed, I kept my back to him, unmoving. Until then it had been Mom who made the first sallies into the storm, trying to sympathize, trying to talk me down.

He sat on the edge of the bed. When I stole a glance at him his shoulders were slumped in defeat.

"You can quit," he said finally. "You haven't left us much choice about that one. But I need my bunny back. I need you to put yourself back together. Okay? This is… I don't even know what to do with this. It's crazy. It's not you."

I wanted to tell him he didn't know me. That he'd snipped out some magazine daughter and pasted her over me. But shame trickled in, and fear, cold and smothering.

"Your mom and I...we're going to take a little break. I'm going to be gone for a little bit. Not forever, okay? We just need some space. You know, to calm down and work things out." I stared at the wall, my whole body locked and rigid. He was mouthing something about how this wasn't my fault, but I knew better. I'd smashed and burned my family like a Molotov cocktail. I was breaking them apart. And for what? If he went, what would be left? Could he really want to be rid of me that badly?

"You're growing up, Marianne," he said. "This is your chance to decide who you're going to be. And this family can't take another hurricane."

And I nodded. One little jerk of my chin. He squeezed my shoulder, left the room. When the door closed behind him, I sat up and looked around at the drawers hanging open and the dance posters in shreds on the floor. The wreckage after the storm.

He was right. Of course he was right.

I picked up all the disastrous pieces. I apologized to my mother. She offered the yoga class—timidly; pathetically—as a mom-and-daughter thing. A way to calm down, a way to reconnect. When I accepted she brightened the tiniest, heartbreaking bit.

I was stronger than I knew. I was sharp as a knife. I had to watch myself.

But in the end it didn't matter how carefully I tiptoed around them. He still left.

16

THE TV REFUSES TO WORK. My computer won't boot up, either. It doesn't even get as far as a blue screen of death; it sits whirring uselessly, the screen blank. There's no escaping the vast quiet of the house. Sleep drags at me, irresistible. When I open my eyes the windows are starting to dim, but there's still no sign of Mom, no noises from upstairs. She said her medication makes her sleep a lot, too. Maybe I should wake her up, make something to eat.

I pass Dad's office on the way to the kitchen. The door is slightly ajar and I stop in front of it, hesitating. It swings open silently at my touch. The room is strangely bare; the bookshelves are still mostly full, but there are wide empty patches that stand out like missing teeth. The rolling cart full of paints and brushes that Dad called his five-minute project station is empty, the latest half-finished canvas landscape vanished from the easel standing next to it. The desk has been swept clean of its usual heaps of paper; the laptop and the huge monitor are gone. The only thing left on the wide black surface is a framed picture, one I drew when I was little: a stick figure etched in crayon, with a zigzaggy beard and a lipstick-red smiling mouth.

It's sat on his desk forever. And he didn't take it.

I don't know what I'm doing in here. There's nothing left of him here, nothing to help me, and why would there be? Was he ever really here in the first place?

I pull the door closed behind me, grind tears away with the heels of my hands. This won't do. I won't think about it. Mom can't see me like this. Will she know I've been crying? I should wash my face. I try to draw a steadying breath and walk slowly to the bathroom, slapping at the light switch.

It doesn't work.

Icy fear blooms in the pit of my stomach. I resist the urge to yank the switch back and forth a few times in denial. I stand up straight in the dark, the thin light from the hallway spilling over my feet, and clench my fists.

"Go away," I say aloud, as steadily as I can.

Fuck you, says a voice in return.

It seems to come from all around me. My reflection in the mirror is a thin wash of light along one cheek, the gleam of an eye, surrounded by undulating shadow. I shrink back against the door, the handle jabbing into my back.

The reflection, staring back at me, doesn't move.

"Who are you?" I try to make my voice as authoritative as Ron's was, the other night, a lifetime ago. I try to show I'm not afraid.

Pretending you don't know isn't going to help you.

"But I don't!" I cry. "I swear!"

Well, I know you. The words are laden with poisonous contempt. **You think you can lie to me?**

"You're the one who called Ingrid, aren't you?"

Oh. Her. Is it smiling?

"What did you *say*?" I cry.

The truth. She's a fake. She's a hollow shell. She thinks she's so kind, so generous, but all she ever sees is her own reflection. All she does is take. Maybe you're content to follow her around like a dog. I'm sick of being ignored.

I'm ice on the water. Cracking. Every word hits me like a stone. That's what Ingrid heard coming out of my mouth?

"She's not like that. You don't even know her."

Listen to you. You're pathetic. You deserve each other. You'd just run away if she wanted you. And she never did, you know. Go drown in the dark and see if she saves you. Give the rest back to me. It's mine.

"I don't understand." I will stay calm. I will not run from this. "What is it you want?"

The figure in the mirror steps closer, a twisting silhouette. It lifts its hands to press them against the glass. I cringe away from it and almost fall. Its voice drops to a scant breath, shivering with rage.

What you have. What you stole.

I don't even know how to answer that. What could I possibly have taken? Did I pick something up, unknowing? Ron's half-smiling question flashes through my mind. *No cursed antiques or anything?*

"What is it? What did I take? I'll give it back, I swear!"

Liar!

"I never meant to take anything from you!" I wail. "This has to be a mistake! Please just tell me! What is it?"

Everything. Everything you have you took from me. The wind. The sun. Your beautiful friend with the painted face. Your mother! Where is she?

"Leave my mother alone." I try to make it a command; it comes out pale and weak.

It's me she wants. Not you. You're an imitation. A replacement! You'll leave her just like he did. I'm the one who loves her. I'm the one who's real.

"Listen," I begin desperately, but it ignores me, speaks over me.

She told me she wanted me. She said so. The words are a keening moan. **She said she'd stay with me. I want her back!**

"You can't have her! Don't you get it? She ended up in the hospital because of you!"

You took her from me. The hands on the glass are fists now. **You took it all! And it's MINE!**

The voice spirals into a scream, shriller than a human voice should go, and I can't take any more. I run, pausing only to slam the door behind me, ignoring the sound of smashing glass as I bolt back to my room, to refuge. I retreat to the very farthest corner of my bed, where I can't see the mirror, willing the ghost away, willing it gone. For a long interval the only sound is my blood thundering in my ears, the rattle of the wind at the window.

Knock knock knock.

I jump at the sound, although it's not loud. *Knock knock knock.*

"Mom?" I quaver. Like I'm a kid again, waking up from a nightmare. It's not her, of course. The sound echoes down from the ceiling, from the wall beside the bed. *Knock knock knock. Knock knock.* Covering my ears doesn't block it out. *Knock knock knock.*

"Stop it!" I scream.

And it stops. But instead there's a scrape and a crash as the books sweep themselves off a whole set of shelves. They lie scattered over the floor with the pages still fluttering.

I edge my hands down from my ears, waiting for something else to happen, but there's only one final, mocking noise. *Knock. Knock. Knock.* And then silence, broken only by the rain, and nothing else moves.

Mom's door clicks open down the hall, and I scramble over to scoop the books back into place. I've only gotten an armful of them back on the shelf when the door opens. Mom's brows quirk, puzzled, when she sees me crouched guiltily on the floor. I want to throw myself into her arms, I want to cry until I can't anymore, I want her to pet my hair and tell me everything will be okay. I look up at her and I don't move. I don't move.

"Do you want some dinner, Marianne?" she says eventually.

Which prospect is worse, lying here waiting for it to do something else or waiting for it to do something that Mom might see? But the hurt and weariness growing on her face as I stay silent decides it.

"Sure."

The house is full of echoing silence as we pad through it, the rainy light fading by near-visible increments. In the kitchen, Mom slides into a perch at the peninsula, resting her head on her arms. There's not much in the fridge, but I manage to put together two ham sandwiches, skipping the mayo on Mom's, and bring them both to the counter. Mom hasn't moved; she only looks up when the plate clinks against the stone surface.

"Thank you, sweetie," she says, with the shadow of a smile. "You're taking such good care of me."

I sit down next to her and take a bite. It's glue in my mouth. There are lines on Mom's face I've never noticed before. Everything seems so upside down. How many times have we sat here together with a snack *she* made while I worried about high school, complained about the idiots in my class, cried about Ingrid moving?

The ghost's words whisper through my thoughts. *It's me she wants. Not you. She told me so. She said so.* That can't be true, can it? When would she have spoken to it? That night I can't remember? I can't ask her. I don't know what to say to her. I'm afraid I'll make it worse.

She pushes the plate away with the sandwich half-eaten. "I'm sorry, Marianne, it's delicious. I just can't eat very much lately."

"Yeah. Me neither. Mom, listen. Can I ask you something?"

She shrugs.

"I'm an only child, right?"

She looks up at me, squinting. "Did I hear that right?"

"I didn't have a twin who...who died at birth, or anything like that?"

Mom's eyebrows have gone up in a look that's half bafflement and half amusement. "Why on earth do you ask?" I can't answer, and after a moment, her faint smile fades back into a weary line. "No, Marianne. It was just you." She puts a hand to my cheek; her fingers are chilly against my skin. "You were all I ever wanted."

I try to smile back, but something changed around us as she spoke, some quality in the air. She pulls her hand away.

"Have you spoken to your father?"

Her voice is very low, but I stiffen. Here we go. There's a shivering, musical sound from the cabinet—the wine glasses jittering against each other—and I look up in alarm, but they fall silent again. Still, I can feel the presence seeping through the room, thick and cold, the weight of its regard. Is it my imagination?

Mom doesn't look at me, doesn't speak. She's waiting for an answer. I have to say something.

"No. Well, yes." And then, unwillingly, "He sent me an email."

"An email. God." Mom pushes herself up from the counter,

swipes her hair back from her face. "His only daughter, and he can't even be bothered to *call*? Did he explain himself, at least?"

I pick up the plates and turn toward the sink, trying to figure out a safe answer.

"He tried. I guess."

"He didn't explain it to me," Mom cries. "What am I supposed to think? What am I supposed to do with this...this nothing? If he's seeing somebody else, why doesn't he just tell me?" Tears well up in her eyes. "I know he's seeing somebody. I *know* it."

"I don't think he is, Mom. Really."

"Why?" She pounces on this. "What did he say?"

I take a deep breath. "I don't want to—"

"Never mind." She closes her eyes; the words are dull and flat. "It doesn't matter. He wouldn't tell you if he was, would he."

One of the plates jerks from my hand and falls to the floor, smashing in pieces on the smooth red hardwood. I jump back from it, my heart hammering. *Go away. Go away.*

"Watch your feet!" Mom exclaims, distracted, thank God. She jumps from her seat. "Let me—"

"Never mind!" I put out a hand, not wanting her to come closer. "Never mind, I'll get it."

Mom watches me pull the broom from the closet and then sits heavily down again, buries her face in her hands. "I'm so sorry. I'm such a mess. You don't deserve this."

I tip the shards of china into the garbage.

"He's your dad. I understand that, Marianne. Even if we're not together anymore, you still need to have a relationship with him. Of course you do. Okay?"

I nod, hoping she won't pursue it any further.

"I'm just so afraid. I'm afraid of what will happen if he finds out about what's been going on with me, since he left." Her voice has gone weepy again. "I'm afraid he'll try to take you away from me. I'm afraid this makes me, I don't know, an unfit mother. And you're all I have left."

"I won't tell him, Mom."

"It's not on you to keep secrets. I know that. But I can't bear losing you."

Around us, the room is filling up with a wintery silence. "Mom. Please—"

"You're the sun in my sky. Nobody's taking you from me! I can't lose you too. I can't."

The glasses in the cabinets rattle and chime, and the green numbers on the stove clock flutter into indecipherable dashes and lines. I wheel to face my mom, but she's not looking at me, she's staring in horror into the air between us, and when I follow her gaze I stagger back a step against the counter.

Knives. Dad's kitchen knives, lovingly sharpened. All suspended in midair above our heads, gleaming in the dim light like icicles.

Pointing at me.

"Marianne," Mom whispers. Her eyes flick toward me, then back to the knives. "Marianne, I think I'm—"

But in answer, like arrows from a bow, like axes, the knives fall. All at once. I don't even have time to put my hands up; by the time I've lifted them the knives have landed all around me, a ragged chorus of hollow thunks. It takes me a few rabbit heartbeats to realize that they haven't touched me. Something tugs at my hair and I flinch away, finally opening my eyes. The biggest one, the one I've always been afraid to use—its point has bitten into the cupboard door, barely an inch from my face. It stands in place, not even quivering. The others are lodged in the polished floor at my feet and scattered over the stone countertop.

Mom sits frozen for a moment with her arms outstretched, then slides off her stool and runs over and clasps my hands, pulls me gently away from the counter and, once we're clear of the blades buried in a little semicircle around where I was standing, throws her arms around me. She's saying "oh my God" over and over again, a near-voiceless whimper. I stand rigid, barely breathing.

Mom finally lets me go and bends to retrieve the closest paring knife. She hisses in surprise when she touches it, snatching her hand away, then pulls her sleeve down over her fingers. She can't budge it and quickly gives up, shaking her hand out.

"It's *cold.*" She fumbles backward till she bumps into me, and wheels to face me, her eyes pleading. "Marianne, was that me? Was that *real?*"

Here it is. The proof I've been waiting for: something objective. And a witness. Another one. Someone who might believe me.

"It's real." The words rise up with tears close behind. "It's real. And I'm so scared. It's getting worse. I don't know how to make it stop."

Mom's lips tremble as she pulls me back into a hug, and I cling to her, let myself sob into her shoulder. I'm making awful sounds and I don't care, I don't care.

"What do you mean?" she whispers. "Are you saying…this whole time… Marianne, what's going on?"

"There's a ghost," I wail. "Some sort of ghost. And I don't know what it *wants*."

A cabinet door slams open so hard its glass face cracks. Wine glasses tumble to the floor, one after another. Gravity seems to lose its hold on their shattered remains; broken stems and curved, sparkling fragments of glass ricochet into the air, spinning in all directions. Mom cries out, clutching me tighter, trying to shield me from them.

I can't explain any further. I don't have time. I'm putting her in danger.

"I have to go," I choke out, pulling away. "I have to go before it hurts you."

"Marianne, no, please, wait!"

But two steps around the corner and I'm already gone, running for the front door.

I don't stop running until I reach the busy street where I usually catch the bus, surrounded by swanky cafés and little boutiques, traffic rushing indifferently past. I stagger to a halt and collapse onto the bench, gasping for breath, bent over a searing stitch in my side. My thoughts are locked in a churning loop of *what do I do, what do I do*, without answers or direction. I don't have any money. I don't have my phone, and even if I did, it probably wouldn't work. I don't even have my coat, and the wind is quickly slicing through the last warmth from my flight.

Where do I go now? I can't go back to my aunt's, and I can't call my dad. What would they think of the knives lodged in the floor? Would Aunt Jen have a reasonable explanation for that? And Dad... If Mom's afraid that a visit to the hospital would make her sound unfit, then what about this? Would anyone believe me if I said it wasn't her?

I shiver and cram my hands in my pockets. My fingers meet a slip of cardboard, and I pull out Niobe's business card: a little purple rectangle inscribed with a new-agey rainbow star design and a phone number.

After a moment of frozen indecision, I pick myself up and push through the door of the Second Cup on the corner.

"Can I use your phone?" I ask the ponytailed guy behind the counter.

"Uh—"

"Please?" He looks a little alarmed, and I swallow, try to moderate my voice. "It's kind of an emergency."

"Oookay," he says, frowning. "Is everything all right?"

"Yes, yes, I'm fine. I just really need to make a phone call."

Reluctantly, he leads me to the far end of the counter and hands me a cordless handset. On the other end of the line, the phone rings and rings. My flare of hope is starting to congeal into fear again when a familiar voice picks up the call.

"Hello?" Ron says, and then again, more cautiously, "Hello?"

"Ron. It's me."

There's a long silence.

"Ron, I really need to talk to you." More silence. "*Please*. I listened to the tape. And more stuff has happened."

"Look, Marianne… The other night. That was really… Look, I don't know what to do with this. You know? I think I'm in over my head. No, I *know* I'm in over my head. I don't know if I should—"

"I know. I-I really think I need to see your mom." Silence. "I can't talk about it here." I cast a glance at the barista, who's frowning at me. He looks away. I turn my back to him and lower my voice, half whispering. "But she was right. And it's after me now. I don't know what to do!"

I close my eyes, listening to the static hissing in my ear, to the ordinary coffee shop clink and clatter around me, waiting, waiting.

"Shit," Ron sighs at last. "Okay. We're at 745 Stirling. Do you know where that is?"

I repeat her directions back to her, trying to cement them in my mind. The guy behind the counter slides me a pen and half a sheet of paper. I shoot him a grateful smile.

"*Thank* you," I tell Ron fervently, stuffing the directions in my pocket.

"Yeah," she says unhappily. "See you soon."

17

IT WOULDN'T SEEM LIKE SUCH a long walk if it weren't for the rain. Buses roaring past send water fountaining over the sidewalk. By the time I turn on Stirling I'm so soaked my clothes aren't even absorbing the rain anymore; it just rolls off me, like down the sides of an overflowing barrel. I've been walking so fast that when I reach Ron's house I'm almost warm despite the clammy flap of my jeans against my ankles.

The address she gave me is half of a small but solid brick square with four windows, their warm golden light spilling out from under the boughs of a looming tree, and two heavy wooden doors that share a rickety porch. Two little dormer windows peer down on the street from the roof.

I hesitate on the porch, twisting my hands. Ron won't be the one answering the door. Of course she won't. I hope she won't. All I can see is the look on her face under the streetlights. The fear in it.

I'm not going to think about it. I'm here, aren't I? Niobe will fix everything.

I lift my hand, drop it again, wipe it against my sodden jeans. Then I take a deep breath and knock hard on the door.

Footsteps creak toward me. There's a long pause before the door opens a fraction. And it is Ron looking out at me. Her red-and-black hair hangs limp and straight around her face. I don't think I've ever seen her without makeup before. It makes her look a lot younger.

"Hi," I manage. Just to break the silence. But she speaks at the same time, speaks over me.

"Jesus," she says, "you're not even wearing a coat? Come in already."

She ushers me into a disastrously cluttered living room, moving a basket full of colorful yarn and half-finished crochet project off a battered armchair. I sit gingerly on the very edge, trying not to get it wet.

"Mom's just upstairs. She said she had to get ready, so she's meditating or something. I'll go tell her you're here, okay?"

Her footsteps go thumping up the stairs; floorboards creak overhead. I hear a few words of low-voiced conversation.

I'm not going to think about what they're saying. I fold my arms, look around the room. In the soft golden glow of an old-fashioned, shaded lamp, amid a clutch of dirty coffee cups and beer bottles, is a picture in a wooden frame. I recognize Niobe by her cloud of hair, although she's rounder in this picture, younger, her smile bright and daring. Standing in the circle of her arms is a little girl in a dress, her mousy hair in pigtails, scowling at the camera. I lean closer, a smile stealing onto my face. Is that Ron?

"Here."

I jump a little and look up. Ron is standing in the doorway, a bundle of fabric in her arms.

"Thanks," I manage as she passes the clothes to me. She keeps her distance. We stand there for a minute in charged, awkward silence before she speaks again.

"I suspended my disbelief before, right? Well. Not anymore. Now I full-on believe you."

"Yeah. I know. Me too."

Her lips tilt into half a smile, there and gone again, as fleeting as the sun glimpsed through clouds. I want to ask her not to go, to forgive me for whatever happened in the park, but she clears her throat.

"You should get changed. There's no way this stuff fits, but at least it's dry. Just hang yours over the bathtub."

The clothes smell a little bit like cigarette smoke and a little bit like perfume, a faint, summery smell, like lilacs or roses. I breathe it in deep on my way up the stairs, trying to hold on to it. In a few minutes I'm shuffling out of the bathroom in a faded, swishy black skirt that I have to roll up at the waist so I don't trip, and a hoodie emblazoned with tour dates for a band I've never heard of. There's no help for my socks and shoes, which are still wet and cold, but I keep them on. At least they hide my feet.

To my surprise, Ron is still in the living room when I return, curled on the couch and worrying at the edges of her black-painted nails.

"So you listened to it," Ron says. I nod. She folds her arms. "I can't get the file to play back on my phone."

"Figures. My phone doesn't work at all lately."

"So." She looks at me, finally. "I guess you don't remember any of it?"

"No. I mean, I didn't hear any of it then, while it was happening. I was somewhere else. That place from my dream, I think." I try, brokenly, to describe the roaring in my ears, the pull of the water, my useless attempt to run away from it. "Until I heard you yell my name. And then I saw... There was something *horrible* there, just for a second. And I think it saw me too. But then I was back in the park with you."

"What was it?"

I shake my head. "It was person-shaped, I think. It was hard to tell. I saw it in the bathroom mirror today too, but the light wouldn't work. All I could see was this...shadow." I tug nervously at the drawstrings at the neck of my sweater. "It *hated* me."

"It said something about you drowning it. Did that tell you anything?"

I shake my head. "I've definitely never drowned anybody."

Although in a dream-logic sort of way the accusation makes sense, somehow, with the water at Aunt Jen's and the water in my dreams.

"Could you tell what it was?" I ask. "What was it like?"

"I don't know. At first you were just acting weird. You took your shoes off. And my necklace. You laughed a little bit, and threw it away. I didn't start to get really scared until you undid your hair. It was floating." She waggles her fingers expressively. "Like, like seaweed, all twisting around. And—I don't know how to explain it. It was dark, but still, it was like your whole face had changed. And it was you talking. I mean, it was coming from you. But, well, you heard it. And after a while... I didn't know what I was seeing at first, I thought you were getting taller or something, but it had lifted you right off the ground; I could see your feet hanging there in the air."

Just like what Mom saw. I lean back on my heels a little bit, feeling for the reassuring pressure of the floor.

"I asked what it wanted, and it just said that same thing again, about 'this is mine.' I think maybe it meant your body? It sort of..." She makes a raking gesture across her arms and chest. My fingers steal to my shoulder, to the little bruises still lingering there.

"And I—" She breaks off, closes her eyes for a moment. When she continues, her voice is ragged. "It was a bad mistake, Marianne, the whole thing. It was stupid of me. I should never have tried it. I didn't know what the hell I was doing."

"We had to try something," I protest, but Ron shakes her head.

"You said more stuff happened," she insists. "Like what?"

Reluctantly, I tell her about the water in my room at Aunt Jen's, the knocking, the pins, the writing on the mirror. And then at home, the books flying off the shelves, the pictures swirling in the sink. The knives hanging in the air.

Ron hides her face in her hands.

"I made it worse. Oh God, Marianne, I'm so sorry."

"I don't know. It was already looking for me, I think. I could feel it. Maybe it was just a matter of time. I'm just afraid it's going to hurt me. Or someone else." I swallow as something occurs to me. *Your beautiful friend with the painted face.* "Maybe I shouldn't be here. It... I think it remembers you."

There's a tense silence, but nothing happens.

"That's kind of weird, though, isn't it?" Ron says slowly. "I mean, with those knives. It *could* have really hurt you. It could have killed you. Why didn't it? If it hates you that much?"

"I don't know. If it's just trying to scare me, it's doing a pretty good job. But why, then?" The voice from the tape drifts through my mind. *I want what is mine...this is all mine!* "I have something it wants. It said I stole something. But when I asked it what I took, it just went on about the sun and the wind. And my mom." And Ron. I don't want to tell her that. My hands go to my shoulders again. "I don't get it."

"Maybe it's just jealous of you. Maybe it really is a ghost. In the sense of someone that used to be alive. Maybe it wants to have the world back."

"I guess. But then why me? I don't know anybody who's died. If it wants the world back, why does it think I'm the one who took it away? How could I have done something like that?"

"And where did it come from?" She's frowning now, as puzzled as I am. "Is it just the kind of creature that does this to random people, or what? It's definitely acting like a poltergeist now, but I never read anything about—"

The light flickers, comes back on with a faint rattle and buzz. Ron and I exchange a look.

"I should go," I whisper.

"Don't," Ron protests, jumping to her feet. "You can't go back out there alone with this thing after you!"

"You don't understand. It was talking about you."

"It's my fault it saw you." She pauses, lifts her chin. "I'm not running away this time."

We both jump as one of the mugs from the side table crashes onto the parquet, but Ron doesn't hesitate; she grabs my arm and hurries toward the stairs.

"Mom? Mom!" She bolts up the stairs ahead of me. Picture frames rock back and forth on their hooks on the wall as we pass, a sway more pronounced than our footsteps could possibly cause. At the top of the stairs a door swings open, a waft of incense rolling toward us. Niobe stands there, beckoning for us to hurry.

She slams the door shut behind us, makes a sweeping gesture with one arm, as if to bar the way or beat something back. A volley of knocks comes rattling down from all around the room, and then subsides into quiet. My heart thunders in my ears. The room is lit by candles, little tea lights quivering in jars and shallow bowls on artfully ornamented bookshelves. The ceiling, the walls, are all draped in fluttering swaths of fabric, ranging from plush to gauzy, some spangled with patterns that catch the light.

Niobe turns slowly, squinting, and peers at me for a long moment without speaking.

"I thought so," she breathes. Her gaze travels to a point over my shoulder. To Ron, I think at first, but Ron's across the room, fists clenched, looking back and forth between the two of us.

"There's someone…" Niobe reaches out to grasp my arm, her voice an urgent whisper. "Listen. Do you know anybody who's drowned?"

And then there's a loud smack and abruptly, with a cry, she lets me go, staggering back a step with her hand to her face. Her eyes, meeting mine, are wide and shocked.

"I should go. I have to go," I choke out, and push blindly toward the door, but Niobe's hand clamps down on my arm again.

"I *think* that would be unwise," she says. "Someone's terribly angry with you."

I stare at her. She doesn't let me go, but massages her cheek with her other hand.

"Well," she says peevishly, shooting an accusing look at Ron, "you sure put your foot in it, didn't you."

Ron looks away, scowling, and folds her arms. "We've been over this already," she mutters.

"We certainly have! Just because *you're* a cement bunker doesn't mean you can't put other people in danger!" She turns to me. "Rhiannon's gotten a little too used to being invulnerable, I'm afraid. She's very grounded. But being made of solid clay has its disadvantages."

"Um," I say.

"She means I'm about as psychic as a fence post," Ron puts in flatly.

"Not to put too fine a point on it," Niobe snaps. "Now you had better tell me exactly what it was you did so I can try to undo the mess you've made of it!"

"I was just trying to get it to talk to me."

"By yourself."

"I didn't think it would work!"

I shift uncomfortably and try to catch Ron's eye, but she's glaring at her mother, who scrubs her hands over her face in a give-me-strength gesture.

"That was a profoundly stupid thing to do."

"Look, I get that, okay? I tried to tell it—"

"There, see," Niobe interrupts, "that was your next mistake. Never argue. Just listen. You need to just be with it."

"Yeah, sure. Take it on a meditation retreat, that ought to do it."

"This is a task that demands a certain amount of empathy,

Rhiannon. Cultivate it. I can't believe this. You should have known better."

"Fine. Great. Now that we've established that, can we please—"

"Did you do anything about protection?"

"Of course I did! Marianne had my necklace. The obsidian one. We burned sage, I cast a circle, the whole nine yards."

"Did you try silver? Amethyst?"

"Well, no, but I don't see why those would work if the other stuff—"

"And what about Marianne, did you show her how to defend herself at all?"

"I thought all that *was* defense!"

Niobe massages her temples. I should say something, anything, but Ron rolls her eyes, and Niobe erupts again.

"Don't start with me, Rhiannon! Did you at least teach her the blue star exercise? Or how to ground herself? They're very simple visualizations, even you should have been able to—"

"Give me a break!" Ron yells. "It's throwing knives at her and you think—"

"It's *what?*" Niobe's voice goes up half an octave. "You told me this was about doors slamming and—"

"What good are blue stars supposed to do? How the hell do you even call that defending yourself? Or are you just mad because you didn't get the chance to hand her a bill?"

"Back off!" Niobe yells. "Haven't you done enough damage here already?"

Ron, who was opening her mouth to interrupt, subsides, her chin stuck out, breathing hard. Her eyes are bright in the light of the candles.

"If you want to do something *useful*," Niobe continues, the words biting and brittle, "get out of the way. Go smoke or whatever. I need to focus."

Ron meets my eyes for one long moment, then lowers her head and stalks from the room, slamming the door behind her. The little flames on the shelves and the shifting drapes of fabric tremble in her wake.

Niobe shakes herself, exhales long and slow, then makes some fluttering motions with her hands like she's brushing herself off.

"All right," she says at length. "Come over here, please."

"I'm sorry," I stammer as she draws me into the middle of the room.

"Not your fault," Niobe says gruffly. "Except that I wish you'd made that appointment right away. I tried to warn you."

"Do you know what it is?" I ask, swallowing the rebuke. "Ron said it sounded like a poltergeist."

"'Poltergeist' is more like a set of symptoms than an actual type of entity." Niobe looks me up and down, pulls a black-silver stone from a nearby shelf. "Here, hold this."

The stone is cold and slick in my hands, drawing the warmth from my fingers. "Can you make it go away?"

"It's not quite that simple," she sighs, rummaging through a drawstring bag sewn with bits of sparkling mirror. "It's been a long time since I tried anything on this level, but despite what my daughter may have told you, I *can* manage some real witchery occasionally. When I have to. I'll do my best to help, all right? The first order of business is at least some basic self-defense. So you have a better chance at fighting it off."

That phrasing isn't exactly reassuring. I clutch the stone. I have to ask.

"Do I...do I have a chance?"

"Everyone has a chance." But she gives me a troubled look. "You really can't think of anyone who drowned?"

I shake my head. "Does that mean it's a ghost? A ghost of someone who drowned in the river?"

She squints into the distance, like she's searching for something. "Maybe? That's not quite it, but..." She shakes her head, letting her breath hiss through her teeth. "Never mind. It's hard to explain this stuff. It's like trying to tell somebody what color Tuesday is. Or what justice tastes like." She glances back to me, and the candles carve deep lines of shadow down her cheeks. "I...haven't done a very good job of explaining to Rhiannon. As I'm sure you've heard. Here, sit down. Right here, please."

She pulls a silky green cushion from a basket, drops it on the floor. While I settle myself awkwardly onto it, she snaps open a pair of spectacles and perches them on her nose, folding out a third lens to rest in the middle of her forehead.

"No smart remarks about the glasses, please," she says crisply, rolling up her sleeves. "All right. Listen up. Where you're sitting is the very heart of my defenses around this house. I don't suppose you can see the lines?"

I glance around the room, but there's only flickering candle-light and shadow. A cold draft pours across the floor from one narrow window, sending the shimmering bronze curtains into a slow, trembling swirl.

"Right. Well, they're there. So you're safe here, all right? But I need you to stay put. Got that?" She waits for me to nod. "So that's the first thing. Now. What you're going to do is close your eyes and imagine a bright white light pouring down on you. All right? Go on, close your eyes. Bright white light. Concentrate on your head, your face, your neck, your arms being wrapped in white light, all down your body, until it gets right to the ground. Or you could imagine growing roots down into the ground and sucking it up. Use your breath. Draw it into you."

I set the black-silver stone in my lap and reach down to touch the cool, ridged floorboards. Outside a car splashes by. Voices talking and laughing drift in and fade again. And waiting underneath is an evening quiet, a soft, breathless quiet, full of the trickle of water in the eaves trough, the roar of traffic like the distant voice of the river, the sound of my blood in my ears. I shake myself a little, clear my throat, afraid it might swallow me again. It's like standing on the edge of a cliff, looking down into the dark. Like the road running the wrong way, down toward the water.

White light, white light, I'm supposed to be thinking about white light. I flex my fingers a little against the floor and seize on Niobe's idea about tree roots, imagining my fingertips growing like green twigs, pushing down through the cracks in the wooden surface, through the brick walls and the old stone foundation, seeking soft damp earth.

But again there's only water—and the dark. I try to imagine the sun blazing down from a sky thin and white with the heat of a summer day. But in my mind's eye, when I look back down to earth I'm standing by the river. Under my feet the sand is cold, and the water is black, stretching out into emptiness. I can feel it rising all around me, stealing the feeling from my fingers, surrounding me like an embrace: ghostly arms winding around me, invisible hands clasping across my chest.

I snatch my hands from the floor. "This isn't working," I gasp.

But my lips move without sound. And around me the room has changed. It takes me a second to figure out what's different. The light is still soft, diffuse, a golden flicker, but it's sourceless; the candles have disappeared. The cloying smell of incense has been washed away. It smells like rain. Like the river. The curtains, the fabric draped from the ceiling have gone limp, perfectly motionless, catching the square of orange light falling through the window.

The weight of Niobe's silvery stone has vanished from my lap. And I'm alone.

18

I CLUTCH THE EDGES OF the cushion, trying not to panic, resisting the urge to call out to Niobe. She's gone. She's worlds away. She told me to stay put. Do I still need to stay put?

"Well, hello."

Niobe's voice makes me jump, leaves me twisting around looking for her. It's muffled, like it's coming from the next room, though I can hear the words clearly enough. They're casual, but guarded.

"Niobe?" My lips shape the word, soundless. "Ron!"

And another voice speaks over me, clear as if it stood beside me. Clearer. Clear as a thought unbidden. There's nowhere to hide from it. I hunker down on the cushion.

What are you doing? the ghost demands. **Is this a trick?**

"You're not Marianne, are you?"

Obviously.

"What's your name, then?"

Don't fuck with me, it snarls. **Whose side are you on?**

"I'm not on anybody's side," Niobe says soothingly. "I'm here to help."

You're here to help her, you mean. You're here to help that stupid, worthless waste of space. You just want to get rid of me!

"Now let's be reasonable," Niobe says sternly, and Not-Marianne lets out an awful, wordless banshee shriek, a sound that stabs through my ears, leaves them ringing. I flounder away from it, scrambling backward till my shoulder thumps into the edge of a bookcase.

And now I can see them. On the green cushion in the middle of the room, someone is sitting in my place. Something. Wearing the same shapeless sweater as I am, the skirt I'm wearing pooled around its knees. Its hair is floating, a restless, writhing shadow around its head. Niobe stands a few paces away with her hands on her hips, shining so bright I have to raise my hand to shield my gaze. As I watch, the thing sitting in my place hefts the stone I was holding in one hand and whips it at her. It moves almost too fast to see, like a video skipping forward. I can't hear when the missile hits the wall, but it leaves a gash punched into it, a crescent of shadow.

I will not! I WILL NOT. You think you can control me? You think you can trap me here?

"Of course not," Niobe says, adjusting her spectacles, brushing her hair back from her face. She sounds calm, but her hand is shaking. "You're obviously very powerful. Very strong."

I am, Not-Marianne says fiercely. **I am. I'm taking back what's mine. And you can't stop me!**

Niobe studies it for a moment.

"It's hard, isn't it," she says softly. "Being strong."

Silence.

"You're fighting so hard. You've been fighting for so long. Don't you want to rest? Even just for a little while?"

I can't, it says wildly. **I can't. I can't.**

"There must be someone waiting for you," Niobe says, her voice even gentler, a mother's voice.

No. There's no one. Never. I'm all alone. I've been alone for so long. They've all abandoned me. They only want her. That good little fucking Barbie doll!

"I'm not talking about her," Niobe says firmly. "I'm talking about you. There are people you love, aren't there? I can help you find them. That's my job, all right? Tell me about them. I'll find them for you."

You can't help me, Not-Marianne whispers.

"Try me. Come on."

I don't remember. She stole so much. There was a place with tall windows. It wasn't for dancing. And it filled up with water, she filled it up to the top so I couldn't breathe, I couldn't breathe!

Niobe crouches down beside the thing, wraps an arm around

its hunched shoulders, reaches out to tame the swirling cloud of its hair.

I thought I made it back. My mother was right there. She held me, she sang to me. Like she used to. She sang me to sleep. But when I woke up I was *there,* **I was alone.**

"Where do you mean? Where did you wake up?" Niobe murmurs.

That horrible place, it breathes, and I shrink back against the bookshelf, goose bumps tingling over my arms. **That dark place. I haven't seen the sun in so long. The water's always waiting. And she pushes me down. Again and again and again.**

It reaches out, suddenly, to clutch Niobe's arm. Niobe winces, but doesn't pull away.

There was a girl with a painted face, it says urgently. **She called me. She showed me the way back. She had a smile like the sun. I don't need the sun back if only she'll smile at me again. She doesn't understand. It's me she wants. I know it. I just have to make her understand. I'm the one who's real.**

It's Niobe's turn to stay silent, stricken.

If you're here to help me, Not-Marianne begs, **help me find her. I have to see her again. I need her. I** *need* **her.**

"And what will you do," Niobe says, failing to be nonchalant, "when you find her?"

She'll stay with me. I know she will.

"You sound very sure of that."

Of course I am. Suspicion clouds its voice. Niobe leans back a little; it yanks her closer. **Why are you looking at me like that?**

"I need to know she's not in any danger."

I just have to make her see. It's pleading, which is somehow more threatening than its scream. **I just have to persuade her. She has to love me. She called me.**

I push myself slowly to my feet, every muscle taut and trembling. I reach, fumbling, for the door. I have to find Ron. I have to warn her. Any second it will turn and see me. Does it know I'm here?

But the doorknob won't turn under my hand. It's not slippery exactly. Somehow I just can't make contact, though my fingers seem to close around it. They told us in math about Zeno's paradox: how the hare should never catch up with the tortoise because all it can do is halve the distance, and halve it again, and again into infinity.

Behind me a giggle rises into a mean and cheerless laugh. I bite back a sob and hammer against the door; my fists are as mute as my voice. When I steal a glance over my shoulder I'm looking into my own face, transfigured by a hard-eyed smile I've never worn. I recoil from it, the corner of the bookcase sharp against my back.

Fun, isn't it? Not-Marianne whispers.

"That's enough," Niobe says, but fear has crept into her muzzy voice, she can't pull away, and the ghost makes a noise of scoffing disgust.

I'm done talking to you. You're a fraud. You can't keep me here. A pause. Its eyes don't reflect the candlelight. **But you do know where she is, don't you?**

Beside me, the door swings open, a mouth opening wide into inky darkness. And then Ron blinks into view as she steps across the threshold, not so brilliant as Niobe, but uncannily bright, like she's been snipped from a sunny picture and pasted onto the surface of the night. She speaks in a murky, underwater jumble, with some words still submerged, unintelligible.

"Shut up," she says. "…here, all right?…alone!"

Not-Marianne's smile turns radiant.

I knew it, it whispers. **I knew you'd come back.**

"That's enough!" Niobe repeats, terror a knife-edge in her voice. She closes her eyes, reaches her hands out to either side as if she's going to pull the walls down. "*MARIANNE, COME BACK. I CALL YOU BACK.*"

It's like someone's caught hold of my sweater, jerked me forward; I can't catch my balance, and I throw my hands out, trying to break my fall—

—and my hand, my elbow, jars against the floorboards. I yelp as sparking numbness travels up my arm, and I hear the sound as it leaves my lips, a pathetic bleat. When I push myself up, my legs are still folded over the green cushion. I breathe in patchouli. Niobe kneels beside me, limned with flickering shadow, clutching her head.

A pounding starts on the wall, the wild, frantic hammering of someone trapped in a room with water rising around their knees. The candles gutter out as if in a single gust of wind, but the air is still except for the same chilly draft creeping across the floor. And all around us comes the sound of smashing glass, a furious staccato like popcorn, little objects from the shelves hitting the floor with an impact that vibrates through the wood. The window implodes, the curtains lashing, shards spraying out toward us, muffling Ron's scream.

When silence falls, Niobe, a hunched silhouette, hasn't moved. Her breath is ragged. Ron slaps at the light switch, but it doesn't work; the bulb must have gotten smashed with everything else. Her face springs into the light of a single wavering flame. A lighter.

"Jesus fucking Christ, Mom," she says faintly. She takes a couple of long, crunching steps toward Niobe, but Niobe puts out a hand to stop her, shrinking down a little, her other hand cradling her face.

"S'okay," she pants. "Migraine. Oh. Ow."

Ron turns to me instead, sweeping debris out of the way with her boots as she makes her way across the room. She takes my elbow, pulls me up.

"Watch your feet," she mutters.

"Don't touch her. Stay where you are!" Niobe's voice is a whip-crack, making us both jump. She hauls herself to her feet, one hand still pressed to the side of her head. She wavers there for a moment, then squints at me. "You. Need to leave."

In the shattered room I can hardly argue. I shrink from her stare.

"Mom, what the hell!" Ron cries.

"I'm not strong enough." Niobe's words are quiet, pained, but as final as a door falling closed. "It's already got its hooks into you. It's already *inside* you. It couldn't have gotten in here otherwise. I can't help you. And I can't risk my daughter. You need to leave."

"Uh, excuse me?" Ron waves her hands in the air. "Hello! I'm right here!"

"You," Niobe breathes, stabbing a finger at her, "have messed this up worse than you know." She looks at me, then closes her eyes again, like the sight of me hurts. "There was a time I could make sacrifices. And it was a long time ago. I'm sorry. I can't help you."

I pull away from Ron, who makes a sound like she's going to protest, but she doesn't. I take long, awkward strides to the door, glass crunching under my shoes every time I put my feet down. Niobe ignores me, rocking back and forth a little bit, her face twisted up in pain.

Once I've closed the door behind me I can run. I pelt down the stairs, away from Ron's voice rising furiously behind me, and throw the door open with a bang.

I fly down the sidewalk, past hedges and fences covered in trailing grapevines, but it's been a long time since I was any kind of athlete, and I'm exhausted. Eventually I stagger to a halt, leaning over my feet and bracing myself against my knees, waiting for my breath to stop burning in my throat. The streetlights are on, glinting from chain-link fences, bleeding other colors from the world, leaving only the murky remnants of the brightest reds and blues. It's a false light, a netherworld light that lets you see but doesn't push back the darkness.

I can't go home. What do I do now?

Eventually I lurch back into motion, following the sidewalk without caring which direction I'm going. That was it. My last hope, the last person who might have helped me. And her one defense, the one thing she said might give me a better chance, only invited it in. *It's already inside you.* It felt like a sentence. Dead girl walking.

I could lie down right here in the street, just let it wash over me. Let go and sink. But the dream is a chilly breath on my neck: the memory of fighting for air, knowing there's only water there to breathe. Animal panic prods me forward, hurries my steps.

I think of Mom's lined, tired face. If—when—the ghost takes over for good, will she know it? Or will she just think it's me, turned wild, lashing out, becoming Hurricane Marianne? Would anybody see the difference?

Ron would. She would know.

She must have been listening at the door that whole time. This time she heard it, all that demented rambling. The naked want. She should have run. But she thought her mom was in danger, and she opened the door. She told it to shut up. Would I have defended my mom like that, if our places were reversed? Could I?

It's a stupid question. I know exactly what a hard, cold moment of truth like that would reveal in me. I've already seen it. I would crumble; I would run. I would hide. It's all I know how to do.

There was a reason it was the adage that I couldn't master. "There's no faking the adage," Miss Giselle always told us. "You need a lot more than strength to make it flow." When you slow everything down that much there's no disguising your weakness, your lack of center, the quaver in your leg that threatens to unbalance you.

There's no faking control. And there's nowhere to hide from the mirror, not with the merciless line rotation pushing you forward.

The day I gave it up was all wrong from the start, and stuck in front of the mirror I couldn't turn away from any part of it: my leg too high, my arms chicken wings, stiff and brushed with goose bumps. I'd been up later than my parents the night before, practicing the same stupid thing over and over again, the long languid moves.

"Long lines, Marianne," Miss Giselle called. "Extend!"

And I wobbled, stumbled out of step completely, had to fumble for my place again. No one met my eye in the mirror. I could feel their stares on my back.

It broke like a bone, whatever was holding me together, and I thumped down onto the flats of my shoes and ran from the room. The only place I could think of to come unglued was the bathroom. I slammed into a stall, curled up on the toilet seat, sobbed into my arms. The echoes bounced off the tiles. They hid the sound of the door swinging open.

"Are you all right?" someone called. I choked on my sudden panic, swallowed it down. Too late.

"Yes," I called back. Utterly unconvincing. And they left: there were two of them, two voices, giggling in embarrassment as the door fell shut behind them. Soon everyone would be talking about it. How I was falling apart. How I didn't have what it takes.

I left the stall, splashed water on my face, looked into my red-rimmed eyes in the mirror. Under the fluorescents I was skinny and sallow, my lips purple-tinged, my breastbone an ugly shadow under my skin.

That was when I knew. I couldn't do it. I was never going back.

I don't know what's more pathetic, the memory or that I'm thinking about it now. I shake my head, hug my elbows, and blow out a long, trembling breath, like they taught us in yoga, exhaling everything negative like a stream of silver bubbles underwater.

But the sound of it sinks away from me into rushing silence. It's lost as the sun. And a weight settles into the backs of my legs, though I stumble to a stop, leaning back against it.

"Not again," I whimper. Or try to.

Everything around me is the same, but immobile, breathless, the windows of the houses blind and dark. I stand there hesitating on the sidewalk, panic beating through the murmuring noise in my ears.

That horrible place, the ghost said. *That dark place. The water's always waiting.* It pulls at me, calling me northward like a compass needle, to where the river should be. I turn my face away, fight to take deep breaths I can't hear. I have to get away from it.

I force myself to take a step. Another. And another. Into the middle of the empty street. Which way should I go? How far can I get? I think all the roads here must lead to the water eventually. I can feel the weight of it bending all the paths, a black hole drawing down the stars.

White light, I think desperately. White light. I stare straight ahead, trying not even to blink, fixating on the dark, empty facades of houses, the way the orange light shines on the wet asphalt, so that it can't slip back toward the water like it did in the park. And I walk.

Stirling leads to one street, then another, and I'm forced to turn, though I'm afraid to, afraid to find the street suddenly sloping down toward the same empty beach. Even the main arteries, usually bustling with traffic and restaurant-goers, are silent and dark. The quiet there is so uncanny I give up and turn back onto the side streets, at random, just to get away from it. I pass empty chairs on dark porches, wind chimes hanging motionless, the leaves of trees hanging wetly down, gleaming in the streetlights. Above the rooflines on one side, a church steeple slices into the sullen sky, pale sea green in the glow of a floodlight shining up from below.

I creep on and on, the only moving thing. Maybe I've been walking forever. The street corners are featureless lakes. A tall, wrought-iron gate leads into a playground where a bright white streetlamp shines like a star, illuminating the slides and monkey bars with a pale wash of color. The swing set stands as if in midair, its whole shape made alien by the flawless reflection underneath it.

I give the water a wide berth, but I'm drawn like a moth to the brilliance of the light, drifting silently along the paved path. The rose window of the church looms on the far side of the park. The halo cast by the streetlamp fades into murky shadow under the trees, across the black swath of a submerged lawn. How long will I be wandering here, waiting for the current to build, for the water to pull me down? How long have I been gone? Will this be the time it doesn't let me come back? Is it still in the real world in my place, like it was before?

If it's in my place…if we've switched places…is this where it came from?

I turn slowly around, seeing the silent world with new understanding. *I'll drown her instead. She can rot in the dark.* Is it ever daytime here? When I look back through the gate, the dark tunnel of the street beyond seems to stretch out forever, and time gapes open with it, bottomless, an eternity without sunlight or sound or warmth. An eternity fighting the current, fighting for my life, all alone.

Yes. That's it. I know I'm right, like I know my name. This is where it came from, this dark, silent, unchanging noplace.

And it thinks I'm the one pulling it down. Into the water. Into that icy, mirror-smooth surface from my dream.

I put my hands to my mouth. No. That can't be it, that can't be true. What power do I have to do something like that? This has to be a mistake. There has to be some way to tell it so, to convince it, whatever it is. Can it hear me from here?

It wasn't me, I try to shout, and then again. *It wasn't me!* It's no good, there's no sound, not so much as an eddy in the air. It's like I'm not even breathing.

Think. I sink down on a bench, ignoring the chilly bite of water soaking through my skirt, and put my hands over my eyes. *Come on, think.* If this is where it came from, then there's some way to affect the real world, the daylight world, from here. It must have found a way. Right? I think of the books sweeping themselves off the shelf, the knives hanging in the air. It can find me. I should be able to find it too.

I sit there for a moment, quailing, but then I think of Ron, her plain pale face in the light of the candles; her fearful eyes, the thin determined line of her mouth. Bit by bit, as if I'm edging around a corner, I force the image of that half-glimpsed figure to coalesce in my mind, its floating hair, its rage like lightning. Come find me, I think. I'm waiting.

And when I open my eyes, there it is, stepping into the circle of fish-cold light, its face—my face—a narrow, shadowed moon emerging from the shifting cloud of its hair. I'd hardly know my own form, draped in Ron's too-big clothes, if it wasn't for the hair coiling languidly around its head as if it's drifting in some underwater current. I shrink back from it, but it ignores me; its attention is fixed on something in the playground. I watch it reach out to touch one of the slides, running a hand over the bright red plastic.

And behind it, crouched at a wary distance next to one of the trees, is Ron. She's clearly visible in the darkness, still shining, a scrap of cheerful sunlight gleaming on water fathoms deep.

She came. Just like she came for Niobe. She followed me.

Like it's heard the thought, the ghost looks up, looks right at me, stopping my breath in my throat. And then it turns to see Ron, who freezes in place, wincing.

Wearing my face, the ghost smiles.

It's you. Of course it's you.

It's hard to look straight at it; it looks like me, but somehow it doesn't inhabit my features the same way I do, and a shadow of malice shimmers from it like heat from pavement. Ron shrinks back a few steps, splashing ankle-deep into the wide pool that surrounds the tree, but then holds her ground. Not-Marianne takes a step toward her, another.

You found me. You came looking for me. That's so sweet.

Ron's hands fly up, her lips move. Her voice doesn't carry through the underwater silence like Niobe's did, but I remember it on the tape. *Stay away from me! Stay back!*

You still think you can tell me what to do? Its smile widens. Another step, and another. Another. Ron falters, falls back a little further. **I'm stronger than you.**

Run, I yell at her, soundless. *Don't be stupid! Run!* But she stands fast, fists clenched, watching Not-Marianne stalk closer. Its hands close on her arms. I watch helplessly as it forces her to her knees in the water, leans over her as she struggles to break its grip.

Mine, the ghost croons with its face inches from Ron's. Hungry. Closing in. **Mine.**

Not-Marianne's long black Medusa hair eclipses them both for a moment. And then, abruptly, the ghost withdraws.

Why should you care? It sounds…hurt? Is that possible?

Ron closes her eyes, says something through clenched teeth.

Why are you still talking to her? I'm the one who's here with you. The words are tender, almost pleading, but its fingers tighten around Ron's arms. Ron turns her head, leaning as far away from it as she can as it bends toward her. **I'm the one who wants you.**

Ron twists in its grip.

Don't say that, it moans. **Don't you see? You saved me. You're the only one I want.**

She's speaking again, fists clenched, but before she's finished it's already shaking its head, its hair lashing.

No. No no no. The air seems to crackle as its voice rises. **Why would you say that? You don't know her. Not like I do. She's nothing. She's useless! This is all wasted on her! She doesn't deserve it! It's mine!**

The ghost gives Ron a shake, shoves her away. She tumbles backward into the water, pushes herself up far enough to flounder back a few more splashing paces, falls again.

She's not coming back! The shadow around it deepens, congeals, lifting it into the air. Ron cringes away from it. **I won't let her! Are you going to run from me? Go on, run! I can tell you want to. See how far you get!**

She doesn't run. She huddles in place and doesn't move.

Isn't that cute, the ghost snarls. **Isn't that adorable. You don't even know her. If you did, you'd run. Go! Do you want me to hurt you?**

Ron lifts her head, seems to steel herself. I see my name on her lips. *Come back.*

But the ghost's rage twists my face into a mask I barely recognize, and though it's nowhere near her, I know it's what knocks Ron sprawling. She's trying to get to her feet as I run toward her, but invisible blows rain down on her; she staggers under each one, reeling. I try to grab her arm, to help her up, but it's like there's a glass wall between us, fitting close to her as a second skin, and though my hand seems to close on her shoulder, I know I can't touch her, some distance will always remain. I try to stand between her and the ghost, flinging my arms wide to block its attack somehow, but it kicks Ron's feet out from under her without my feeling so much as a whisper.

You're in over your head, it says softly, stepping slowly, deliberately toward us. **Aren't you. Stupid. Naive. You think she'd come back for you? You think she'd even try? She's right here, you know. I go where she goes. She's been here this whole time. She's standing right here doing nothing. She's too afraid to stop me. Too weak to stop me. She can't stop me from taking. What's. MINE!**

Leave her alone, I wail. Ron is on her hands and knees in the water, and her expression crumples, her shoulders shake as she starts to cry. But she doesn't move. *Ron!* No sound, I have no voice. *Rhiannon! What are you doing? Run!*

I can't look straight at it, but I know it's turned to look at me again. I heard somewhere that people used to think there were actual rays that come out of your eyes, unseen particles with an impact you can feel.

I know you can hear me, the ghost says.

Leave her alone! I scream.

Make me, the ghost replies coldly. Beside me Ron curls up small in the water, trying to shield herself from another onslaught, rocking under impacts I can't shield her from. She pitches to one side, barely catches herself with an elbow.

Give it to me! the ghost rages. **You will give it to me, or I will make it not worth having!**

Desperately, I turn away and throw myself across the distance between me and the ghost—a vast gulf, a few steps—reaching out to seize hold of it. To my astonishment, it shrinks away from me.

And then the world whirls around me, and I hear the splash of my hands connecting with the marshy ground before I feel it. I'm panting like I've run a race, and I huddle there for a long moment, listening to my breath, to the rustle of the leaves, to the sifting drizzle of the rain.

To someone crying.

When I look up, Ron is still kneeling in the water a few meters away. Her hair trails into it, hiding her face.

"Are you okay?" I croak.

She nods jerkily.

"Ron—"

"I'm fine. I'm fine, I'm okay."

I lever myself to my feet—my bare feet, numb with cold—and splash toward her, but she puts a hand out to stop me and starts to wobble upright herself. She half laughs, then sniffles and lurches a bit as she stands, wincing. "Shit. I'm soaked."

"Oh my god, Ron. Why didn't you run? Were you *following* it?"

"I didn't know *what* to do, okay? When I caught up with you your hair was floating again. And it didn't see me, it just went on up the street, so I thought maybe I ought to…I don't know. I don't know what I was thinking." Her voice thins into silence. She presses a hand to her side, lets her breath out slow and trembling.

"Ron—"

She dismisses the horror in my voice with a shaky wave of her hand. I swallow the hundred apologies I want to blurt out.

"Here," she says. "You'll need your shoes. It left them on the sidewalk a while back."

They're stuffed in her coat pockets; she pulls them out and shoves them at me as she splashes past, limping a little.

"C'mon," she mutters. "Let's walk. I'm freezing."

19

WE COME OUT ONTO THE sidewalk, under the glow of the streetlights again. I drink in the sounds of distant traffic, our hurried footsteps, the mutter of the wind. Ron has become smaller somehow, folded into herself. She doesn't look behind us, but her eyes flick back and forth across the road, and she jumps when a car turns onto the street just behind us. I don't know what to say. I want to tell her to go home, I want to tell her she doesn't have to stay, but it seems cheap, ungrateful. I want to tell her how amazing she was, facing it down. I can't believe she did it. I can't figure out *why*.

"Is your mom okay?" is what I eventually come out with.

"She's just got a headache," Ron mutters. "That happens when she overdoes it."

"She was trying to teach me a thing about white light," I stammer, though she probably heard that. "I tried. I really did. That other place just...dragged me in."

"Figures. Well, so much for visualizations."

"Ron. Listen, I tried to stop it, I couldn't touch you, it—"

"Fine, yeah," she interrupts, her voice pained. "I get it."

"I'm not like you," I say tightly. She has to know this about me. I can't face her disappointment when she finds out. "I would have run. The ghost was right. I'm too scared. Maybe I shouldn't even have—"

"Just. Just don't," Ron says sharply, silencing me. It's a long minute before she sighs and speaks again. "Look, don't listen to it. Okay? That's what it wants. You can't believe the shit those kinds of things say about you."

I nod, digging my fingernails into my palms.

"Seriously," she says, putting a hand on my arm to pull me to a stop. "I get it. You tried. Look, I'm here, right? I'm fine."

God, it just beat her up and she's trying to reassure *me*. I nod again, looking away down the street, trying to keep my mouth an iron line. I wish she'd stop looking at me so I could get my face back under control.

"Let's keep moving, okay?" I whisper.

We walk in silence for a while. I have to keep hitching up

the borrowed skirt; it's heavy with water, slapping and clinging icily against my legs. We could be ghosts ourselves, hurrying past hedges and fences covered in trailing grapevines, the warm glow of kitchen and living room windows, the occasional car splashing past. I cling to the little sounds around us, holding them close, hoping they might be an anchor, a lifeline to the real world. The chirp of a car alarm, jingling keys. A muffled bass beat drifting from someone's window.

"That place I was in," I start, too quietly, and have to repeat it before Ron looks around at me. "I think that's where it comes from."

"What makes you say that?"

"I just have a feeling. I don't know."

Ron's lips quirk.

"Now you sound like my mom." She gives me a searching look. "Was it the same as last time? The other place?"

"Yeah. It was a little different at your house. Maybe because your mom's psychic. She was all...I don't know, lit up. I could hear her. And you, a little bit. But out here...it's kind of a mirror of the world. Everything's the same. The road, the streetlights, all the buildings. Or even inside. But you can't hear anything, and there's no one else around. Just the river. Or something like the river." I fumble for words to describe it, clench my teeth to keep them from chattering. "Being there is like... It's like you're treading water. All the time. And if you stop you'll go under. And I think that's where the ghost is, usually, when I'm here. When it says I drowned it... I don't know if this makes sense. I think it means I trapped it there."

"How is that even possible?"

I shake my head. I don't want to think about it.

"Right." It's heartening to see her eyes narrow thoughtfully, a shade of the detective returning. "I guess it doesn't matter. It *thinks* you trapped it there. And it wants to be here instead, all the time. So it hates you. And when it says 'this is mine'—"

"It means my life," I whisper. "It wants me to let it live my life. While I stay there, in the dark."

The thought has that same unquestionable weight, like swallowing a stone.

"Well," Ron says, "on the bright side, it said you have to give it. That means it can't take it from you. Right? It can't keep you there forever."

I nod, because I want there to be a bright side, but the ghost's last threat hangs over me, and even if Ron is right, I'm not sure it matters. How long before it comes back?

"Maybe we can find somewhere to hide from it, at least," she mutters. "There has to be someplace it can't go. Or something that'll ward it off. Salt didn't work… What about iron?"

"Knives," I sigh. Ron looks at me, frowning. "It was throwing knives. Don't those have iron in them?"

"I guess so. I don't know, does steel count?" She shoves her wet hair back from her face. "Maybe if we lit a fire, since it's all about the water? Or is that too obvious? Dammit, we need to figure out what it *is*."

"Your mom said 'poltergeist' is more of a set of symptoms than a real thing."

"Mm," Ron says, maybe conceding the point. "Well, there was this one famous case in Nova Scotia, from the 1800s. It's all over the internet. This girl had, like, lit matches dropping out of thin air around her, that kind of thing. I guess there were six ghosts after her all at once."

What a horrible thought. "It's definitely only one that's after me. I just don't know why."

"I don't know if there was ever really a reason for the poltergeists in the stuff I read. With this girl in Nova Scotia, they thought maybe it started because her fiancé tried to rape her." She stops in the middle of the sidewalk and looks at me, suddenly diffident. "Um…listen. This is a really personal question, but…I mean, did anything ever—"

"What?" I blink in surprise as I sort out what she's getting at. "No! No, nothing like that. This ghost is…pretty much the only bad thing that's ever happened to me."

"Well, good. Okay." She frowns, though, like she's trying to place a puzzle piece. "Anyway, it sounded like they came and went on their own. Pretty much out of nowhere."

"After how long?"

"I don't know. A couple of years, I think."

I turn blindly away from the thought. Ron catches up with me in a few long strides, and we walk in silence for a few moments while I find my voice.

"I kind of wish you hadn't told me that."

Ron winces. "Sorry. Full disclosure, right? I don't know if it even means anything."

Years. It already feels like years, and it's been how many days now? There has to be something I can do to stop it. Doesn't there?

"I don't see how it helps," I admit, my voice small. "That doesn't tell us anything about what it is, or how it got there, or how to make it go away."

Ron shivers and looks away. All I can see of her face is a pale crescent.

"Yeah. I know." She sounds beaten, bewildered. Lost. "I'm out of ideas."

"I'm glad you're here," I whisper. "I wish I could go home."

Ron says nothing, but she slips an arm through mine, offering half a hug. I lean into her a little, grateful for her solid warmth, inhaling flowers and cigarette smoke.

"I wish I could at least call, you know? To explain. To tell Mom I'm okay."

Ron digs into her pocket, offers me her phone, but I shake my head.

"It won't work."

Frowning, Ron pushes a button, holds it down. "Right. Fuck. Do you figure it does that on purpose?"

"I don't know. Probably."

"Well, maybe we can find a pay phone. It should be harder

for it to mess with an analog connection, right? I mean, the tape recorder worked."

"I guess?"

"Come on," she says, new purpose filling her voice, and pulls me forward. "They can't have gotten rid of all of them."

Arm in arm, we scuttle past stately apartment buildings, their stone facades topped with crenellations, stained glass windows glowing and through strings of little midcentury houses interspersed with slick, skinny infill buildings, all angles and demurely dramatic lighting. Images wheel through my head: Mom's face as she looked up at the knives suspended in the air. The glittering shards of glass whistling past us. God, it can't have hurt her, can it? It's followed me everywhere so far. It can't have stayed behind. I gather the hem of the skirt in my fist so I can walk faster.

The street runs underneath the highway. A sound barrier muffling the noise makes a high, blank wall looming over us. We hurry through a broad, echoing concrete tunnel; the spiderwebs strung from the orange lights on the walls billow and tremble. The rain has thinned to a fine mist, and our passage is visible in the saturated air, leaving a faint, spiraling tracery. All around, blending into the constant far-off roar of traffic, there's the sound of water running, running, running downhill past us toward the river.

"I thought maybe I could stop it," Ron says eventually, keeping her eyes on the sidewalk. "That's why I followed you. I thought I could make it go away."

"It could have killed you. You know that, right? It seriously could have killed you."

Ron puts up a hand to deflect this. "I know, I know. I guess it's just…" She sighs, taps her temple with one finger. "Cement bunker, remember? Mom used to have these…panic attacks, or something. After my dad left. When I was little I could stop them. I could make it go away. It was like my superpower. I'd wake up and find her curled up next to me in my skinny little twin bed." She laughs a little as she says it, but with her arm in mine I can feel her going drawn and tense. "This isn't that simple, obviously. I don't know. I had to *try*."

"Did it stop working? Your superpower?"

"I don't know. I guess I just…grew out of it." Her lips go thin. "I didn't turn out the way she thought I would. No psychic gene. And I got tired of her hauling me around all the time. I'd get stuck handing out her cards at the psychic fairs and everything. And then I'd get bitched at for ruining her vibe. For pushing customers away with my negative energy." She grimaces. "Well, I guess she might have had a point. A kid sulking over a phone in your booth isn't exactly great marketing."

"But you were a kid," I say, surprising myself. "Looking after her wasn't your job." The words become my father's in my ears, a resonance that hurts. *Don't put that on your plate.* "And I know it's kind of your job anyway. I really do get that. But that doesn't make it your job to protect *me*. You don't have to come with me. Really."

Ron pulls us to a stop, looks at me.

"Of course I do," she says.

The silence is dense with all the words I can't find. She hugs my arm tight against her side; I can feel the rise and fall of her breath. Miss Giselle's voice flashes absurdly through my mind. *Softness and strength.*

I'm back on that summer beach with the stars falling from the sky, possibilities welling up just out of reach. I can't make this mistake again. I have to drown this now, sink it as deep as I can before I start to hope, before I cling too tight. Everything screams at me to look away, to break eye contact before she sees through me.

But she smiles. Just a little bit, an awkward quirk of her lips. And she doesn't look away.

And then she jerks away, throwing her arms over her head with a sudden cry. I reel back a couple of steps, my heart lurching, but slowly she straightens up, runs her hands carefully over the back of her head.

"Sorry," she stammers. "Sorry. Something...I think it...grabbed my hair."

Knock knock knock. The sound is metallic, this time, as if someone's tapping on the barrel of the streetlight with their knuckles. It's faint, but Ron shrinks from the sound, looking wildly around for its source.

"You don't have to come with me," I whisper again. Ron lifts her chin.

"Come on" is all she says.

We walk with a little distance between us now, me with my

arms folded, trying to focus on the shapes of the stones in the retaining wall running beside us, the spiky swaths of juniper spilling over its sides. I can't think about what I maybe imagined passing between us, an impossible minute ago, what it might mean. I don't dare. I'll fall apart if I think about that.

Ron's face is full of sharp shadows. Without her usual whorls of eyeliner and dramatic lipstick she looks pale and fragile.

"You look really different without makeup," I say, inanely, breaking the silence.

Ron snorts.

"I don't bother with it if I'm just at home," she replies and sighs, hunching her shoulders. "I wish I had today, though."

"What, so you could scare the ghost away?"

"I don't know, something like that. It's war paint."

I remember her straddling Farrell, fist raised to strike, and I look at her curiously. "What do you need war paint for? I mean, you were on the rugby team. Nobody bothers the jocks. They're the ruling class."

"You'd think." Ron looks away, fumbling in her pockets, patting her coat. "It doesn't matter. Life in the jungle. Show a second of weakness and they'll tear you down. Ugh, I hope these didn't get wet. I *seriously* need a cigarette right now."

She slides one from a slightly crumpled box and turns to light it. I wait for her to elaborate, but she's silent, blowing smoke away from me.

"It's not that hard, actually," she says in the end, her voice low.

"Blending in with them. You just have to kind of tack into the wind, you know? Adjust your camouflage a little bit, depending on who's looking. But not so much that they can tell you're faking it."

"That's sort of what Ingrid said." She'd said Luke and Farrell and the rest of them were just doing the same thing, an insight so depressing that it's probably true. "I never understood how she did it, though."

"But that's something I always thought was cool about you." She gives me an appraising look. "You don't buy into it. You're the same person from every angle. You've got...what's the word. Unity? Integrity. I'd almost forgotten what that looked like, you know?"

I'm absurdly flattered, but the compliment itches, feels untrue. "Maybe you're just not seeing all of me."

"Well, you're not *faking* it." Ron's smile twists. "Trust me, I know what that looks like. From personal experience."

"What, meaning you did that? Faking it to blend in?" She raises her eyebrows at the surprise in my voice. "I just thought, I don't know, you act like you couldn't care less what they think."

"Well, I don't!" she flares, but a few steps later continues more quietly, "but that's not really true. I want to make goddamn sure they know I'm not one of them. Right? I used to be pretty good at it. Blending in." She puts the cigarette to her lips, speaks around it. "I was a fucking pro."

"At your old school?"

"Former lifetime. Yeah."

She falls silent. I'm trying to think of some way to ask what happened without prying. The street starts to slope more sharply uphill. We pass a tennis court, dark and empty, flanked by trees. The lights of the houses on the next street wink through the leaves.

"Sorry," Ron mutters at last. "I don't mean to be a drama queen, dragging this out. It's just a long, stupid story that I'm not proud of. And I haven't told anyone about it before."

I nod, still not speaking, afraid I'll dissuade her from confiding in me if I say the wrong thing or sound too curious.

"Yeah. Well. There was this girl at Lebreton last year. Mikayla. She wasn't one of the queen bees, but you know, up there. She'd sung the lead in the musical for two years straight. And she was Gertrude. In the play. We were... I don't know what we were. A thing. There was this party where we both had a lot to drink, and I kind of...well...I kissed her." She clears her throat. "Okay. More accurately, we made out. And at first I was on cloud nine. Like oh my God, I kissed *Mikayla*. But afterward...she acted like it never happened. She was *somebody*, right, she couldn't afford to get branded with the L-word. You know. Lesbian." She draws the word out—*lezzzzzzbian*—and makes jazz hands before rolling her eyes and lifting the cigarette again. "The horror."

She scowls for a moment, exhaling a long stream of smoke, then looks away, the corners of her mouth turning down. The silence stretches until my ears ring. I keep my eyes on my feet. I should say something, but I can't think of anything that doesn't sound absurd. Fake.

"Instead she got together with this...this virus. Elliott. He didn't even like her. Not like I did. He was always 'teasing' her." Ron puts air quotes around the word. "Tearing her down piece by piece. Trying to make it look like *she* was the one who was lucky to be with *him*. I can't have been the only one who noticed. But it was always jokes, right? God forbid anybody take something too seriously. Everyone would smile and laugh and join in. Including her. And I got a little emo over it, I guess." She runs a hand through her hair, grimacing. "You know that scene in *Hamlet* where Ophelia is ranting at Gertrude about flowers and shit? Yeah. I was…convincing. It was pretty bad."

I can feel the space between us like it's a solid object, a thing with edges and weight. I could cross that distance, put my arm through hers again, or around her waist. Like she reached out to me.

"So I dropped out of the show and started hanging out with Tristan Olivier. Nihilist goth boy, most disreputable company I could find." She waves the cigarette. "Started smoking. Which was when Mom, the great psychic, finally started to worry. God."

"Is that why you switched schools?"

"Well. Part of it. People noticed me turning into a freak show, obviously. They couldn't figure out what my problem was. Total fall from grace. And maybe I was watching Mikayla and Elliott a little too closely. You know, staring while goth. I guess I freaked her out. It morphed into, like, a million different versions, but basically the story went that I was turning into this psycho stalker. They said I'd been leaving used tampons in her gym shoes. That kind of thing. I was pretty creative, apparently.

"So the last time I saw them, they were just walking across the parking lot, all nauseating, preppy couple of the year with their arms around each other. Me and Tristan were out there smoking. I was already having a bad day. And Elliott says to Tristan as they walk past us—I swear to God—he says, 'Watch it, man, never stick your dick in crazy.' And I kind of lost it." Savage satisfaction creeps into her voice. "I broke his fucking nose. And he's a lot bigger than Farrell."

"Come on, are you kidding? That's amazing."

"Yeah, I guess it sounds good, doesn't it?" Ron looks away. "But it's not like it accomplished anything. Except scaring Mom into sending me to Pearson. I can still see her face. Mikayla. The look she gave me. Part of me was still hoping, you know? Stupidly. Right up until that look." Her fingers are trembling when she takes the cigarette from her lips to exhale. "Anyway. There you go. The sad origin story of Emo Rhiannon."

"You can't blame yourself for any of that," I protest. "They were horrible to you."

"You weren't there," she sighs. "Trust me."

I watch her smoke, trying to find the words to argue. I want to tell her about Ingrid, but self-consciousness keeps me silent. I'm no braver than Mikayla was. And anyway, there was never anything between me and Ingrid. Just my own inability to face reality.

"How do you do that?" I ask instead, mostly to change the subject. She gives me a quizzical look, and I mimic her gesture with the cigarette. "Doesn't it make you cough?"

Success; she smiles lopsidedly at me.

"You get used to it. Don't, though, it's a stupid habit. Here, see, you go like this." The point of the cigarette glows as she takes another drag. She blows the smoke out in a long, stage-whispery hiss: "Biiitchy-bitchy-bitchy-bitchy."

I burst out laughing, and then half choke trying to stifle it, afraid the sound clattering down the street will bring the ghost down on us again. But the echoes run out ahead of us and fade without incident back into silence and the sound of running water.

"How's that supposed to help anything?" I ask, keeping my voice low. Ron grins.

"No idea. It just does. It's a trick I learned from Tristan." She levels a warning glare at me. "Don't use it."

"Are you kidding? My parents would kill me."

"Yeah. Mom too. Didn't stop me. I think she's pretty much resigned to it by now. It was just badassery at first—war paint—but they get to you, you know?" She folds her arms across her chest again and blows smoke out through her nostrils, then makes a face when she intercepts my admiring look.

Ron flicks the butt of her cigarette away as we crest the hill. Ahead there are cars passing back and forth, harshly lit by tall white lights looming from the median. Beyond is a long, dark stretch of park or field and a handful of dimly lit, blocky government buildings. We hurry by more regal-looking houses and jarringly vivid blue recycling bins overturned near the sidewalk. On the corner, there's a glowing blue-and-white sign: Ottawa Hospital, Civic Campus.

"There's got to be a phone around here somewhere, right?" Ron throws over her shoulder. I follow her into the parking lot, past a stand of ambulances, past the glaring red letters marking the door to Emergency, through a warren of cars. And next to an antique-looking bus shelter, a pay phone stands in a pool of light.

"Here." Ron tips two quarters into my hand. The brush of her fingers against mine reminds me of something.

"Wait. There was one other thing. About the ghost. It didn't want me to touch it."

"What do you mean?"

"Before I got back. I saw it hurting you. I couldn't touch you, there wasn't anything I could do to help. And I tried to grab it, make it stop." I shift a little under Ron's stare, drop my gaze to my feet. "I know. I wasn't thinking very clearly."

"Jesus, Marianne," she says weakly. "Who knows what could have happened; it could have *eaten* you or something."

"But it didn't. It pulled away from me, I felt it." Ron's eyes haven't left my face; she looks so impressed that I feel a little awkward, my head full of protests I don't voice. She's the one who stood up to it and didn't budge. "Does that mean anything, do you think?"

"I don't know," she says, rubbing her eyes. "It seems like it should. I don't know. I can't think straight anymore."

"Yeah." I sigh. "Seriously."

The streetlight over the phone booth stutters, blinks back on as I push through the plastic doors. My fingers are numb and clumsy, and I have to hang up in the middle of the number and start over again.

It goes through in the middle of the first ring.

"Marianne, is that you?"

It's a woman's voice blurting out those words all in a rush, but not my mom's. I stand there stupidly, trying to figure out who I'm talking to.

"…Aunt Jen?"

"Oh my God. Thank God. Are you okay?"

"I'm fine," I say automatically, a knee-jerk response to the frantic edge in her voice. "I'm just out with Ron."

"Why didn't you pick up your phone? I called you about a million times!"

"It's not really working lately," I stammer. There's barely any static this time. Just the faintest crackling hiss. It's barely different from the normal sound of a phone line. It should be a relief; it's not. Somehow the silence is not empty. There's a tension in it, an attentiveness. Like someone listening. I clutch the receiver's chilly silver cord. Fear skates over my skin.

"What happened?" Aunt Jen is demanding. "Where are you?"

"What's wrong?" I counter instead of answering. "Where's Mom?"

"Oh, Mare-bear." There are tears in her voice. I wait, paralyzed, while she fights for composure.

"I don't want to talk about this on the phone," she says finally. "Where are you? I'm coming to pick you up."

"I can't come home," I whisper.

"What was that?"

I have to force the words out.

"What happened? *Where is my mom?*"

"Marianne," she says at last, deliberately, obviously steeling herself. "Your mom is back in the hospital."

"What?" I choke.

"She called me earlier, and she was…pretty incoherent. Worse than before. This time she didn't even seem to know what was real. I was so worried. She just didn't sound safe."

I close my eyes.

"I had to call someone," Aunt Jen pleads. "She was talking about knives and ghosts and I don't know what all else. She said you were in terrible danger. I was so afraid for both of you. I had to call the police."

I hunch over the phone, hugging one arm across my midsection, my forehead resting on the black plastic of the case. Too late. My fault. Maybe I shouldn't have said anything. Maybe I should have stayed, waited out the storm. I left her alone.

"They took her in for a seventy-two-hour evaluation. Given her history, and…and the state of the house."

The tide of static is still slithering, subdued, under her voice. If I let myself, I think I can feel the weight of the ghost still with me, like it's holding a rope tied to my wrist, standing behind me somewhere. Waiting to see how I react.

"Marianne? Are you still there?"

I nod at first, then shrug my shoulders, trying to shake off the feeling of being stared at. Is it my imagination? I don't think so; I'm starting to recognize it. Like recognizing the sound of someone's footsteps, or the way the house creaks when the door opens. Sounds you don't notice until they start to become familiar. I will not turn around. I clear my throat.

"Yes. Yes, I'm here. Aunt Jen, listen, I have to talk to her. Okay? I have to explain."

"I don't know if that's such a good idea right now, Mare-bear. I...I think we need to wait until they tell us it's safe for you. And for her."

I want to protest, but she's right. Just not in the way she thinks she is. I can't let the ghost get near Mom again.

"Just a phone call," I plead. "That's all I'm asking for. Won't they let me call her?"

"Listen, where are you? Let me come and get you, okay?"

I knew I was going to end up crying. I let the tears run hot down my cheeks without bothering to stop them. They send little ripples shattering across the puddle at the bottom of the phone booth.

"Marianne?"

"I can't come home," I say again, hoarsely. "I can't."

"Of course you can. It's safe now, sweetie, it's safe to come home."

"It's not! You don't understand, I'm so scared—"

"Now listen," she interrupts in that firm, no-nonsense way adults get when you've really alarmed them. "I don't know exactly what happened over here tonight, but I can see it must have been pretty upsetting, okay? I get that maybe you don't want to be here right now. So we'll go to my place."

"But—"

"Marianne, the police are still here, do you understand? If you don't tell me where you are this instant, I have to ask them to go find you. Please. Just let me pick you up."

And I crumble. I knuckle under. Like I always do.

"Fine," I whisper. "Sure. I'm at the Civic."

"Where? Reception? What's the closest door?"

"No. No, I'm outside. At a bus stop."

"All right. Look. Go wait by the big sign at the front entrance, okay? And then stay put. I love you."

How long will that last once she figures out what's really going on? "Yeah."

"Okay. Stay put! I'll be there in ten minutes." She hangs up.

I stand there with the phone beeping insistently in my ear. This is my fault. Because I caved and told Mom the truth, I've ruined everything. They've all written her off. Even if the hospital lets her out, custody will go straight to Dad after this. I'll never see her again.

I have to tell them. I have to tell them what she saw was real. If she has a witness, they'll have to believe it.

Or maybe they'll just assume it's something that runs in the family.

I shouldn't go with Aunt Jen either. I'll be putting her in danger. Sooner or later it will set its sights on her too. But where else am I going to go?

This is what it meant. *I will make it not worth having.* I remember the darkness stretching out into forever, a tunnel studded with streetlights, utterly empty. Just now, the real world doesn't seem so different.

Carefully, carefully, I put the phone back on the hook. Ron is sitting on the curb, smoking. She looks up as I step out of the phone booth hugging my elbows in close, holding myself together. Her eyebrows quirk sympathetically as she takes in my expression, and then the sympathy shades into alarm.

"Is everything okay?"

"It's my mom," I say tonelessly. I can't look at her. I speak to the empty street. "She's in the hospital again." It sounds melodramatic and false in my ears. "She tried to tell my aunt what happened. And my aunt called the police."

Ron gapes at me. "Oh my God."

I shake my head, sinking down onto the curb beside her, resting my head on my knees. She crushes out her cigarette and scooches a little closer to me.

"I can't really blame my aunt. I mean, how would it sound? They must have found the knives, they were stuck right through the cupboard doors. And there was broken glass everywhere. Nobody's going to believe it wasn't her. And my aunt said she was...talking about me. About how I was in danger. That's why she went to the hospital in the first place, because she was afraid she might hurt me."

Ron waits for me to continue, her knuckles pressed to her lips.

"I don't know what to do," I whisper. "I should run away. Somewhere far away from everybody, so it can't get to any of them. But Aunt Jen is coming to get me. She said she'd send the police after me otherwise. And I can't go with her. I can't. I can't even..."

Hesitantly, Ron puts her arms around my shoulders. A stupid, ugly sound escapes me before I can choke it back. She hugs me closer, gathering my tangled, dripping hair away from my face with one hand. Her fingers brush my cheek.

"Listen," she says by my ear, her voice urgent and gentle. "It's up to you. I'll come with you either way, okay? I'm not leaving you alone with it. All right?"

I press my hand to my mouth, fighting for my voice, fighting to keep it together. Ron's hands slide over my cheeks, turning my face toward hers. Our foreheads almost touch. Her lips are a breath away from mine.

"I'm not leaving you," she repeats. "I promise."

I don't know what it is that warns me, but by the time I hear the deafening sound of smashing glass I'm already on my feet, stumbling forward, my hands knotted in Ron's sweatshirt, pulling her with me. Little glittering cubes pelt down all around us, and a chorus of car alarms shrills into the air. Ron scrambles to a stop, staring at me, the glass crunching under her boots.

Behind us the glass panes of the bus shelter are scattered in a sparkling spray over the sidewalk, over the road. Through the metal frame I can see the line of cars behind it, their windshields gaping, jagged holes, the edges of the fractured glass curving out toward us like reaching hands.

"God *damn* it!" Ron yells into the empty air. "Back off already!"

"Ron," I plead. I'm still clutching her, can't seem to let go. "Don't."

"Come on." Gently, she pulls my grip loose from her clothes. Keeps one of my hands in hers. "We have to go. They'll think it was us otherwise."

"Yeah. Yeah, okay. This way." I refuse to look over my shoulder as we hurry back the way we came, but the wail of the car alarms follows us, cutting through the night like a searchlight.

20

AN ETERNITY LATER, AUNT JEN'S little car comes to a halt beside us where we're perched together on the curb. I turn my face away from the glare of the headlights. Defeat and relief and shame and fear spin through me, blurring into each other. I wish I could just lie down and sleep for a million years.

I hear the door slam; hurried footsteps. And then Aunt Jen is hugging me tight.

"I've never been happier to see anybody in my life," she whispers into my shoulder, and then pulls away to look at me anxiously.

"Are you okay?" she pleads. I can't meet her eyes. "Look at you, you're soaked." She notices Ron and manages a wavery smile. "Hello again. I almost didn't recognize you." Ron smiles back a little, looking awkward. "Would you like a ride home? It's the middle of the night; I can't just leave you to wander the streets by yourself."

"Actually, I'd like to come with you. Please." Aunt Jen looks a little taken aback and opens her mouth to reply, but Ron hurries on. "I'm sorry. I don't mean to impose or anything. Really." Her gaze meets mine for a second. "It's just that I promised her I'd stay."

Aunt Jen looks up at Ron in silence for a moment, then wipes her eyes quickly with one hand.

"I see," she says and sniffles a bit. "Okay. Sure. Thank you. Get in, then, girls, let's go home."

The night slides by the windows, streetlights whipping past. I put a hand up to my face to block the view, keep my eyes down. I don't want to see the water. I don't look up until I hear the building's ancient garage door growling as it closes behind us.

I'm peeling my feet out of my wet, icy shoes, wincing at the blisters they've left on my heels, when I hear the living room couch creak, making me jump.

"Marianne?"

Dad? I stumble back against Ron as he steps into the foyer, but he gathers me into a hug anyway. He smells different than he did before, like different laundry soap or something. He smells like a stranger.

"Thank God you're okay!"

"What are you doing here?" I breathe. He lets me go, looking hurt.

"Jen called me," he says. "When she couldn't find you at home.

We were so worried. Jesus, bun, there was glass everywhere. There were knives stuck in the floor! And the downstairs bathroom's all smashed up. What happened?"

I sag in place, holding my head in my hands. I should never have agreed to this. I should have run, I should have left them all behind. I can almost feel the ghost's satisfaction crackling through the air: all the rest of the people I love, all right here, all at once. Hostages it can pick from. And I can't explain. They won't believe me.

"You have to go." I try for stern, but it comes out broken, desperate.

"I know you're mad at me, but—"

"You don't understand!" I wheel to face Aunt Jen, who's stepping through the door. "You called him? Why did you call him?"

"He's your dad, Mare-bear," she replies helplessly.

"Listen to me. The knives—that wasn't Mom. Okay? You have to leave before—"

Dad and Jen just exchange a look.

"What?" I demand. Ron's hand steals around my shoulder, a reassuring weight.

"Mare-bear, your mom's not well," Aunt Jen says gently.

"She'd be perfectly fine if it wasn't for what's been happening to me!"

"You can't blame yourself for this, bunny. Your mom's a grown-up. She has to take responsibility for her own issues." Dad sighs, then casts a look at Ron standing behind me. "I'm sorry, maybe you should go; we've got kind of a family emergency on our hands here."

Ron doesn't budge. "I know," she says evenly. "That's why I promised I'd stay."

"I appreciate that," Dad says, unmoved. "I do. But this really isn't a good time. One of us can give you a ride. I have to take Marianne home."

"I'm not going!" I cry.

Dad heaves a sigh and rubs his forehead. I take a deep breath. He won't listen unless I'm reasonable. I have to stay reasonable.

"Listen," I try again. "I know you don't believe me, but you have to—"

"I understand if you don't want to be at home," he interrupts, and his voice is getting that implacably patient sound that means he's digging in for a fight. "But I think you need to stay with me for a while. I'm really concerned about all this. I need to know you're safe. I brought your things, you're all set." Sure enough, there's my backpack and my suitcase sitting next to the stairs. I didn't even get to unpack them at home.

"You don't understand," I cry. "Please, please just listen! It's not safe to be around me, there's something following me, something dangerous!"

But they've stopped paying attention; they're trading that *see-what-did-I-tell-you* look again.

"I should never have sent her home," Aunt Jen says to him tearfully.

"Don't worry," he tells her, and then turns to me, his face grave. "Have you been taking your pills, bunny?"

"That's not my name!" They think I'm off the meds. Of course they do. I can't back away from them; there's nowhere to go.

"Come on, Marianne, let's go home." Dad holds out a hand. "I'll make us some hot chocolate and we can work this out. Okay?"

I stare at him. He crooks his eyebrows, waiting for a response. Waiting for me to give in.

That's all being reasonable has ever meant.

Silence rushes in as I inhale. Rising all around me. *No. Oh no. Not with all of them here!*

"Marianne." Ron takes a step back. "Marianne, your hair—"

"No! Not here!" It turns into a scream. "Go *away!*"

There's a sudden flare of light, a volley of sharp pops; the apartment plunges into darkness. Aunt Jen cries out. But I can still hear my breath rasping in my ears, stumbling footsteps as Dad backs away. Their silhouettes are still there in the dark as my eyes adjust.

"Marianne?" Ron's voice is shrill. "Marianne, say something!"

"It's me," I gasp. "It's still me." And I burst into tears.

"It's all right, it's all right," Aunt Jen says unsteadily. "Hang on, let me get the flashlight."

The closet door scrapes open. Dad's hand brushes my arm, reaching for me, but I shrink away.

"What was that?" he says to Jen. "Is the power out?"

"Looks like." Aunt Jen clicks her flashlight on, spilling a wide cone of warm light. "There we go. It's okay, see, nothing to cry about. Everything's all right." She turns the light on my dad. "Look, she's obviously at the end of her rope. Let's just let her stay here for tonight, okay? They have to let her see Laura soon, I'm sure of it. I'll take her for a visit, and then she can go with you."

Is it just the light, or is Dad's face pale? He turns out his hands in defeat.

"All right. All right. If that's what you want, bunny."

"Please go," I whisper. He bends over to kiss my forehead and obeys without another word. The door falls closed behind him.

My room is in pieces, Aunt Jen explains as I trudge after her up the stairs. Drywall is ruined when it gets wet, so half the walls have been ripped apart. She's not really sure where to put Ron, but assures me we'll figure something out. She pulls out a pair of jogging pants and a threadbare T-shirt from her dresser, collects a fluffy robe from a laundry basket and a colorful quilt from the storage closet, and pushes the bundle at me. And then she stops talking, turns away.

"I just don't understand," Aunt Jen whispers, and when she looks back to me her eyes are swimming with tears. "I don't understand what happened. She's never fallen apart like this before. Never like *this*."

I clutch the clothes to my chest and can't think of a word to say.

Downstairs, Aunt Jen lights a couple of candles and sets them on top of the piano as Ron and I take turns in the bathroom getting changed. When Aunt Jen eventually emerges from the storage closet with a musty-smelling air mattress, Ron drags the coffee table out of the way while I pump it up next to the couch.

"It's like we're setting up for a scary movie night," Ron muses, watching me. "We should order a pizza."

"I'm so not hungry."

"Yeah. Me neither." She collapses onto the couch with a sigh. "We should, though, sometime. When this is all over. Just hang out. Like normal people."

I can't imagine a time when this might be over. There was a time before it started, and it seems unreal, hopeless, lost.

"Yeah," I manage. "Normal would be good."

"Marianne." I jump a little at a touch on my hand, but it's just Ron; her fingers have closed around mine. They burn against my skin, warm and dry. In the candlelight her face is half in shadow.

"I'm okay." My voice breaks, betrays me. "Really. I just have to—"

"Seriously. We *will* figure this out."

I don't trust myself to speak. We. It hangs in the air between us. She doesn't let go of my hand.

I sink down onto the couch beside her. Our knees are touching, her body a line of warmth alongside mine. I rest my forehead on her shoulder. I can smell her hair. Smoke and roses.

"Your hands are freezing," she murmurs, and she folds the one she's holding against her cheek. Like it's the easiest thing in the world.

Knock knock knock. Knock knock knock.

Ron's grip tightens on my hand. And with a long, shuddering scrape of wood on wood, a jangling thrum, the piano inches over the floor toward us. The candles topple onto their sides, then roll off entirely; the fern sitting on top of it jitters, dances toward the edge, and falls to the floor, its green ceramic pot breaking like an eggshell, startling me into a strangled shriek.

The piano comes to rest a couple of feet from the wall it's usually pushed up against. There's another volley of knocks, and then silence descends again. Colder than before. Ron and I scramble to our feet, diving for the candles on the floor. They've left puddles of wax and black scorch marks on the parquet.

Aunt Jen comes flying down the stairs, looking wildly around the room, taking in me standing and Ron still crouched on the floor. Her gaze finally comes to rest on the plant lying smashed beside her.

"Good lord, Mare-bear, is that all that was about?"

But she stops short, frowning, as she notices the piano.

"Now, what on—how did—" She looks from me, standing there with the candle in my hand, to the piano. Back to me again. I can see the gears turning in her head. Because we couldn't have moved it, obviously. How many hundreds of pounds does it weigh?

"Aunt Jen." Maybe it's worth a shot. I have to try. "You have to believe me."

"What are you talking about?" Her voice is sharp, a little frantic, reminding me of my mom's. "Are you trying to tell me—"

"I'm trying to tell you that Mom didn't throw those knives. It was something else."

She stares at me, then turns toward Ron. Ron shrinks down a little bit, looking back and forth between the two of us. I can practically hear what she's thinking; it's written all over her face: *oh, shit.*

"It's been happening ever since Dad left." Her expression doesn't change. I plow on. "You heard the maintenance guys, the water didn't make any sense. There's something after me. It's been after me this whole time. That's what Mom saw, that night. That's what happens when it gets control."

"Oh, come on," Aunt Jen says weakly, but stops there.

"I have to get out of here," I cry. "Before it does anything worse. Don't you get it? It's still here!"

Aunt Jen draws herself up, lifts her chin.

"Marianne. I don't know what your mom said to you. But there's no such thing as…whatever it is you're talking about. Ghosts."

"But—"

"There's no such thing!"

"But the piano!" I fling my hand out toward it.

"I don't quite know what happened there, that's true," Aunt Jen says resolutely, "but that's no reason to fly off the handle and—"

"Are you kidding me?" She flinches, but I can't moderate my voice anymore. "What's it going to take?" I turn around and around, looking for some sign of the other presence I can feel in the room, in the guttering of the candles, in the hissing silence underneath. "Well, come on! Do something already! *Do something!*"

Aunt Jen starts forward, making a soothing *shhh* sound, her hands out, beseeching. Behind her, Ron is shaking her head frantically, mouthing something, making emphatic negative gestures. I turn away from them both, twisting around again, scanning the room. In the patio door I catch a glimpse of a pale shadow, its features awash in fury.

It only takes a step to reach the armchair. I snatch an empty teacup from beside the radio. Before I can hurl it, Aunt Jen makes a clumsy snatch at my sleeve, pulls my arm back, and the teacup crashes to the floor instead.

"Marianne!" Aunt Jen cries. "Stop it!"

The figure in the glass is still there, staring at me, wild-eyed, arm half-raised. Next to a phantom Aunt Jen. Shaking, I pull my hand back to my side, and watch it mirror me.

It's just my reflection. Of course it is.

"I thought—" But I can't come up with any sane way to finish that sentence and close my mouth on silence instead.

"Listen," Aunt Jen says, with careful, heavy precision, "do I need to call your dad?"

I bury my face in my hands and shake my head, mute, defeat washing over me. Because it doesn't matter what I say. She'll call him anyway. She'll tell him all about this. They'll tell Dr. Fortin. How long before they decide that the medicine isn't working, that I'm dangerous? Just like Mom?

If they stick me in the hospital, it won't be any kind of break. I'd be more trapped than ever. At the mercy of something they don't think is real.

Wordlessly, Ron ducks into the kitchen; after a moment she returns with the broom and sweeps up the remains of the teacup. Aunt Jen is still holding my arm, like she's not sure what's going to happen if she lets go.

"I'm okay, Auntie," I whisper. Like I'm five again. "Really. And I'm sorry. About the teacup." About everything.

"It's just a cup." She releases me, reluctantly, watching my face. A long pause. Is there fear in her eyes?

"It's been a long night, Mare-bear," she says eventually, and hugs me tight. "Get some sleep, all right? We'll talk in the morning." After one last troubled look at the piano, she disappears upstairs.

I take the dustpan from Ron and dump its contents into the trash can under the sink. Just as I throw myself back down on the couch next to the pile of blankets, the silence is shattered by a siren whistle starting in the kitchen, low at first and quickly ramping through the scale into a shriek. It's a few endless, noisy seconds before I figure out what it is: the kettle. I jump to my feet and round the corner to find steam jetting out of it, little bits of water splashing out of the spout.

It's sitting on the counter.

I make a couple of abortive moves toward it, not sure how to make it stop without an element to turn off, afraid of burning myself.

Finally I unhook an oven mitt from the cupboard door, shove my hand into it, and snatch the kettle back onto the stove, dancing back from the hot water that splashes on the floor. Only then does the sound start to skirl back downward, fading as the steam slows to a trickle.

I stand there panting, the oven mitt still dangling from my hand. I can't stop listening. Waiting for the next blow to fall.

Ron's voice at my elbow makes me jump. "Here." She holds out one of the tea towels that had been hanging on the stove handle, drops another on the floor, and sinks to a crouch, pushing it gingerly over the wet tiles.

"You shouldn't have told your aunt," she says, not looking at me. I shake my head, unable to summon a better response. "She must think you're going completely off the deep end. That's what it wants. It just totally played you."

"I wasn't thinking," I mutter.

"No shit."

"I didn't hear you saying anything!"

"Well, of course not!" Ron sits back on her heels. "How do you think she'd react if I tried to mix into this? Your dad was already looking at me like I'm some sort of cult leader!"

I pick up the wet towels, still hot, between pinched fingers and drop them in the sink. "I guess it's a good thing you weren't wearing the war paint, at least."

"I guess," Ron snorts.

I flop down on the couch again, and Ron sinks down beside me, although she keeps a careful distance between us this time.

"I don't know," she sighs. "She might surprise you. Your aunt. I mean, there's only so long she can deny it, right? If it keeps on like this."

"Yeah. And then what?" I lean into the blankets, away from her. "I should never have come back here. It almost had me earlier. Again. It almost came through."

"It can't," Ron protests. "Look, when that happened it was because we basically invited it. So we'll just be super careful from now on. Right?"

"Don't try to make me feel better," I snap. "It doesn't help. I heard you, you didn't even know who you were talking to."

She doesn't answer.

"Sorry," I say after a moment, my voice small. "I shouldn't have—oh God. I'm sorry."

"I get it," she says stiffly. "It's okay."

It's not, though. Obviously. I'm an idiot. Niobe's words hover in my ears: someone who will go to hell and back for you. That's what she's been doing all night, and look how I'm repaying her. I don't deserve her. The ghost was right.

But so was Niobe.

I rub my eyes, trying to think, trying to wring some answers from the memory. She said…maybe this was more than a friend. The thought hurts, like a light too bright to look at, and I hurry past it.

She said not to be a victim. Take action. That makes about as much sense as ever. Although the part about me bringing this on myself is starting to sound scarily accurate. Like those red shoes from Ron's story are welded to my feet, carrying me spinning out of control. Why did I ever open my mouth?

A hitch of a breath from Ron drags my attention back to her. She grimaces and swipes a hand hastily across her face.

"Ron—"

"It's okay, it's okay," she croaks. "It's not you, all right? I just had this awful fight with my mom. Before I left. I said…some things you just don't say, you know?"

If I were as brave as she thinks I am, I'd reach for her hand. The ghost will never let me. I fold my arms instead.

"God. This is stupid," Ron says. "You've got enough to worry about." I just look at her, and she pushes her hands through her hair. "It's just…what if she's been the real thing all along? And I was just too mundane and jealous and…and chickenshit to see it? What if it was me pushing her away, all this time? What if it's my fault she can't read me, what if it's because I gave up on her?"

"I don't think your mom would let you push her very far." It's like the ghost is sitting between us, a gulf I don't dare cross. "And you would never give up on her. Not really. She's your mom. I mean, how long have you known me? And you're still here. After all this."

"Yeah, and a fat lot of good it's done anybody." She rests her head wearily on her hand. When she moves I catch a glimpse of livid bruises darkening on her upper arm; she follows my gaze and tugs the sleeve of the T-shirt she's wearing down a little. I look away.

"I should never have dragged you into this."

"I was the one who got all cocksure and called the thing," Ron counters. She sniffs. "It's not your fault it listened to me." Her eyes close briefly. "Maybe I could get it to follow me somehow, distract it. Maybe that might persuade Mom to do some ghostbusting."

I fight down a flash of panic at the idea. "God, don't do that. What if it caught you? I don't think it would work anyway. It didn't follow you before, after the other night by the river."

"Yeah." She shivers a little, pulls her feet onto the couch. "It was like it was starving. You know? Like a black hole. I wasn't sure if it wanted to eat me alive or... I don't know."

"You should go." The echo of the ghost's words is ugly in my mouth, but I have to say it. "You should go home. It's still here. It's already beaten you up enough."

Ron shakes her head, emphatic, unmovable. "No. I'm not going anywhere. Not until we figure this out."

I'm not going to cry again. I'm not.

"Why?"

Ron hesitates.

"It's not like I wasn't tempted, believe me. I almost did, when I saw you walking down the street with your hair floating. It walked away, and I stood there, and I thought, I don't have to follow it." She looks at me, her lips twisting. "But then I thought, if I ran away...

that's all I'd ever be. The kind of person who runs away. The kind of person who does nothing. And goddamn, I refuse to be that. I'm *not*."

"No," I agree faintly. My smile is wobbly, but it's real. "You're not."

21

I TOSS AND TURN ON the couch, trying to get comfort-able. I forgot to take the pills tonight, and the moths are back, my thoughts reeling in frantic, jittery loops like they're swirling around a light bulb. I stare at the shadowy ceiling, trying to quiet them enough to make sense. The wind roars and whistles outside. What now? What am I going to do?

Maybe I sleep for a couple of hours. I'm not aware of drifting into it, but there comes a point where I can feel it slipping away from me, like water inching down the beach. It leaves a deeper, chilly silence in its wake.

I try to speak, to sit up. The farthest I get is clenching and unclenching my fists at my sides, my fingers cold and numb, scratching soundlessly, uselessly, against Aunt Jen's afghan.

When I open my eyes a figure sits at the other end of the couch, a murky silhouette. If it was a real person it would be sitting on my legs. If it was a real person I would hear it breathing, the small noises of its movement. But it's motionless like no living thing is motionless, except for the restless, swirling shadow of its hair. Its presence is its only weight, and it flattens the air against my limbs, my chest, my face. Binding me in place. Every breath is a slow, drowning gasp.

Give up, Not-Marianne whispers. I'm not sure if its lips have moved. I can't look at it except in stolen glances. Why does it still look like me?

I won't, I cry. Or try to. My lips form the words.

You will. I'll make you.

Please. Please just go away.

You'll fold like a paper doll. That's all you are. A pathetic, wispy little doll mouthing other people's words. There's not a single piece of you that you own.

But you didn't want to touch me! I shout soundlessly. *Why not?*

You think it matters? it sneers. **Who would want to touch you? You'd crumble into pieces. You'd blow away. Who would bother?**

I think it means something, I insist. *I think you were afraid of me.*

Without transition, like it moved impossibly fast, it's on its feet, towering over me, its hair snaking and weaving around its face.

You wait, it breathes. ***You wait.*** **You think I can't hurt you? You think your girlfriend can save you?**

She's not—

Listen to you! it rages. **You don't deserve her! You don't deserve any of this! None of them even want you. I'm the one who's real! If you won't give them back to me I will make you!**

Ron doesn't want you! I hurl the words at it. *Can't you see that? You can't make her want you!*

There's a vast silence.

If I can't have her, Not-Marianne whispers, its eyes wide, unblinking wells, **nobody can.**

Stay away from her!

The deep-water weight against me eases enough that I can heave myself upright. But in pushing my fist against the couch cushion I realize my fingers are curled around something hard and rectangular. I look down and find I'm clutching the red plastic handle of Aunt Jen's bread knife. The faint orange glow from the streetlights gleams on every serrated point on the long blade.

What are you doing? I want it to be a demand, but the breath has been crushed out of my lungs.

What would happen, it muses, **if she woke up and found you standing over her with that?**

I swallow. The ghost leans over me, drops its voice to a heavy whisper.

What do you think would happen?

I can't let go of it. It's like I've forgotten how. The handle's edges dig into my fingers. My hand rises, slowly, like I'm losing an arm wrestling match, though I'm pushing back with all my strength.

What if you put this to her throat and started sawing? Do you think she'd have time to scream?

Stop, I whimper, my bravery gone. The knife tilts in my hand. I can't even make it tremble.

Do you think they'd listen to you then? Would they believe you?

Shadow thickens around the thing that still wears my face, the streetlights outside dimming, the wall behind it receding from my sight, sinking into a darkness that stretches out forever. Suddenly there's a cool breath of air on my face, the green, weedy smell of the river rising up around me.

This is your last chance, it whispers.

I try to shrink back against the cushions, but instead somehow my feet slide off the couch, my toes jamming painfully into the ground. I stagger upright like something shoved me, almost losing my balance; I'm still clutching the knife in one flailing hand.

Do you think I can't do it? Do you think I won't?

I try to bolt for the door; instead I pivot toward Ron. One of my feet slides forward. I try to scream, to warn her, but I can't open my mouth.

If you want to run, there's only one way you can go. It doesn't point, but the void behind it draws my eyes anyway. Its bare feet, its black-marked toes, hang in the air over gray sand. **That's where you belong. That's what you deserve.**

It's the dream again. I'm back in the dream. My steps shamble toward the water despite my flailing attempts to resist. If I manage to stop, my arm lifts again against my will, raising the knife.

Go, Not-Marianne snarls. **Go!**

I shuffle forward a few helpless steps, as small as I can make them. Toward the ghost; almost past it. I can feel its eyes on me, alight with triumph. The smooth wood floor turns gritty and soft under my feet.

Ron's words suddenly echo through my head. *You have to give it. It can't take it from you.* There's a way to make this stop, this death march into that horrible otherworld, into the icy water.

It can't make me.

With a desperate, soundless shriek I pitch myself sideways. Toward my shadowy double. And it falls back with a cry of its own: a sound of disgust. Of fear. And then I stumble into the arm of the couch, four pale walls in their proper places. There's no one there anymore, just trembling orange shadows and the whisper of the wind.

But I'm still holding the knife.

I force my fingers open and it clatters to the ground. I sit down hard on the floor and huddle there, trying to breathe, sweat standing icy on my skin. A few feet away from where the knife lies gleaming on the parquet, Ron's hair is an inky tangle across her pillow. She's snoring a little bit.

I can't stay here.

I hurry into the kitchen and pull the peanut butter jar down from the top shelf of the cupboard. Inside is a fat wad of bills: Aunt Jen's emergency money. I stuff the roll of cash inside into my pocket. That ought to buy a bus trip to somewhere a good long way from here.

The sweater Ron loaned me is still damp, but I pull it on anyway. Ron stirs but doesn't wake as I pad past her, and I pause, looking down at her. She's flung out an arm, throwing off the blankets. As I watch, she pulls her hand back to her chest, curling up a little bit, shivering. Carefully, afraid I'll wake her, I pick up the edge of the covers and lower them back over her. I don't smooth back the hair that's tumbled over her face.

I'd be the kind of person who runs away, she said earlier. I guess that's what this makes me. Like that girl she kissed. She's stood by me through all this, and all I'll be is one more thing she'll blame herself for.

I don't have a choice. It doesn't matter what she thinks. It doesn't matter what any of them think—Aunt Jen, my parents. It's better than a knife in the dark. They'll be safe, away from me.

Right. How noble of me.

I pull open the patio door slowly so it doesn't squeak. Aunt Jen's money is a hard lump in my pocket. Deep down, am I just hoping that if I run fast enough, or far enough, I might escape it for a while? Because I know that's stupid; it would never work. Even now I can feel the ghost waiting somewhere behind me. Watching.

It doesn't matter. I step out into the garden, slide the door closed behind me. I'm going. I have to. I have to take action. I have to do *something*.

The clouds are shredding, and the moon winks fitfully in and out among them, sinking into the black arms of the pines beside the seawall. The streetlights are still on; there's enough light to make out the gray shape of the garden path, the hedges trembling in the wind. When I step through the gate it yanks itself out of my hand, slams closed behind me with a clang.

"Shhh," I hiss desperately.

The wind in the pines, the roar of the waves, is the only answer. Over the treetops, dawn is starting to show red and gold against the clouds. And slowly, I turn around to look at the bay, a shade darker than the sky behind the barricaded seawall, little white crests rising and falling out into the distance. This time I don't flinch from it. The fear falls away from me like water running through my hands, leaving a horrible, empty clarity.

The money, a weight against my thigh in my pocket, is useless. The beginnings of my flimsy plan crumble around me. There's no point. If I run from it now, away from Mom—away from Ron—it's still won: I'll be running from it forever, running into fear and loneliness without end. Treading water.

There's nowhere I can go. Nowhere it won't follow.

And into that emptiness boils something white-hot, incandescent, radiating through my chest, stealing my breath. Propelling me into motion, lengthening my stride until I'm running, tearing down the street toward the park, my steps slapping on the pavement, through the wide marshy puddles that fill the park, under the roaring trees. My lungs burn, my feet turn leaden. I stumble, but I push myself forward, don't stop. The river has crept up even farther over the beach, leaving only a thin crescent of sand beyond the last row of poplars standing guard beside the path. I plunge across the sand into the water, cold as steel, and I run until it drags me to a stop, thigh-deep, the waves tugging at me.

"*Here I am!*" I scream at the horizon, throwing my arms wide. The wind whips ribbons of hair across my face. "*Here I am! Come and get me!*"

Squinting into the wind, gasping for breath, I watch the world before me tremble and thin, fading into transparency, draining the faint light from the sky, swallowing the moon. And it stands in the water, that thing that isn't me. Except for the twisting halo of its hair, we could be standing on either side of a mirror. If we raised our hands our fingers would touch. There's a wavering line between us where the water flattens into glassy stillness, stretching away behind it without end, rimed with a dim crust of ice. Unflinching this time, I look into my own dark eyes, my own face, thin and pale, luminous against the waiting, featureless, unchanging dark. The depths tug at me, a current as relentless as the waves pushing against my legs.

I wait for Not-Marianne to cross the distance between us, pull me down. But it doesn't move.

"What are you waiting for?" I grate. "Come on!"

But it pulls back from me as I start toward it, casts a look over its shoulder, into the emptiness. I'm alone with it this time. There's no one it can use against me. And there it is again, suddenly plain to see beneath its venom and rage: a desperate fear.

"*It's not fair,*" it moans. "*It's not fair, it's mine, give it back!*"

I edge forward, past the waves. Into the darkness where the river meets the icy lake, where reality gives way to the dream. The water slices into my thighs; silence closes over my head. But Not-Marianne shies back another step with a wordless cry of mingled fury and despair.

I could make it keep going. I could bury it forever. That's what it would do to me if it could.

But it can't.

It's a ghost. It's just a ghost. It's never been more than a shadow.

And I'm made of light, molten and pure: a rage like I've never known. A certainty. I'm the one who deserves to live. I'm the one who's real.

I'm the one who crosses the distance between us in one lunge.

My hands close around its throat. Numbing cold seeps through my fingers, up my arms, but I ignore it. I won't let go. Not-Marianne lets out a single sobbing cry, clawing at my arms, but I'm as ruthless as the invisible tide eddying around us, crushing it down, submerging it bit by bit. It struggles to lift its chin above the surface, powerless as a moth pinned to a board, the water devouring its snaking hair. It will never break the surface again. I'll walk away from here serene, untouchable. Perfect as the moon.

"Marianne!" The shout comes ringing out over the water from behind me. "*Marianne!*"

It's Ron, her booted feet flying across the crescent of the beach, charging heedless into the water.

"*Help*," the ghost splutters, choking, sobbing. "*Help me!*"

The rage pulses through me again and I push it under. The water closes over its head. It flails, manages to fight its way to the surface again for a frantic gulp of air. It will be the last time. I will make it the last time.

"Stop it!" Ron screams.

I twist to look around at her, bewildered. And a shred of black drifts across my vision.

My hair. Floating.

I snatch my hands up to quiet it, to pull it back down around my shoulders, but my fingers have gone numb, and my hair sifts through them as if I'm underwater. Not-Marianne flounders desperately away from me, splashing back toward daylight.

Toward Ron's open arms.

"No. No!" I hardly recognize my own voice as it ramps into a scream. "That's not me! It's a *trick!*"

The ghost stumbles toward Ron, but its hair isn't hanging wet around its face the way it should if it were real; it's still a swirling cloud, defying gravity. Ron grips its outstretched arms, holds it away from her, though it begs and leans toward her.

"*You can save me,*" it pleads. "*Don't let her drown me. It's me. You know me. You saw me!*"

"Don't leave me here!" I wail. "That's not me! I'm the one who's real!"

And Ron looks frantically between us, back and forth.

She can't tell us apart.

The hot white light that's been filling me, insulating me, bearing me up goes cold and clotted. The chill winding up my arms seeps into my chest, into my bones, sends shards of ice slicing into my thoughts. Images vivid as nightmares flash through my head, crystallizing around and through my last two years. Memories that fit into mine like the other half of a split piece of wood. Double memories.

Shadow memories.

Did I get up and leave the yoga studio with Mom? Or did I open my eyes to find the room dark and silent, the doorknob untouchable? Did she tuck me into bed that night, or was I trapped, left behind, hammering on the door and screaming for her in silence while the water rose past my waist?

Did I drift through school, a placid nobody, or was I drowning? Like in all my dreams? There's no time when you're drowning. Ten seconds could be a year. Two years. A thousand. Clawing for the surface. Pounding on the underside of the ice. Without thought, without sound, without breath, without anything but the purest terror.

The night I thought was missing is knife-sharp in that shadow memory: when I finally broke through into the light, into the air, gasping and choking, stumbling against the railing on the roof. And Mom found me there as I sobbed in bewilderment and relief and exhaustion. The daylight part of me faintly remembers stumbling along a dark and silent beach. But the shadow memory says I let loose a torrent of rage and betrayal on my mother, let my fury bear me into the air like it was water, finally in control. Her face was pale and terrified at my feet.

But she reached for me. She caught my ankle. Pulled me back to earth, wrapped her arms around me. I clung to her, couldn't let her go, made her promise over and over that she'd save me from the invisible hands that had held me down for so long, that she wouldn't let me drown. She stayed with me for hours, sang to me like she did when I was little, until I finally fell asleep.

I thought I woke to her sitting on the side of my bed, head bowed, hands clasped between her knees. But the shadow memories say I found myself alone in a world gone silent and dark, become a nightmare copy of itself. It was bordered everywhere by silent, icy water, no matter where I went. And just out of sight, there was always someone with me, someone who dragged me into the water, pushed me under, over and over again. I screamed for help, for my mother, and couldn't make a sound. There was no one to help me. I fought for every second above the surface. Even the dark was better than drowning.

What I remember as Ron's silly incantation…in those shadow memories it was someone calling me. Summoning me back to sound, to the mesmerizing swirl of the wind, to her. A girl with warm dark eyes in a beautiful painted face. She lit the way back like the sun. She heard me when I spoke. And she told me who my enemy was. The one who had taken my place in the sunlight. Who had taken everything.

They spin through me like snowflakes, like a tide, a torrent of snips of moments seen two ways. Dad leaning across the table...or leaning away from me, toward a stiff, pale copy of me sitting statue-like across from us, while I watched over his shoulder, boiling over. He never wanted me. He wanted me drowned and gone forever, he wanted that frail, fearful ghost instead. The one who would cooperate. The one who'd be reasonable. Watching a movie with my mother... or watching my mother put her arms around the impostor, forgetting me. Niobe calling me back...or Niobe, for all her lying, gentle words, shoving me back into the dark so that the *other* could take over. Ron struggling in my grasp because she's come looking for the *other*, not for me, never for me. Ron, who wanted to hear my voice.

Who sees me.

Ron's hands are on my arms, burning through my sweater, shaking me. My hands are folded uselessly over my head, but I can't block out the tide of double memories flooding over me; I'm stagger-ing under their weight.

"Marianne? Marianne! What the hell! Tell me this is you! What's going on? Fight it! Stay here! Stay with me!"

I can't keep the two strands of memory separate, the daylight and the dark, they're blurring together, the world is blurring together. I can't tell which memories are mine anymore, which set is real. I can't hold onto the rage anymore, and underneath it there's only fear, bottomless and icy.

There was only ever fear. Fear of the water, the silence, and the dark. Fear of never being seen. Fear of an eternity alone.

My own fear.

When I open my eyes again Ron has vanished, her voice smothered into roaring silence. All that's left in the world is this ghost, this shadow, standing face-to-face with me in the glassy black water that sucks hungrily at our legs, waiting to pull us down. Which one of us is real? Does it matter?

We've each pushed the other underwater, tried to banish each other; we've been fighting for so long. But I have both our memories now, and we both remember the cutting sweetness of the wind. The brilliance of a red slide.

I remember.

I remember being desperate for the sun.

"It's okay," I whisper, and my voice cuts through the silence and the dark, ringing clear as thought. It—she—stares at me, uncomprehending.

"I'm sorry. I'm sorry. I won't leave you here." I lift my hands to touch her icy face; she reaches up to grasp them. Our fingers blur into each other. "You don't have to be afraid."

And I press my lips to hers. Drink her down. Like ice melting on my tongue; like water too cold to taste. Until the mouth on mine is warm. Until the sound of the waves is crashing in my ears.

The wind is like a slap, colder than the waves shoving at my thighs. I reel dizzily backward, but someone is gripping my arms with both hands, and my lurching motion overbalances us both, topples us together into the water. When I flounder upright again I find Ron already back on her feet, staring at me, water plastering her hair flat against her head and dripping down her face. Around us the sky is lightening, the river gray-brown, stretching out toward the hills on the other side.

"Is it you?" she gasps, sloshing toward me. "It's you, isn't it?"

She clasps my face between her hands, her eyes searching mine. Her fingers tangle in my hair; it hangs dripping and ordinary, subject to gravity again. When I don't speak, she takes a sobbing breath.

"God dammit," she says. "You can't just give up, Marianne, what the hell!"

I barely notice as she drags me to my feet. The sound of the waves rushing past and the wind lashing the trees is like music, an endless, unconscious chorus, a layered galaxy, every piece in motion. It's mesmerizing. Beautiful.

"Say something," Ron demands.

"It's me," I whisper. It's so easy to lean against her, to let her hold me up, hold me close, keeping a glow of warmth between us against the slice of the wind. "It's okay. It's over. It's just me."

I'm curled on the couch in Aunt Jen's fluffy robe, finally warm, barely awake, when Ron emerges from the shower, her hair wrapped in a towel, wearing the skirt I borrowed from her what seems like a million years ago. She kneels on the floor next to the couch, her face level with mine.

"You said it's over," Ron says softly. "Are you sure?" I nod. "What the hell was that? What happened?"

I turn away, shake my head.

"I don't even know where to start."

"Try me. What did you do? What was it?"

I hide my face behind my hands.

"Look," Ron says, a little desperately, "I know this whole thing has been weird and horrible. It's just that after all that, and with Mom, and… I need to know, you know? Can't you tell me?"

"Don't ask me. Please don't." The words break into pieces as they fall.

"Hey," Ron says, pulling my hand away, folding it in hers. "It's okay. Really. I'm sorry. Never mind."

But I have to tell her. It's too heavy a secret to keep, and I'm not drowning myself anymore. I'm leaving the icy lake behind.

If she's going to hate me I need to know. I need to know now. I lean my head against our clasped hands.

"It was my red shoes."

"It… What?"

"Remember that story? With the red shoes? That's what it was. The ghost. This piece of me I tried to drown. Because no one wanted it." Stupid tears drip down my face, leaving searing tracks. "I did cut off my feet."

She doesn't let go of my hand, though she frowns, sorting through this.

"So you...have your feet back now? Is that what you're saying?"

"Does that make sense?" I scrub my eyes with the heel of my hand. "I don't know how else to explain. It's okay if this is too weird. If you have to go. I understand. It's just..." *You're the only one I want.* "I don't want to lose you."

She reaches out a tentative hand, brushes clinging tendrils of hair away from my face.

"I woke up," she says, "and you were gone. I thought I wasn't going to reach you in time. I thought for sure you were just going to let go and...and give in. But you said something to me. I was pretty sure it was you. You said, 'I'm sorry. I won't leave you here.'" Her eyes are bright, suddenly, and she swallows. "'You don't have to be afraid.'"

"I'm afraid," I whisper. "I'm still afraid. Your mom was right. It's *in* me." All that want. All that rage. Everything that lashed out at Ron, held her down, knocked her sprawling. The knife-edge between love and hate. "What do I do with that?"

"Well," she says, "drowning it didn't work, right? So what did?"

What worked was plunging in. Drinking it down. A kiss like standing under a waterfall. When the wind yanked me back to reality it came with a mouth warm on mine. Ron watches me in silence while I teeter on the edge of asking.

"Ron. This might be a stupid question, but...did you kiss me?"

She shifts a little and rearranges her arms before meeting my eyes again, a little wary, a little defiant.

"You kissed me first."

Silence wells up between us, alive and humming. Her hand in mine, fingers wound tight together. The impulse that wells up in me is as nameless as the ghost, but it has the weight and momentum of a breaking wave, impossible to stand against. Slowly, I lean toward her, pull her to me. I taste smoke and summer as our lips meet. The room spins gently around us, time dissolves.

It's nothing like kissing the ghost. It's the opposite of drowning.

When we draw apart she gives me a tentative half smile.

"You mean this, right?" Her voice trembles. "You're not going to…pretend it didn't happen? I mean, I'd understand. It's been a weird night."

I rest my forehead against hers. When was the last time I wanted something? When was the last time I let myself?

"This is everything," I tell her. "This is everything I want."

This time she's the one who kisses me. Tender, hungry, like she's challenging me to prove it. And wordlessly, with my whole heart—the sunlight and the dark—I promise to, I promise, I promise.

22

I FOLLOW AUNT JEN DOWN the hospital hallway, hunching my shoulders against the subliminal whine of the fluorescent lights. My shoes, still soggy, squeak on the linoleum with every step. Somewhere an intercom crackles.

I want to explain. I have to, somehow. But telling Mom what it really was… I run aground on the idea, stumbling into blank anxiety. How can I tell her?

I told Ron.

I feel for the crinkle of paper in my pocket. Ron. The note says to call her later. There's a glow of warmth to the thought, like a promise, like a piece of solid ground, somewhere to stand. If the ghost was real, Ron was too. Her lips full and soft against mine. The whisper of her breath.

"Marianne?" Aunt Jen's touch on my arm makes me jump. "How are you doing? Are you okay with this?"

"I'm fine," I say, not looking at her. She puts an arm around my shoulders.

"I'll be right with you, okay? I'm right here. There's nothing to worry about."

Chaperoning me. Protecting me—or maybe protecting us from each other. She's barely spoken to me all day, although I've caught her watching me. I scared her last night, I think. Maybe she halfway believes me.

But it doesn't matter what she thinks, I tell myself as she holds open a door for me. Not anymore. It's over. It's just me now.

Sunshine is pouring through the window, a dazzling river over the floor. Mom is a shadow against it, curled up against the tilted end of the bed, facing away from us.

"Laura?" Aunt Jen says. "I've brought Marianne."

No response, but the line of her back is tense, listening. When I lick my lips and try, "Mom?" she flinches from the word, just a little.

Aunt Jen shoots me a helpless look, but I don't return it. I clench my fists. Courage is a rope I can hang onto. I stepped out into the icy lake, didn't I?

One foot, then the other. I wade into the light, toward the bed with its plastic rail.

"Mom. It's me."

She doesn't move. I watch the shivering lift and fall of her ribs under her flannel pajamas. If I reach out to her, will she pull away?

But as I stand there working up the will to try it, she turns, finally, by slow degrees, like she's afraid what she'll see.

"Mom, listen," I begin desperately, but she squeezes her eyes shut, shakes her head. Tears drip down her face onto the pillow.

"I'm sorry." She barely makes a sound, mouths the words. "I'm. So. Sorry. I'm so sorry."

She raises her arms to cover her face, turns away as if she can't bear for me to look at her. Keening the same words over and over, even as I scramble onto the bed and put my arms around her. She barely lets me, all bones and hard edges in my embrace.

Aunt Jen looks like she's debating coming closer, pulling me away.

"I'm fine!" I fling at her. "Can you just give us a minute? Please?"

She seems about to speak, but just stands there, shifting unhappily.

"Well," she says finally, "I'll be right outside, okay? If you need me."

I wait for the door to click shut behind her. Wait for Mom's sobs to ebb.

"Mom. Listen. It's—"

"Don't," she chokes. "Don't tell me it's okay. It won't ever be okay. How can I ever let you be alone with me after this? How can you ever trust me now?"

"But it wasn't you. You know it wasn't you."

"I should never have let you come home. I should never—"

"Mom. *Mom.*" I put my hands on her damp cheeks, trying to force the knowledge through on contact. "Listen to me. Seriously. The knives. That wasn't you, okay? You didn't throw the knives."

"You don't understand," she moans, pulling away. "You can't just ignore this, Marianne, you can't just pretend this away!"

"I'm not pretending. I was there, remember? I saw what happened. It wasn't you."

"It must have been me," she says doggedly. "They said so. The police. The doctors. There were knives all over the kitchen, there was one stuck right through the cupboard!"

"You couldn't throw a knife that hard, Mom. I told you what it was, remember?"

"But it can't have happened the way I remember, Marianne. I was hallucinating. I was seeing these impossible things."

"You saw the knives all hanging in the air," I interrupt, and she goes rigid, statue-still, staring at me. "Like they were hanging from invisible threads. Right? And then they fell. All at the same time, so fast you could hardly see them."

She just looks at me, open-mouthed, her eyes darting back and forth, searching my face.

"You really saw that?" she whispers.

"I saw it too, Mom. It was real. I should have stayed with you. I was just so scared." My voice breaks. "I was afraid it would hurt you, and it would be my fault."

"But that can't have been real!" she cries. "How is that even possible?"

"There's been…something…kind of weird going on with me lately," I say. "I tried to tell you. There was this…kind of a ghost. Something like a ghost. It's hard to explain. But it's gone now, Mom. For good. I took care of it."

"I don't understand. There's no such thing as… What do you mean, a ghost? A ghost of who?"

I close my eyes. The answer is still there, waiting: one syllable. The simplest truth.

"Me."

"What?" Mom says blankly, but as I fumble for some way to elaborate she turns away from me, buries her face in her hands. "No. I can't trust this. I can't tell, Marianne, I can't tell what's real and what's not anymore. What if you're not even really here?"

"I'm here." I reach out to take her hand. She swallows hard. She doesn't look at me, but her grip is so tight it trembles. "I promise I'm really here. It's true. If you're seeing things, I must be too. Ask me again next time I see you. Or ask my girlfriend. She'll tell you." My fingers steal to my pocket. "I think she's my girlfriend now. Her name's Rhiannon."

There's a long pause. Mom frowns. Opens her mouth. Closes it again. Turns fractionally toward me.

"Wait." The words are slow, careful. "Hold on. You mean… *girlfriend* girlfriend?"

Maybe I should be worried. Afraid of how she'll react. But

instead I feel a smile bubbling across my lips, impossible to suppress. She looks so shocked, and it's so weird and awkward. So *normal*.

"Back up," she says, her voice a little stronger. "I'm obviously missing something here."

"There's this girl," I say. "She…really went to hell and back for me, the last few days. I kissed her earlier. I'm supposed to call her." The smile wells up. "She's amazing, Mom. You'll like her."

"Oh." She leans back against the pillow, blinking. "Wow." A beat. "So…does that make you…a lesbian, then? Or, um, bisexual?"

She says the words cautiously, like she's not sure how to pronounce them. Totally weird and awkward. *Peak* awkward. And I start to laugh. It escapes me in giggles and muffled snorts that just make me laugh harder.

"Oh my God, Mom."

A smile, trembly and hesitant, dawns on Mom's face. "Sorry. Maybe I'm not using the right words."

"No, no, it's okay. I don't really know what to call this yet. I just want—"

Hesitations clamor for my attention. I'm oversharing. This is going to sound starry-eyed. Stupid. Sappy.

Who cares.

"I just want *her*," I finish. "I just want to be with her."

"Well. That's fine." She squeezes my hand. "That's wonderful, sweetie. I can't wait to meet her."

I drink it in: the sun pouring over us, Mom's hand in mine. The lightness filling me like a balloon. I could do anything.

"Is this something I should have figured out before?" Mom says.

"I don't think so. I didn't."

She watches me, her smile fading. Her jaw tightens.

"Did you already tell your dad?"

"Mom."

"I'm just asking," she protests. "I just need to know. How much he gets to have while I'm *stuck* in here. I hate that he gets to hear these things before me, I hate that—"

"*Mom.*"

She falls silent, looking at me. It's anger, I realize, that just washed over me. Not fear. But it's sinking away, leaving me standing in some cold, rocky place. Breathing clear air.

"Mom, you can't do that anymore. I can't listen to it."

She shrinks back against her pillow.

"I know. I know. I'm sorry." The tears spill over again. "I'm just so afraid. I'm afraid you'll choose *him*."

"I'm not choosing. You can't ask me to do that. Neither of you gets to ask me to do that."

She puts a hand to her mouth to smother a sob, turns away from me.

"I just don't want to lose my family," she cries. And I pull her close, put my arms around her. Hold her tight. I have to swallow before the words can get through.

"We're still a family, Mom," I whisper.

"Do you think you could call your dad?" Aunt Jen asks timidly as she closes the patio door behind us. "If you don't, I'm going to have to."

"Yeah," I sigh. There's no escaping it. "Just a sec."

I pull the medicine bottles from my backpack, tip them into my hand: one, two, white and yellow. I stand hesitating over the pills. If this is over, really over, do I need them? Can I leave them behind, walk away from them? I'm walking away from the water, aren't I?

But it was fear, that moth wing panic, that brought me there. That's what I was trying to escape.

I'm not getting back on the hamster wheel of anxiety.

In the end I head to the kitchen, fill a glass with water, and toss back the pills. How am I going to tell Dr. Fortin about everything that's happened? Maybe if I call it a dream?

I'll figure it out.

My phone is still at the bottom of my backpack. It powers up without complaint, of course. Outside, I push through the gate in the hedge to scuff slowly down to the end of the street, looking over the seawall. The sun shines gray-gold through the crests of the waves slapping at the concrete, leaving a wide, sparkling trail across the bay.

I can't tell Dad about any of this. There's no way he would understand; he'd just think I was losing it. Or even worse, blame Mom. Somehow I have to convince him the knives lodged in the floor were a misunderstanding. Nothing serious. Not worth fighting over.

I told Ron about the ghost. I told Mom. This is going to be way harder.

I guess I'm going to have to stay with him at least part of the time, after all this. I clutch the phone, fighting a wash of dread. Life after divorce. Mom's not done ranting, and Dad will be watching my every move. It almost feels like they're the ones who've been possessed, replaced with raving aliens I don't recognize. But maybe now there's someplace I can stand, between the two of them. A place of my own.

The phone buzzes in my hand.

Hope you're ok. Call me when you get a min, Ron writes. And then, a moment later: Miss you. Is that weird?

I'm grinning. Like an idiot. I can't help it. I read it over and over, testing the idea, not quite daring to believe it, torn between euphoria and terror. Oh God, I have no idea what I'm doing. I'm going to screw this up, I know it. And even if I don't there will be a storm of a different kind to brace myself against; something tells me I won't be invisible anymore next year.

But from somewhere else, from some quiet depth, a part of me says coldly, *Well, bring it on.* I stepped out into the icy lake; I made it back. None of them can touch me.

I climb up on the seawall and squint into the golden light, let the wind whip my hair away from my face as I type out Dad's number. I stand there waiting as it rings. The water is beautiful, spread out before me, its surface a million shifting points of light.

ACKNOWLEDGMENTS

It's not every day you get to put a check mark next to a dream you hatched when you were five years old.

Chief among those I have to thank for this privilege are Annie Berger, Sarah Kasman, Cassie Gutman, and the whole team at Sourcebooks Fire. The book you're holding is a testament to their editorial insight, enthusiasm, and TLC. *Mesdames*, you have made every step of this process a delight.

Before she found this wonderful home for my little ghost story, Lana Popović, agent extraordinaire, saw straight to the heart of the book it could be and challenged me to dive for it. I stand in awe of her wizardry.

This project would have foundered utterly if it weren't for the literary midwifery of Allison Armstrong and Zélie Bérubé, both of whom have been cheering for it since it was naught but an evil twinkle in my eye. Their belief in me, their encouragement, and their detailed critique of many drafts got me through highs, lows, and a few freak-outs. Wendy McKee has also been an amazing cheerleader through the editing process, volunteering to read the manuscript closely again and again—whole or in pieces—when even I was sick of it. Everyone should be so lucky in their writing buddies.

Nova Ren Suma and the writers at her 2016 Djerassi YA Novel Workshop—Bree Barton, Aimee Phan, Catey Miller, Melissa Mazzone, TJ Ohler, Jacqueline Lipton, Wendy McKee, Shellie Faught, and Rachel Sarah—cracked the literary world wide open for me and provided the most inspiring and nurturing setting possible for rewriting. I am so glad to know you all.

Many wise and generous people read this story at various stages and offered their insights to help me take it to the next level: Ilana Masad, Nina Fortmeyer, Liana Bérubé, Karen McManus, Linsey Miller, Jacqueline Lipton, Chang Hong, Sarah Sambles, and Madeleine McLaughlin all planted seeds that bloomed into a better book.

I'm deeply grateful to Angéla Hacquard, Jessica Bayliss, and Natasha Razi, who each gave thoughtful feedback on critical aspects of this story. I'm also indebted to Eric Workman, Lisa Barleben, and Darlene Bamford for applying their professional expertise to my weird questions. Any errors remaining are my own.

I maintain that YA Book Twitter is the best Twitter: for making me think, for offering wonderful feedback opportunities, and for all the online friends and editors who gave me tips and helped me hone my pitching chops. You're too many to name here, but this book wouldn't exist without you.

The knowledge and experience of my fellow Electric 18s has been endlessly helpful and reassuring—I'm thrilled I got to share this journey with you. Cheers as well to Averill Frankes and Sanna Guérin, my indomitable Wednesday night Ravenpuff support group. You give me courage.

Hugs and kudos to Heather Bostelaar, who kept the home fires from burning the house down while I chased the rainbow. My beautiful, bookish daughters, Rose Bérubé and Deji Yanofsky, continue to warm my heart with their pride and excitement. Corey Yanofsky— who read everything first, took the household reins, and calmly, repeatedly reminded me that all of this has happened before and all of this will happen again—remains my rock.

And finally, all my love and thanks to my parents, Louis Bérubé and Marilyn Weixl, for their unflagging support, understanding, and love.

ABOUT THE AUTHOR

Amelinda Bérubé is a writer and editor with a small department in the Canadian public service. She holds a bachelor of humanities from Carleton University and a master of arts from McGill. *The Dark Beneath the Ice* is her debut novel. Visit her online at metuiteme.com.